Praise for Sometimes You
"This unpredictable, surreal n(
literary modes from science fiction
exploring space and the spaces between.

- Ted Zorgon

"This enigmatic tale of (in no particular order) love, AI, gods, giant chickens and rock stars will leave you scratching your head in wonder and yearning for your own trip through a labyrinth filled with emotions and revelations."

- Rebecca de Boudewijn

"This is a crazy, mouth dropping, awe inspiring ride through the interstellar universe with characters that make you laugh and then cry – on the same page. Douglas Adams would have read and loved this book".

- Vivien Snodgrass

"So I read your book! It is, I don't know how to put it, an absolute mindf—-! And I mean that in the best possible way."

- The Pummel Review

"An immersive, glorious and slippery sci-fi romp that could only have slithered from the wise and devious brainchild of Verhoeven, Cronenberg, Frank Herbert and Douglas Adams. If you can imagine it. Which you can't. So you'll just have to read it, won't you? Probably twice."

- Lesley Halm

"Be prepared to plunge into a kaleidoscope of galactic proportions to confront the most peculiar, yet strangely familiar characters who will echo through your mind for a long time. A fast-paced rock 'n' rollercoaster for your brain."

- Andreas Jäger

"Thoughtful and insightful grown-up science fiction – Noir is the Asimov of the 21st century!"

- Alexandra Maxwell

Sometimes You Just Need a Break

le wiggle noir

Published under the auspices of The Flat Mars Society.
© 2024 le wiggle noir
All rights reserved.
This is a work of fiction. Similarities to real people, places or events are entirely coincidental.
Cover artwork by Daniel Reed.
Logo for The Flat Mars Society by Daniel Marshall.
eISBN 9781763502000
ISBN 9781763502017
Contact: lewigglenoir@yahoo.com

For Karl, Rachel, Joseph and Twinkle

"Writing is just inky wiggles on a page"
le wiggle noir

Contents

Prologue
Chapter 1: The Man in the Euclidean Server
Chapter 2: I Just Love to Sit in the Dark
Chapter 3: Breaking on Through
Chapter 4: Skylah, and Unbuckling The Belt of Orion
Chapter 5: Ho Ho Ho Little Hobbit Where Have You Been?
Chapter 6: The C-beam and the Damage Done
Chapter 7: Whispers Down the Wires
Chapter 8: Consolations of a Digital Life
Chapter 9: Hi-Jinx Mired
Chapter 10: Well, of all the Space Monkeys
Chapter 11: A Hen's Revenge
Chapter 12: The 1001 Personalities of a New Norse God
Chapter 13: Not Everything Beautiful is Far Away
Chapter 14: You Cannot Run
Chapter 15: The Missing D
Chapter 16: A Terminal Case of Pareidolia
Chapter 17: A Blizzard on Second
Chapter 18: Fly Fishing in the Yukon
Credits

Prologue

"Sometimes you just need a break," interrupts the Virtual, her spatio-temporal stream as faultless as her skin, her voice as silky as her long chestnut hair.

My Full Immersive Reality experience is broken but you get what you pay for with the free account.

There are notes of sympathy in her voice when she says, "The same old, same old isn't doing it for you anymore?"

No, I can't say that it is.

No matter the quality of the cinematic experience, it's just stay in movies these days – and being tormented by ads and dreams of faraway, exciting places.

I have suggested to Norman, "Nepal is still viable, we could fly in and out. They don't recommend stopping anyway."

She does not glide as glistens to sit beside me on the couch to lay an ephemeral hand on mine, "Your other half holding you back?"

Their market research is personalised.

"We have a range of holiday experiences to suit the adventurous soul including trips to ..."

You have my almost undivided attention though I would like to get back to the movie sometime.

Yes, freshen the relationship up, get away from the madness of it all rather than letting the resentments build and build until they reach a heated, fiery crescendo which would not be a healthy outcome for anyone – especially Norman. I guess I do blame him for the bored, circumscribed life I live. He had always been utterly obsessed with mathematics. It is the air he breathes; it is how he loves. As a boy, he had ridden his bike up to the university to sit in on lectures to worship at the feet of the mystic Pythagoras. But that is his life, and while I suffer it as best as I can, I do not want the rest of *my* life to be wasted away as only one spoke in his academic career. I want to waste it on parties and sun and drugs and women. I *so* wanted women. I want all the things that I'd missed out on, and my bucket list is extensive.

I want Ibiza. I want to blow my mind out in a car. I want to try for the kingdom and to sail the wine darkened seas a thousand years ago. I want the worms to eat my brain. I want to choose life.

And this is not it.

I guess that's always been me. Flaky, petulant, scatty, tempestuous, impulsive, work things out on the run, live like there are no consequences.

Ostensibly more interested in achieving an academic career Norman is, in reality, *off with the pixies*, dreaming of worlds beyond human consciousness, worlds of artificial intelligence. Maybe he is made as somnolent by the mundane as I am.

I have taunted him, "If the only way you can think is as a computer do you want to become one?"

It's interesting how some people's idiosyncrazies can land them a well-paying job. Just choose your crazies wisely. And it must be said that it has also landed us a very nice apartment in the spectacular Old Ball, a building wrapped in an elliptical bronze latticework that glows in the late afternoon sun and is just such a short walk from all the city's tempting diversions. But what good is living this close to the city when we never get to experience any of those diversions? Norman responds by calling us "mutually exclusive". But despite our turbulent relationship, this is how we have been of others since infancy. We had played together as babies. My first memory is of us running through a field of wildflowers together. We are so small and the grass is so high. We stop to look, amazed at a blue flower, the first blue flower ever to exist so far as we know, and the sun comes out from behind a cloud, flooding the meadow in a soft, silver light. If only we could have stayed together, inseparable in wordless wonder.

Chapter 1: The Man in the Euclidean Server

"How did I get here?" Norman muses as if waking from a dream.

He had been thinking about the China brain conundrum again. He is sitting under a willow that droops over a pond surrounded by reeds. The sun is overhead. He had forgotten his hat again and, though it is a gloriously soft spring day, feels that what hair is there is too thin on his head. In Norman's opinion, the willow could do with some more foliage. A rivulet flows from the pond down into another one. Insects skim the water, touching and creating ripples. From somewhere above, he can hear a skylark's song. Norman loses himself in the reflection of sunlight on water until the birdsong wakens him.

"And more importantly, how do I get back?"

He ponders his options.

"When lost in the wild, doesn't one follow water?"

Reaching into his pocket he thinks to call someone to come find him or, at least, ask the maps app to take him back to the Centre ... if he had brought his phone. He has a vision of it sitting on his desk by his raffia summer hat.

He notices an ant crawling up the valleys and hillocks of his trouser leg. He places his hand in the creature's path, but it turns away. He tries again and this time it goes onto his hand. He raises it up to eye level to purposefully study the ant for all its antness. He turns and twists his hand this way and that as the ant traces its way upside and down around his hand.

Norman squints at the ant, his eyes made bigger by his horn-rimmed glasses.

"What, little ant, are you thinking?"

He smiles his lopsided smile as he has never quite mastered the art. The ant bites Norman and in outrage he flicks it towards the pond.

Norman follows a dirt path that runs beside the rivulet and under a canopy of willows until he comes across the Wandering Albatross Café set just beyond a marsh in a garden. He knows where he is now as he has a liking for the little bohemian café. He prefers it to the very modern Go Café that is further on from here. He orders inside then sits on a folding canvass chair in the garden. He looks up to see the new buds of flowers on the tree that he is sitting underneath and wonders if they will bloom or whether, with the spring, they will be killed off with another chaotic cold snap. He shakes his hand. It is still throbbing from the ant bite. It prompts him to take out his pocket watch to check the time.

"Oh blast!"

He still had to check the compliance certificates on the Pythagorean and Euclidean servers before checking his presentation for the wine and cheese this evening. It was an important presentation, maybe his most ever – all the Friends were coming to be charmed, he hoped, by sharing in his Vernian sense of technological wonder. He did not have time for afternoon tea.

Five minutes after he leaves, a waiter comes with Norman's order. The waiter goes back inside the café to charge Professor Greenwood for a pot of tea and two scones. It is not the first time that Norman has absently left without paying. It is a first for not having eaten and drunk it though.

Norman follows a network of dams and weirs that channel the glacial melt from the mountains behind Tywndale to the servers for the Centre for Advanced Artificial Intelligence Research. While not today, he does sometimes pause at the bottom of the rise to gaze up at this capsized ocean liner of a building. From there, the twenty storeys of the CAAIR loom even higher. He would consider all the spreadsheets, streams of figures, terabytes of data, visualisations and models, and the few token pieces of art that were hidden behind the reflective windows of the Centre. From his office on the nineteenth floor, he sometimes gazes out over the campus towards the city of Twyndale as if the Centre were a beacon of light to the world. Not too near the full-height windows, mind. He can get seasick if he does. The only time Norman had gone to sea had been on a team building day cruise. The waves had grown larger during the cruise and to begin with, he had enjoyed it until it had become too rough. He had waited though until they reached the fjord before throwing up, attracting little fish to his side of the boat. They had peered up through the green water with their bulbous eyes at the benevolent god who is showering them with the manna of the toast he had for breakfast.

Today he does not pause. A concerned look clouds his face.

"I'm late, I'm going to be late."

It feels like a moment where, if Norman had long hair instead of his comb over, it would fly in the breeze behind him as he scurries up the slope past basking students. As pleasant as the campus is now with students sprawling here and there, it is not that long ago that it had been under a blizzard of snow, and any students lounging on the lawns then would not thaw until the spring. In Norman's rush, his slick soled shoes seem unable to find grip on the grass and he slips and slides his way almost to the top before falling over and landing on his knees.

....

The doors to the Centre open as he approaches up the last few steps. Yet on entering he is ushered to a queue that has formed at the reception desk by what appears to be a security guard.

"What is this?" enquires Norman about a microscope-looking machine on the counter.

"An iris scan sir. Your pheromone signature has already been matched" replies the guard, "for this evening's event."

"Oh, I see. Was I notified of this?"

"Yes, in Warden Akinfeev's newsletter."

"Oh."

Back at his desk, he frowns on finding his hat and phone. He sits to read Akinfeev's latest missive. There had been a plethora of them since Akinfeev had started two weeks ago.

"Indeed, so it was," Norman blinks.

Norman reads the rest of the newsletter for other useful tidbits of information that he may have missed. From a lengthy list detailing the constant electronic assault that they were under at the CAAIR, the one that most intrigued him was a brief on developments in physical security threats. This one described how ants were being retrofitted with cameras for eyes and were able to track targets of interest by inserting a 'bug' under the skin via a bite.

"Hmmm," Norman looks sideways at the red swelling on his index finger before smiling, "What is the likelihood?"

Akinfeev also reported on rumours about development of a kind of dust that could spy on you. He rated it as plausible but at present unlikely.

Time is pressing so Norman grabs his tablet to go check the servers. The server floors are generally devoid of human life. Stack after stack. Bank after bank. Silent with only the flashing of lights to signify the passing of electricity and data. Norman could lose himself in his work amongst them, each server named after a famous mathematician. Having completed his compliance certificate check on the latest Pythagoras server build, he had come down to Euclid when the flash of a clean room suit catches him off guard. He stifles a profanity. His instinct is that he has seen an apparition. No, there they are, tapping into the servers, and they're not one of the maintenance team.

Norman accosts the person, "Who are you and what are you doing here?"

The man stands up. He is marginally taller than Norman, and under the weave of the hood Norman can make out that he has long black hair in a ponytail.

The man removes his mask to say, "I work for Akinfeev."

Unshaven to the point of having a greasy beard, he gives the impression he could have played in an eastern European metal band.

"How did you get the access code? There are no server-access clearance notes filed in the SMS today."

"I work for Akinfeev," he repeats with a hint of contempt for being questioned.

Norman's mind clouds over feeling a violation to the integrity of his servers' configuration.

"Akinfeev does not have the remit to manipulate the data in the system."

The man picks at some food stuck beside his sharp canine teeth in boredom.

"Do you know who I am?" Norman demands.

"Of course we do Professor Greenwood," the man points at Norman's knee. "There's dirt on you."

On this floor full of servers but no people, there is an echo of undeniable though deniable threat in the man's voice. No further conversation shall be entered into. Please exit the floor at your quickest convenience. You may direct all correspondence to the Warden of Security, Centre for Advanced Artificial Intelligent Research, University of East Twyndale.

Closing the office door and leaning his back against its pale wooden grain, Norman thinks that it is altogether easy to dislike the equine-faced Akinfeev. It's mutual. He doesn't like Norman. He doesn't like Georgia. He doesn't even like poor Rodders. He seems to have taken an especial dislike to Rodders. But none of this is personal. He dislikes everyone. And he had started so recently.

He certainly gets about his business quickly, thinks Norman.

In the tearoom, Akinfeev never discloses anything about himself except for general unpleasantries. But that is far from the worst thing – having Akinfeev point the hole where his index finger should have been felt like being cursed by having the bone pointed at you. Except that there was no bone. And even in two weeks since Akinfeev had arrived, Norman has had that hole pointed at him more than he would ever want.

When Akinfeev cannot use voice command on his computer, he has manufactured an interesting style that accounts for the 'm', 'j', 'u', & '7's. While nobody knew what had happened to Akinfeev's finger, it hadn't stopped Rodders from penning a speculative story about the tragic fall of the digit. Outwardly, it had been a fine-looking finger, but one day it became infected. The fingernail had kept the infection secret for too long, until there had been no other choice but to amputate. Rodders is working on a sequel where Akinfeev and his finger are reunited. Maybe that's why Akinfeev really dislikes Rodders.

As nobody knew what had happened to the finger, nobody knew Akinfeev's background. He had been parachuted into the newly created job of Warden by the University. He sounded street, but it was equally possible that he had an education at one of the big two universities. Maybe he was both. Rodders had been working the rumour mill on him. There was one that he used to work IT security for a prison, and another that he had been an inmate. Neither would have surprised Norman for you wouldn't say that Akinfeev condoned violence, but it always seemed to be on the table for him. After all, who do you employ to see if your security is up to scratch but a hacker of said security?

"Or maybe," as Rodders had scurrilously suggested, "he'd been a snitch who pointed a finger – and, as they say, snitches get stitches."

Rodders perhaps took a scattergun approach to truth – sooner or later he'd hit the right story.

So there was an aversion like a paralysis that crept up Norman's spine stopping him from storming into Akinfeev's office to demand to know what was being done to the Euclidean server.

Still, thinks Norman considering the dirt on his knee, *it had been terribly remiss of me not to don a clean room suit to go into the servers.*

He had been in such a hurry.

He sits down at his desk annoyed at himself for another lapse and the contamination he could have brought into the servers. He begins to go over his presentation for this evening. The establishment of the CAAIR had been so monumental, so full of work and risk but tonight, tonight was proof. The first they had that he knew the way. That the hint and glimmer of greatness that the University and the Friends saw in him was no flim flam sham. While the path never exactly leaves him, feeling its reflected golden glow fill him up eases away the doubts.

When the knock on his door comes, he isn't reading over his presentation.

Norman had been reciting a number as if it were a mantra of calmness: "Eighty-three billion, nine hundred ninety-nine million, nine hundred ninety-nine thousand, nine hundred and ninety-nine."

He has said it more than once. He had become distracted from his preparations when he went to scroll the screen and his finger pinged with pain again. His right index finger had swelled red and puffy.

"Same finger as Akinfeev's missing one," observes Norman.

Another knock and Norman casts his eyes back to the screen, "Now where was I?"

Rodders jams his monumental wedge of curly black hair through the door followed by the rest of him in his skinny black suit and skinny black tie. Balancing such hair always seemed so improbable to Norman. It is as if Rodders was spinning a lopsided bowl on a beanpole.

Georgia had sent him to ensure that Norman would go schmooze at the pre-talk drinks with the Friends.

"We don't want him forgetting," she had archly smiled.

Norman sighs. He had hoped to avoid it. He had a distaste to be so blatantly out rattling the can for funding from the Friends. That and the Friends always wanted to talk non-disclosure agreements and partnering arrangements. Such talk had a way of making him drift off. He found the whole thing a tedious and irritating disruption to his work. He wanted to be free and unentangled from such concerns.

As Rodders walks up to his desk, Norman closes his computer.

"There's people downstairs with guns. I think pepper spray too."

"Whatever do you mean?"

"Friends of the Friends."

"Oh."

....

The foyer of the CAAIR where they were having the pre-talk was a great glassed-in void that reaches five storeys above them. The floors above the foyer were cantilevered back into the rest of the building. Rodders shuffles Norman over to long tables bedecked with precariously slight wine glasses, a variety of the very best vintages and canapés. He pushes a glass of sauvignon blanc into one hand and a cracker of wild salmon and dill into the other.

Norman tries to wave the wine away as he seldom indulges but Rodders says, "Cheers," and with a flourish clinks their glasses together.

They step away to stand by one of the pieces of token art that the University had thought to bestow on the CAAIR.

"Indeed, so there is." Norman nods towards the men and women wearing sharp suits and holsters.

Cars crawl up to the front of the Centre disgorging the Friends. They leave their overcoats at an impromptu checkroom that had been set up just inside the foyer. After watching the growing crowd, Rodders clears his throat by downing his glass of wine in one go. He wants to make the most of it as he's on limited time before Georgia arrives. Rodders has no invite to this evening's presentation because he's kept in the dark about the precise work of the CAAIR. He's the victim of a double-blind precaution. It is Rodders' job to come up with spurious academic papers that have nothing to do with the CAAIR's current research because there are companies whose sole job it is to discover what they're up to. So Rodders must remain ignorant about what the CAAIR is really doing and that's maybe why his eyes are always darting in different directions trying to pick up morsels of rumour. Rodders' very appearance in the tearoom has the capacity to silence conversation.

Norman has more than once commiserated, "Poor poor Rodders."

Before departing to get another glass, Rodders whispers, "Did you hear about Yanelt?"

"Has he got another job?"

Yanelt had left the CAAIR last week. Rodders' face slackens, his mouth purses, and Norman is filled with foreboding. Another one gone by their own hand – Yanelt only the latest. There had been others in the last few months. Norman remembers a few of the most recent: Yorke who had supervised him as a post-doc, Satori

Kakemoto at Tromsø who he had gone through university with. Now Yanelt. He had been found by his five-year-old daughter. Had leaving the CAAIR made him so desperate? Yanelt had seemed happy enough in the parting.

"Almost relieved," thinks Norman.

There had been no tears. If only he had got in touch with Norman, he would have found a job for him.

"No note either," Rodders intimates.

Norman frowns. Rodders departs back to the long tables. Norman is rummaging in his pocket for his phone to see if there is a message about Yanelt when an urbane voice interrupts him.

"Ah a Dali. It's strange that he went so out of fashion. This is one of his paranoiac-critical period paintings if I'm not mistaken."

"Huh?"

Norman looks up to see one of the Friends standing next to him.

"I suppose, I don't know," Norman replies unsure what to make of the painting though he can see how the elephant turns into the swan then turns into the elephant and could be both at the same time.

Rodders is back with his next glass then frowns as they are all joined by Georgia.

"Thanks Rodders," she says much to his chagrin.

He plaintively holds up one finger. She smiles but shakes her head.

"The presentation is about to begin," she states.

The Friend places a hand on Norman's shoulder.

"We are led to believe that you have some very exciting news for us Professor Greenwood. Wishing you the very best of luck with it."

The Friend turns to walk down the corridor to the conference room while Rodders skols his to-be-last glass of wine before exiting by the front doors.

"Oh Norman," Georgia exclaims giving him a quick look over, "you and your scruffy suits. There's dirt on you."

Norman turns ashen.

....

From the vantage of the stage Norman surveys the conference room with some satisfaction. It seems that all the Friends did come. Georgia is miked up and pacing the stage introducing Norman and the work of the CAAIR. Her voice is full of engaging cadences that tinkle about the room like bird song in a forest. Her presentation is saturated with phrases like 'elimination of pain points', 'business value' and 'strategic opportunities moving forward'. Akinfeev lurks with a couple of his people behind the chairs under the rear balcony. He will have bolted the conference room doors both electronically and physically – the room will exist in a bubble outside of either.

There is a note of pride in Georgia's voice when she states that, "The Centre for Advanced Artificial Intelligence Research has been at the forefront of mapping the soma of neurons of the brain with nano-scale robots..."

The man standing next to Akinfeev, the one from the Euclidean server, holds a finger up to his ear and nods to Akinfeev. He waits a moment before making a slight thumbs up gesture to Georgia who then gestures for Norman to speak, and there is a cordial round of applause.

"Thank you Director Pietersen. Ladies and gentlemen. We are very pleased to announce the successful completion of the mapping of the soma of neurons of a cockroach. This has never been accomplished before. It is proof of concept and approach. We are now putting together a transition team to ramp up work on a whole-brain emulation of a chicken. This is a many fold leap in complexity from what we have already accomplished and the penultimate milestone before a whole-brain emulation of a human being is attempted."

The applause starts once Norman finishes his presentation and, one by one, they stand to give it. The conference room doors are opened and Norman walks down the steps from the stage to lead the Friends outwards to the canapés and expensive wine. With each Friend who comes to congratulate Norman, another sauvignon blanc is pressed into his hand. Then in the handshake of some iron grip, his finger throbs again, reminding him of the ant bite. Like a first time drunk he is beginning to become very loud as he relates another anecdote, tells another story, makes another pronouncement. He is the child who had ridden his bike up to the university to listen to lectures in mathematics.

Or loudly and elatedly he tells a Friend with a hand on their shoulder, "Enough data and you can predict anything. Everything from the Big Bang to the death of all light in the universe. It's a technical issue not a philosophical one. And," he smiles, "undoubtedly a financial one too."

The Friend frowns at those kinds of sums and the kind of projects that Norman might set his sights on after creating a whole-brain emulation. The stories are all recited to the smiles and laughter of whichever Friend is in front of him until Norman is almost beside himself in contemplation at the absurdity of it all.

All too predictably another Friend is asking about partnering arrangements, but Norman gazes over their shoulder at something faraway though it appears like it is getting closer. The Friend glances uncertainly over his shoulder but doesn't see anything. Then Georgia is there.

"Yeah, great questions," she says thoughtfully leaning her head to one side.

Full of wine, Norman is having troubles following the words coming out of her small mouth until it seems like her mouth blurs to complete blankness. He shakes his head trying to clear the impression. Instead, he tries focusing on her hands, but they are making gestures of ripping something in two.

Norman raises his head to peer into the shadowy void that reaches five storeys above him, and he feels his legs go wobbly. Georgia catches his elbow, steadying him, and smiles at the Friend. As she guides Norman towards the front doors, he begins to mumble a complaint about the man in the Euclidean server but stops short as Akinfeev is standing at the doors with a hat and overcoat.

She assures Norman, "There won't be any funding issues for the next phase of the project," before handing him over to Akinfeev.

Akinfeev guides him down the front steps and the gull-wing doors of his autonomous car float gently upwards.

"Another cockroach," Akinfeev points at the car, "and you presented on another."

Akinfeev lowers Norman into the car and hands him the hat and overcoat. Norman is too drunk to protest that the fedora and coat are not his. Akinfeev laser-focusses in on his swelling finger and Norman feels self-conscious enough to make a fist to cover his finger with his thumb.

"That looks painful," Akinfeev says blandly, "you should be seen to."

As the wing doors descend, Akinfeev's long horse face stretches and bulges in the curved car window. Norman is reminded of a look that Akinfeev had given Yanelt in the tearoom when they were first introduced to one another. With no forefinger, Akinfeev raises his middle finger to his ear as he watches Norman pull away.

As the autonomous car picks up speed, Norman thinks about taking it back into manual control as he has secret dreams of being a racing car driver yet is inured by alcohol not to. The silver cockroach floats along the roads back into Twyndale and, in the flush of his success, it seems to Norman that it also floats along the path towards creating a simulacrum of the human brain. The future where he raises sentience from the silicon substrate feels as concrete as the car he is in and the road he is on. Norman falls asleep with the happy thought that doing so would make him famous in his own lifetime and many after it.

With the mountains behind Twyndale and the city laid out in concentric ring roads, the car takes Norman on a circuitous spiral down through West Twyndale before getting to the city centre. It's so late that even the working girls have gone home rather than try for more business. There are no stars above to draw dreams from. There never are. The light pollution makes it impossible to see anything; anything apart from the moon and Norman revives to see a cloud making a stark gothic cut-out on it.

The Friends have never spent their midnight drearies pondering the China brain conundrum. They may know about art, but they don't have an inkling of what mapping the soma of neurons might entail.

"Their judgements will necessarily be less understanding but," he concedes, "that's why they have their technical advisors."

Norman fumbles with his phone trying to read the message about Yanelt. Georgia is encouraging anyone having difficulties with the pressures of their job or with Yanelt's untimely passing to seek counselling. She also promises that the University will review its policies around the care it provides employees during the termination process. Norman tries to examine the puffy swelling of the ant bite but between the moving car and his drunk moving head, he cannot focus.

He counts: "Eighty-three billion, nine hundred ninety-nine million ..."

Next he wakes, he is befuddled about where he is. Once the car senses that he is awake, it turns on the internal lights and brings Norman's chair gently back to the vertical. As Norman had sunk into sleep, so had the chair lowered to the horizontal. Now above the rim of the window and with the internal lights creating the palest of glows outside, Norman dimly understands that he is in the underground carpark of the Old Ball on the far side from the lift and stairs.

He imaginarily pats it on its dashboard.

Good car to get me home.

Norman feels incapable of taking the double helix stairs that run to the top of the Old Ball.

On the clock ones and twos spin between 1:12 and 2:11.

Or is it early morning?

The lift it is then. The winged doors of the car float up and he sloshes out. He kneels on the ground feeling more drunk than before he had gone to sleep.

"How is that possible?" he moans.

He does not feel well staggering to his feet. His head lightly touches the leather underside of the door. Then in the shroud of the carpark, Norman is suddenly overwhelmed by the feeling that there is someone lurking in the shadows.

"Hallo," he calls out.

No answer. Norman is not reassured. The overhead lights should have come on by now. It could be an electrical fault, but it feels more ominous than that. Being under the car doors, maybe they had not detected his emergence?

"Hallo," he croaks like there is dust in his mouth.

Still no answer. The concrete walls soundproof Norman's calls from reaching friendlier ears. He feels terribly alone and his legs go weak like a forewarning of falling. The suicides of too many purportedly unhappy scientists whirl through his mind: Yorke, Kakemoto, Yanelt. Has news of his cockroach success leaked already? The hands of the Friends are all over him. They are around his shoulders. Their hands sticky from spilt sauvignon blanc, oily from the smoked wild salmon canapé. He feels himself being dragged down into a quicksand of fear.

"They were never suicides," he whispers to the shadows.

He scans the darkness and is menaced by his blindness. It is as impenetrable as it is impossible to remember the faces of the Friends and their associates. Had there been any clues that his faraway, absent mindedness had missed? The subtle knife of an indulgent smile knowing what was to come later?

While blinded by the dark, he is beginning to see very clearly.

"Of course, of course."

He has not paid attention. To be where they are, the people with the oily, slippery hands have to be cunning. Play both sides would be the cleverest thing to do. Collaborate if that seemed likely to work; destroy the other if it wasn't. There are more shadows than light in the carpark. The ant bite bulges red, his knees and elbows are covered in dust from kneeling on the floor. There is dust on the soles of his shoes. He frantically pats his knees and elbows, but the dust only insinuates itself further into the weave of his suit.

Norman jerks his head up. If there is a killer lying out there in the dark then it is too late to rid himself of dust. Then Norman understands that the killer is enjoying this moment of terror before completing the hit. They like their victims petrified. Norman's heartbeat is hammering in his ears.

This is the kind of place that killers kill in.

"What's that?"

The scrape of shoes? The hammer of a gun going back? Another unhappy scientist gone too early by his own hand.

The killer's pleasure in Norman's terror gives him an opportunity to flee to safety. The lift will take too long to come and the flight of steps beside the exit ramp too far. The winged doors of the car take an eternity to gently float down.

"Go," Norman commands the car, "go now."

"Please state your destination," replies the car.

"Go," pleads Norman.

"Go Café? Is this your destination? Please say 'yes' if it is."

"Anywhere but here."

"Anywhere But Here Catering? 'Out of the box solutions for funeral wakes'?" asks the car.

The desire to take the car into manual control is screaming in his ears yet he still doesn't. Eventually he convinces the car of a destination and, as the car's headlights swing around the walls of the carpark, shadows follow them.

Chapter 2: I Just Love to Sit in the Dark

We're in the silver cockroach floating towards West Twyndale. Norman is picking at his finger – it's still sore from the ant bite.

"This place shows films, even at this time of night?"

Yes, it is true that it does do movies. Sometimes even this late. Nothing I've said is exactly untrue but knowing everything can be detrimental to doing anything. I'm just amazed that I've got Norman this far. Shadows swing across the seat as the car banks around a corner.

"What is the name of the cinema?" he says looking anxiously out the window.

"The Sheridan."

An old, withered crone of a place, coughing her last ruby lipsticked, poisonous breath, and as if it had breathed on them, you were only the faintest shade of a shade in the grime on the mirrors in the bathroom. Rub as hard as you might, that stain is never coming out. The makeup on her is plaster-thick, a courtesan's art-deco death mask.

The Sheridan. Lit by an unreliable light bulb, take a walk with her down the corridor to the bathrooms and you might never find your way back. That hallway was a place for the abandoned. You never knew what or who you might step on. The vinyl on the walls bends and pops as you grope your way along and oozes with moisture like a burst pimple. The bathrooms smell like rotting fish. The graffiti on the walls is written in brown Nikko. Probably. Toilets break and aren't fixed until they cause flooding. But, pro tip, whatever you do, don't use the liquid soap from the soap dispenser. Don't ask, just don't.

The Sheridan opened with spotlights roving over its façade and in the optimism of the urban renewal of West Twyndale. That optimism has long since departed along with the spotlights and the people who instead rove to places by the river for entertainment. If spotlights were to strafe the façade these days, it would be only if hostages were taken. Nobody wants to see those crumbling wrinkles. The humiliation would be too much, the fall too terrible.

Leaving the buttery smell of popcorn in the foyer to go down into the ballroom is to descend into an underworld so different to the concrete carpark of the Old Ball. It is an underworld smelling of mushrooms and dirt with a chilly dankness even during a dry summer. During those winter thunderstorms that rage out of the far north, drips come through the ceiling and shower through the dusty chandelier. It's the only time the chandelier ever gets cleaned. There is a mould in the carpets down there so virulent that it fears nothing, not even bleach. And with Norman dreaming his dreams, I sometimes sneak out for a midnight movie here. Movies and ...

As we walk towards the front doors of The Sheridan Norman says, "It sounds rather loud for a movie."

He's not wrong about that but his choice of attire could be. He's wearing the fedora and long grey overcoat that Akinfeev gave him. This should be interesting.

He's pulled the brim of the hat way down low muttering for a kind of explanation, "Iris scan."

He furtively looks around.

"It's not that kind of a place," I reassure him, but he's not interested.

Oh well.

Inside the smoky glass doors of The Sheridan, the noise becomes much louder. Before the descent down the steps into the ballroom is a gnomic man with a pointy ginger beard, dressed all in black. He's smoking a cigarette and looks at Norman's getup up and down. Unsure of himself, Norman grins like a fool and gives him his ticket. The man takes it with a baffled smile, then holds it up to his cigarette and burns a hole dead-centre in it. The hole is ringed by blackened veins. The man hands the ticket back to Norman and we go on our way.

I hear him say behind Norman's back, "Wanker," which upsets Norman.

"Why'd would the ticket collector call me that?"

"He thinks you're a cop. It's the fedora and overcoat combo. And he's not a ticket collector."

Norman can't help but smile at the thought that he's a cop. Maybe anything's cooler than a professor of artificial intelligence. Norman opens the door to the cavernous ballroom and is greeted by a staggering scene.

"What merry hell is this?" he gapes as we walk down the stairs.

Well, it ain't no movie that's for sure. The band on stage is in full berserker mode – they're doing a metal rendition of The End by The Doors and the mosh pit in front of them is heaving. Bodies are being flung about, people are climbing columns and leaping back into the crowd. There's crowd surfers everywhere. A confusion of emotions play across Norman's face as the light show also does: blues turning violet, reds turning magenta, the band turning something else apart from human. He seems at least partly intrigued by it. But if Norman has Pythagoras, then I have Mr. Mojo Risin and I'm off, flinging myself with a burst of repressed energy into the maelstrom of what looks very much like the dammed. I come back with a broad grin after the singer has bid farewell to nights where he has tried to die to find Norman off with the pixies.

Poor thing wants to be anywhere else but here.

Norman though quickly makes to stand behind a column that supports the upper balcony. I meander behind bemused that he is overwhelmed by this. But I am wrong.

"I've been followed. I knew it, I knew it," he half yells above the music.

"Huh, what do you mean?" I ask.

"Him, there. It's that fellow I found in the servers, Akinfeev's man."

He points to a man in the crowd who is whipping his long black hair backwards and forwards to the beat of the music.

"Um, okay, should we say 'hi'?"

Norman looks terrified by this suggestion.

"God sakes no."

"I'll talk to him," I say.

"You most certainly won't."

"Anyway, you can't be sure that he is following you. It could just be an accident. Sometimes you just need an accident," I say helpfully.

Akinfeev's man seems to agree as he smashes his head forwards and backwards.

"There is no such a thing as 'just an accident,'" Norman states.

Norman watches the man for a moment before saying, "I need to leave."

He makes to step from behind the column when Akinfeev's man suddenly turns on his heel and disappears towards the foyer. We watch him go.

"See, we're fine," I say.

I turn back to watching the band hoping to encourage Norman to do the same. And he does for a few fidgety, hiding-behind-the-column minutes. He turns the collar up on his overcoat. Then snap, he goes scurrying up the stairs to the exit.

Oh well, this didn't last long.

I stare wistfully at the band for a few last cherished moments until they finish another song. In-between songs, the acoustics of the room turn the raucous chatter of the crowd into something more primal, like a room full of croaking toads.

I'm frustrated but feel obliged to leave. I find Norman flattened behind a column in the foyer peering from beneath the brim of his fedora out the doors of The Sheridan.

Nice, he's waited for me.

No, it's not that. It's like he's frozen. He doesn't even notice that I'm here. I'm going to flick him on his nose when he pops back into his Norman-shaped place from wherever his fear-induced, out-of-body experience has taken him.

He asks, "Is there an emergency exit?"

I frown pointing, "Like there's the front doors ..."

"No," he almost shouts at me.

I'm not too happy about being shouted at so I suggest the bathroom. There could be a window there.

Norman scuttles across the foyer with his face averted to take the corridor towards the toilets and past the gnomic man who calls out a bit more drunkenly this time, "Wankah."

The light bulb arcs occasionally to register that a voltage is running through it and that there is in fact a corridor. In one of the unsparked moments, we stumble on someone crashed out on the floor. When the light bulb sparks again, we see a man who has an uncanny resemblance to Norman if say seen through one of the mirrors in the bathroom.

Weird.

He complains about being stood on. The water in the bathroom is fortunately at low tide tonight. There is a window above the basin and when Norman stands on the basin craning his head through the opening, he can see an alley outside.

"Is this really worth it?" I ask but he is already trying to lever himself up through the window.

"Okay," I say, "rock'n'roll baby."

....

So we're back behind the column in the foyer scanning the street with Norman having a sore knee because the soap dispenser failed as a leverage point. The street outside is empty. On a table, I spot a pair of dark glasses. They could be lost. There's nobody left in the foyer. Everyone is in for the band.

"Can I steal them?" I ask.

"No."

"They'd fill out your fedora, coat combo you have going."

"Someone will be back for them."

"I'll be quick."

Norman ignores me. I look longingly at the glasses. They are within snatching distance.

"Okay, okay."

"This is serious."

"Yeah, I guess."

If you're going to indulge your fears, then don't be shy about it. Go all the way and Norman darts from behind the column and through the doors leaving me behind. I stand behind the doors looking at Norman, who has squeezed himself into a nook of the portico. From there he is scanning the street. It is empty and Norman's caution gives way to haste. As soon as he steps out from the portico, as if by coincidence, Akinfeev's man appears sauntering up the steps to The Sheridan. There is just a slight nod and faint smile in Norman's direction as they cross paths. Nobody strolls the streets after midnight in West Twyndale. Not these days.

....

What Norman talks about:

- the ramp-up of the whole-brain emulation of the chicken project,
- recruitment of the project team managers,
- transitioning over the cockroach team members,
- pushing Georgia to start planning for the leap to emulating the brain of a human being.

What Norman doesn't talk about:

- the evening at The Sheridan.

He's still a bit angry about that.

It is as though Norman has left me behind the glass doors at The Sheridan. The door has swung shut between us – I on the inside watching Norman from behind dirty, smoked glass. Everything is remote. I feel as if, when he froze behind the column at The Sheridan, he was freezing me out. It's not really that much of a change for us.

There's the physical leaving, then there's the spiritual one, and that's the one which happens first. There were promises made and broken, subtle ones to be sure, important ones of the soul, which I clung to even if Norman had abandoned them. He had abandoned them as surely as he had our play to ride his bike up to the university. Betrayals are subtle to begin with; it is only the consequences that turn bloody.

It's like he has locked me away in our storage room, with his boxes full of notebooks, journals, photo albums and prizes for maths competitions. I go there sometimes to turn the dusty pages of them. In a photo album, I find a photo of toddler Norman on the beach by the water looking out at the impossibly large waves. In among his journals, I find some surf magazines that he had collected after his boat trip. Behind that, I come across a vinyl album of The Doors and the half-shaded face of a one-eyed Jim Morrison looking back at me with all the beauty of a Greek god. From his other eye stares a band mate, a hand on Morrison's cheek pushing away as if spawning from the Lizard King like the others have already. And I have no idea how I have smuggled this home past Norman.

Most of his notebooks are unremarkable, being filled with diagrams and calculations. There are pages of indecipherable equations that have a certain artistic value in themselves. I am sitting on a small stool with a notebook on my lap reading something that is quite different:

> in outer space, solid ice, when heated at a constant temperature passes the triple point and is converted directly to water vapour. It does not pass through the intermediate liquid state. Sublimation is magic!

when Norman comes in.

"You took me to The Sheridan under false pretences. There was never a film showing."

I smirk rather proud that I'd got him there, "Yeah, maybe."

Norman fumes a shade of red – he's been brooding about this for a while. He turns on his heel slamming the door shut behind him. It slams so hard the door auto locks.

I go to the door and yell, "Come on Norman, let us out."

I couldn't help it if one of Akinfeev's peeps was going to be at The Sheridan. Could be just an accident, could be. It couldn't be my fault, could it? I look at that passage about sublimation again and think that we are that piece of ice floating in a chartless region of outer space, and I am beginning to think the only chance to shatter that state is with an ice pick.

....

"Norman," says Georgia, "Norman," she repeats.

He had not heard her come into his office. She had just been there, and he feels unsettled by her sudden appearance while he had been examining the list of server-access clearance notes.

"What's that number that you were saying?" she asks.

He recites, "Eighty-three billion, nine hundred ninety-nine million, nine hundred ninety-nine-?"

"Yes, that one," Georgia cuts him off.

"Oh, it comes from an old problem in AI, the China brain conundrum. If say we were to replicate all the functions and interactions of the neurons in our brain with networked computers, at what point does the human subject that is being replicated change from human to computer? At what point, does the computer become sentient? But that eighty-three billion, ninety-nine million ... represents all the rest of the neurons that you would have to replicate and that, my dear, is a lot of cabling."

"It is, but thankfully, we're not doing it that way."

Norman asks, "Do we receive notifications if a server's access is compromised?"

Georgia apologetically frowns and the wings of her Nordic blonde bob touch her shoulder, "Like the dirt incident?"

"I am as mortified about that as you are but-"

"These lapses," she says, "that you have ... are you're thinking about things like the China brain conundrum?"

"Sometimes," Norman admits.

"You need to be more careful, we can't afford any risk to the project."

Moving to more comfortable topics Georgia asks, "Have you seen the data on the chicken emulation?"

"I just received it, but it looks good."

Norman scratches his index finger.

"I believe we can proceed," he says feeling the unstoppable momentum of the project.

Perhaps, others will take time to spot the issue. Perhaps.

"That's wonderful news," Georgia says and stands to go.

Norman stops scratching his finger after Georgia notices him digging into it with his thumbnail.

"That looks infected."

"Oh, it's just red from rubbing."

After she leaves, Norman collects his tablet and though it's not quite going home time, he leaves anyway. He has left the silver cockroach at home today as he has developed a dislike of underground carparks and goes to the bus stop to catch the bus back into Twyndale with the students. Norman intensely studies the data on the chicken emulation on his tablet until he feels like he is being watched. He turns to notice a man with a crew cut on the seat behind him looking over his shoulder. As if there is no issue, the man slowly slides back in his seat. Norman hunches his shoulders before switching off his tablet.

The bus stops on the far side of the park from the Old Ball and Norman watches as the man with the crew cut wanders away before he turns to cross to the other side. If he gets home before night, Norman often liked circumambulating around the copse of trees in the centre of the park. It is not the same as being by the streams that mark the borders of the campus, but it is a refuge in the middle of the city. Today, he marches straight towards the Old Ball. As he waits at the lights on Second Avenue, he realises that he needs food for dinner and, with a sigh, goes to the supermarket on the corner instead of up the stairs to the Old Ball. On entering though, an exceedingly pale man with an absolutely white shock of hair and vivid blue eyes follows him in. The man seems to have a similar liking of sourdough loaves to Norman and likewise picks up an olive tapenade from the delicatessen counter.

Then as Norman is staring in the window of a freezer door at frozen vegetables, he stands behind him to say, "Imagine being flash frozen yah? Do you stop thinking when it happens," his hands make exploding gestures, "or do you lie there wondering why you pulled that silly face?"

The man reaches past Norman for a bag of brain-like cauliflower while Norman stares at him in horror.

"I'm not a cryogenics charlatan," cries Norman pushing his glasses back up his nose to glare at the man.

"This is meant to be a yoke," he says mispronunciating the 'j', "do not be offended please. Relax, chill out," he nods and, before he continues down the aisle, he places a hand on Norman's forearm, "Take it easy."

....

Back in the Old Ball, Norman has cast himself down on his couch.

He takes out his tablet and mutters, "Eighty-three billion, nine hundred ..."

It's only a matter of time before other people will do the calculations on the rate of capture that he has roughed out. On the cockroach and chicken their method worked, on a human's it may not be fast enough. Eighty-three billion.

If Georgia has ever been definite about anything it's that, "It's critical that an AI is created. The CAAIR cannot be left with a dead person on its hands and no AI," she had repeatedly made clear, "nobody's caring about the destructive scans of cockroaches and chickens."

"Except the cockroaches and chickens themselves," Norman had thought.

He rubs his finger. Since then, ant bites which have clouded his concern for small creatures.

"There's certain," she had smiled, "ethical and legal challenges around the destructive scan of a human's brain. Murky questions of murder become involved."

Despite a heaviness in his legs, he raises himself and goes to the window to look out over to the park. Norman sees his outline in the window and frowns. If the brain's neuronic structure deteriorates before the scan hits the magic point of replicating consciousness, then there will be no AI.

Maybe for the first time ever, Norman is daunted by his undertaking.

"More than 200 neurotransmitters, complex electromagnetic phenomenology, constant fluctuations, independent activity at all levels. It's a damn infinite-dimension machine!"

The sun is setting behind the mountains of Twyndale and Norman can feel the cold air against the window. The heating will start soon. He looks at the ant bite. There is one thing that he could do.

....

I come in to find Norman in the bathroom, the air full of mist from a shower, sitting on a stool, a towel around his waist, with a kitchen knife in his left hand aiming at his right index finger.

He says rather groggily, "I got all the dust off me."

I appreciate he is quite drunk.

"Careful with that knife Norman, you could do yourself an injury."

The knife wavers this way and that. He's not wearing his glasses and the alcohol is affecting his aim too.

"I got to get it out of me."

"There'll be blood."

"Blood?" he pales.

"Yes, lots."

"Oh I say."

That seems to do it for Norman but he fumbles putting the knife down and it cuts his finger and we have to get a bandage on it asap. I smile. I did in truth love this very ordinary man. Wrapping the bandage around the cut felt like an attempt to heal the wounds we had made on one another. Our feelings so scoured, the ground between us scorched, the broken bones of our relationship not reset properly and daily grinding away in agony. We share a momentary glance and it seems as if he still loves me. He raises his finger like he is reaching for me, then I realise he is attempting to write equations on the steam in the bathroom. Is he really trying to capture love that way? He swirls the steam about in a flurry of symbols and letters and seems for a moment happy. Then gone, like his equations written in mist, he frowns. He drops his hand along with whatever else it may have been. I turn from him in disgust. Ruin a genius if you must but break the heart of your soul mate at your own peril.

....

A new box arrives one day when Norman isn't home. I get super excited – ooh, a present – and open it. Well, it isn't a present, that is for sure. It is ... what is it? It has come in a ventilated container as if it is a mail-order puppy, which it is not – though it is hairy. I gingerly lift it up in front of me. It is prickly. Two tendrils uncurl from the main ball and waft about as if they are alive. It's like watching a living, underwater ... beard?

Norman is angry when he discovers the trail of destroyed packaging and the less-than-well reconstructed box. Another larger box arrives a few days later. This one I leave alone. This one is heavier than the first. I kind of fear what might be inside. Ignorance is a plausible alibi. Plausible ignorance is a plausible alibi.

....

Someone's here. I see the silhouette of a large man standing at the end of the hallway to the cinema room looking for something. I'm in the sunken lounge watching the walls, deep in Full Immersive

Reality mode, and freeze. Like inhaling the droplets of a plague, I've suddenly caught all of Norman's fears about Akinfeev and the friends of the Friends. The man is walking up the corridor. Do I stay frozen, or do I slither off the couch to hide underneath? What would the Lizard King do?

Slither- no, too late.

He is standing right behind the couch, looming over me. The man exhales as if he is letting go of a great labour. There is the sound as of someone peeling a bandage – skin and hair go with it. Then there is the sound like a sword slowly being drawn out of a scabbard and I am stabbed with a paralysing terror. My head is poking above the back of the lounge ready for execution. And then, horror of horrors, the man's body transforms as if it is changing states from material to liquid. It hits the floor with a gush. There is still a man standing behind me. Smaller now and I recognise him. The eyes are a giveaway.

"Oh shit my peeps, it's Norman!"

Naturally, I don't say that. There is, of course, nobody ever around on Friday nights. The only posse on the lounge with me would be my imaginary friends. Norman turns off the FIR projector because it will make him seasick if he doesn't.

"Boooo," my phantom crew moan on their way out, leaving me with a bewildered and bitter resentment.

... Which explains the second box. Norman has ordered himself a full-body hazmat disguise to go out in. A way to elude the ants, dust spies and pheromone scans. Yet an iris scan might still find Norman in there.

And so it begins. Friday nights, between 5.30 and 9.30, Norman disappears. Sublimation aside, I know Norman doesn't believe in magic, but this act he pulls surely qualifies. One minute there, next minute he's split. 5.30 he splits, 9.30 he splits again with his reappearing liquefying act. Like any good magician, the audience is completely baffled. First the beard then, goddamn it, the body goes too. He stands there in his singlet and boxers, his comb over matted, his face red from the removal of the beard, covered in a patina of liquid. I never get used to his arrival and the removal of the bodysuit. Whatever the next step is, Norman has taken it along a very dangerous path.

The following Friday night his disintegrating-rematerialising act behind the couch scares me so much, I exclaim, "Oh fuck bubble head stop doing that."

He retaliates by turning off the FIR. This is something more than drifting apart – we're breaking apart. Into our own worlds. Yet, will he spin off, leaving me to wither and die alone in my own dark space or will the worlds fall into a downward accelerating spiral of mutual destruction? If you ask me, Norman hasn't hit escape velocity yet.

....

How will I do it? In the library with the candlestick? I don't want to hurt him too much, but the modern world is a world full of opportunity – and we have some nice heavy pewter candlestick holders. We keep them in the dining room with the good silver, at a table only ever set for one. I hold it in my hands and lurk waiting for him. In the dark, he does not see the face of madness leer at him.

Another late Friday night, another night of wondering where he goes, another night of quiet, seething resentment, but when the moment comes, he turns on the lights, restores sanity, and nothing comes of it. Keeping a box of matches beside the candlestick makes everything plausible.

"What are you doing here?" he asks.

"I just love to sit in the dark," I smile with an innocence full of repressed anger.

After a few more of these nights the surprise gets old for him, too.

....

To freshen up the relationship, I've begun hiding in other places around the apartment. I leap out at him screaming and run away screeching. He turns on every light in the house before he enters. I am enjoying making Norman jump at shadows.

When he shaves, I sit in the bathroom imagining him slitting his throat. Things are getting out of hand. We're spiralling closer to the edge and we both know it. I don't know what would help. Perhaps if we could sync into each other's dreams – maybe then we could properly speak to each other. Or at least have sympathy for each other's nightmares. It would be a very, very, very long-distance phone call.

It goes on until, for all my plotting, the moment of opportunity comes. Norman's Friday night disappearances are getting earlier and earlier and his reappearances are getting later and later until tonight it must have been well after midnight. I am sitting in the kitchen unashamedly reading an entry in his journal. The light from the hallway downstairs only dimly lights the kitchen. It looks like Norman has received an epiphany about the way ahead with the project. He is filled with that golden glow again. It is a paradigm shift. The stars aligning if he flips the model which weirdly makes me uneasy.

I hear the front door open and close. Lights turn on as Norman goes from room to room. I hear the beard being roughly ripped off and what sounds like a cry of anguish, pieces of Norman being left behind. Then a heavy thud as the hazmat bodysuit sloughs to the floor. At least he unzips in the bathroom now. It is easier to clean up the mess. A door slams, and I jump. Slamming doors isn't his jam. With Norman, it's always buttoned-down emotion in a waistcoat and suit. It slams again and again, and I flinch, and flinch again. Norman is trying to work something out of himself. Another cry of anguish and with that the door-slamming stops. The following silence is more ominous. I could easily put his journal back. He need never know. But I want this confrontation now. Back lit, he stops at the top of the stairs. He is wearing his boxers and singlet, and his hair is a mess from being roughly dried. Not wearing his glasses, he squints into the kitchen. I initially think that he is embarrassed about my reading material, but I am mistaken. The feeling that engulfs the kitchen is one of absolute distress.

It is a precarious place for Norman to stop given how I want to hurt him, unleash my anger, slash at him with whatever is to hand. The kitchen is the most dangerous room in any house.

I step into the light and sneer, "You were never good at love were you?"

Norman ducks his head. My words have hurt more than if I had thrown a plate. Pain and horror twist his face and I hate myself for having unleashed those words.

But as he turns away from me, I swear that it will be the last time. All my rage swells up. My old sense of betrayal surges. It is an easy thing to fall down dimly lit steps. So, I give him the nudge he needs to send him on his way. The world is full of opportunity. Pain, horror, distress, all give way to a look of shock on Norman's face that he is falling. Feeling that he is, he grasps for any hold and takes me with him.

Chapter 3: Breaking on Through

When I come to, I have an ant's-eye view of Norman. He is still out, dead cold. He is as crumpled a mess as his discarded Friday night bodysuit usually is. It is like he has been pulled apart and Picasso-ed back together: his legs, arms, neck, and head all at wrong angles. In the spiralling fall, we have become entangled, and we lie half on, half off the stairs. I slowly begin to extract myself from the jumble of Norman, praying that he will not stir. He is so hard to move that I think he must revive. He doesn't. I am sore all over. I stand above him.

Sometimes you just need a break.

I turn from him as he had turned from me, and I do not look back. I rush down the double-helix staircase to find the door to the Old Ball ajar as well. Down the steps to the street below. The avenue outside our apartment is still busy and I run straight across it. The cars do not swerve and neither do I. Breaking is for chickens. Into the park opposite I stop for a moment until the heavy breath of some huge feeling begins to surface. It kicks me forward again. It is on my neck all the way across the dim and dewy grass, long thin claws reaching out for me from a hooded darkness. Heavy, predator footsteps hunting me down. I am a newborn fawn failing to find its feet in a strange and terrifying new world, missing each time I try to put one down. Missing in the half-moon night, stumbling, trying to catch myself before I fall, before I am caught.

Childhood sweethearts no more. Inseparable for life no more.

I flee across the park and hurl myself into what I hope is the safety of the hazy, luminous streets beyond. I run oblivious of where I go. I run amongst the late-night purveyors of hotdogs and burgers. I leap over the bums on the sidewalk. I flit past shop owners pulling down steel shutters. A cop yells a Dopplered blur. I am there and not in a twinkling. I run, and they leer, laugh and leech sideways as I fly by.

Harried by dread, I feel like everyone is watching me, everyone knows that I killed Norman. There are eyes everywhere, cameras everywhere. My righteous anger flees from me as I flee from the scene of my crime. This feeling of being surveilled must be a delusion I tell myself, but I have an overwhelming need to vanish. To get as far away as possible. Now. I run to the closest subway.

The lights are blinding in the subway and in that moment, I feel like I disappear into them. The comfort of that moment passes and then I run through the turnstile, paying no fare – nobody cares. The platform is humming with commuters and Virtuals. The Virtuals are almost as convincing as the commuters until they fudge their spatio-temporal stream and fuzz at the edges. They walk amongst the throng, hawking various offers and are ridiculously too good-looking to be anything other than artificially created sales reps.

One Virtual shouts that their deal is the chance of a lifetime.

"Don't miss this opportunity."

They are scant on details. Each Virtual tries a different angle. Another one is provoking more interest than I would have thought with such a marketing pitch:

"You will get to work in an *actual* factory."

"How quaint," I hear someone say.

That can't be right. I must have misheard. I've come in halfway through. A role-play maybe or a Fair Trade Experience.

Another captures my interest, "Travel the arcane paths to the court of the Lizard King."

I search the crowd for that Virtual and light upon one with deep blue almond eyes and long honey-brown bangs wrapped in a red skirt suit.

I beckon her over and she purrs with a hint of sexual promise, "Or if you don't like that one, we have many other packages to suit any and *every* taste," she says offering me a ticket out of here to a good time.

I try not to excitedly gibber, can you really get me to the court? I keep it chill and start with some small talk. You've got to work up to popping big questions to the *über* women of the world even if she is an immaterial girl. As we speak, her hair starts to go streaky blonde, her face rounder, her figure fuller, and I am sure her breasts are getting bigger. She is undoubtedly scanning me for unconscious non-verbal cues layered on a racial profile – all to get her sale across the line.

It's making that special someone in your life into the person you always wanted them to be.

I know I should be outraged that they should presume to know me this way – it's just that they aren't necessarily wrong.

Before we could get down to the serious business of running away together, other Virtuals, seeing that my travel consultant had got herself a pigeon, start to flock about to sell their wares.

"Live as one of the local indigenous people and pick coffee at altitude in the Andes!"

Another one cries, "Experience the ultimate surfing adventure."

I am being overwhelmed by the swarm. In the bright lights of the subway, I do not want this much attention. I start backing away, which entices them all the more.

I see my original travel consultant petulantly stamp her delicate foot and exclaim, "Oh, *scheisse*."

As their Virtual faces get closer, more demanding, and quite terrifying, I agree, "Oh, *scheisse*."

I am being mobbed by beautiful imaginary people. Their hands, grasping for me, passing through me, giving me the shivers. Then blanching a paler shade of anger than a human being could go, my original travel consultant starts pushing her way through the melee. There is pushback – mostly me towards an incoming train. A security guard starts towards the crowd, asking for authorisation codes. My travel consultant suddenly loses her appetite for a sale and disincarnates. For all her fakeness, that upsets me no end. I have also lost my travel consultant. One after another Virtual dematerialises as the security officer asks for their authorisation code. I don't want to talk to him either. With perfect timing the train doors whisper open, I turn and step onto this train to God knows – anywhere else but here.

It is a train of nose-to-nosers, all doppelgangers of one another. I grip my seat trying to keep the fear and panic at bay. It is all becoming too much. The bust-up with Norman, being on the run, the vanishing travel agent – I had got what I wanted and now reality is biting me on my arse.

"This isn't what it was supposed to be like," I whine, "Where are the tequila shots and lines of coke?"

I feel like I am losing myself in it, feeling lightheaded, dematerialising like the travel agent had done. I grip the seat all the harder to ensure that reality doesn't slip through my fingers. The image of Norman lying at the bottom of the stairs afflicts me. What have I done? Boredom had killed again.

My fellow passengers are putting me on edge. Where do you look? Do you look into their eyes or somewhere else? Get sucked into the gravitational pull of their vacant commuter gaze? Everyone is oblivious, absorbed in their own worlds of entertainment. Only one man isn't. He had been at the back of the travel consultant melee.

Out of all the angelic faces there, he had not been one of them. His face is scarred or tattooed, his smile a scattering of broken teeth. The doors of the train had wanted to close on him, but with a nonchalant use of superhuman strength, he had pushed them ajar and let himself in. They had snapped shut behind him. He gives a little shimmy as if he is adjusting a suit though he is wearing a black hoodie and cap which is like the very incarnation of the fear that had chased me across the park. There are two empty seats opposite me, and I hope, and I pray and pray ... No, of course he is going to sit there, and he takes up both. I happen to catch his eyes behind his dark round glasses and wish I hadn't. Unlike the commuters, it's like I'm seeing eyes staring out at me from the deepest space. It triggers my full, irrational, losing-my-shit fear mode.

He's followed me, he's followed me.

I swing my head from side-to-side and back to the people sitting quietly, sedately on their seats, while I am panicking.

Where are they taking me? Where is this train going?

After taking a moment to scope the carriage, the man starts making comments to people sitting near him like he's cadging for business. The way he speaks, it is difficult to catch what he is saying. He slides into a wheezy drawl, faint transmissions from one of the islands of humanity being made on far off worlds. Everyone on the train is trying hard to ignore him and the nose-to-nosers aren't to be underestimated in their perseverance. They might be ignoring him, but nobody is going to tell him to shut up. It doesn't help him that he isn't one of the pretty travel consultants. And these quiet, complacent, compliant people are my companions on this train that lurches on a precipice, lurching, about to fall into some kind of infinite void of nothingness, a nothingness like the air of a cathedral or the deathlessness of cyberspace, out of which you never return. I am going out of my mind. My face contorts in horror. I want to scream at the docility of those around me, instead, I choke on fear.

I push my heels into the floor and grip the window ledge behind me as if that will forestall the fall. In the anonymity of the train nobody pays me the least bit of attention. As the enticing plunge draws irrevocably closer, I glance at a piece of paper that has appeared on the window opposite me:

Needz to scamper quick bruh?

Call tru eddie

Then there was a phone number.

Yes, yes, I do need to scamper quick bruh, get me off this train.

Under the phone number a crooked arrow jaggedly points downwards. I follow the arrow until I find myself looking into the eyes of the man across from me who seems now to be sizing me up.

Shit, he's seen me looking at him. Shit, shit, shit.

He had spoken to people on either side of him and now he says something indecipherable to me. Everybody else had blanked him as if they too had fled from a hooded darkness in a park. I can't say why I choose to respond to him with a "Huh?" when everyone else had ignored him. Maybe I deeply understood what it was like to be blanked. Even behind his glasses I can feel his gaze sliding into me like a hypodermic needle seeking to find an obscure vein. He says something else equally opaque.

"I'm sorry?" I say and he seems to have made up his mind.

"Whizz you going? Mayb I can help. I's a removalist. We there in a flash. Doors-to-the-doors service. I help people who needs to scamper quick. No dis-tance too big, no dis-tance too far."

I throw places about without thinking too much about them, "How about Spain? Ibiza?" I ask, "Hawaii?"

He makes a gesture of weighing up a set of scales but I know that these aren't viable anymore.

"I recks yous got to go much furder. I recks you look like you have the needs to go much, much furder. Something about you says you needs to do some long-distance scampering."

He presses a button on the arm of his sunglasses and the lenses telescope outwards. There are dials on the side, which he tweaks. Then he makes some gestures in the air, flipping his fingers this way and that, moving his hand up and down as if scrolling through a database or opening a window on a different universe that only he can see through.

"Ah," he nods, "I recks that The Belt is da place for you and we's be in luck, there's a shuttle leaving tonight."

"What's The Belt?"

He holds up his index fingers and thumbs to make a rectangle, "It's pikchur postcard."

And as he describes The Belt of Orion, I know that it *is* the place. Sometimes you have to go a long way to get away from yourself, get away from the madness of it all and make a fresh start. A space island resort standing off the ringed planet of Hyrieus, whose image is perfectly reflected in the crystal waters that lap the beach. The waters are so crystalline that it glows at night, and they sell it in vials as babies' nightlights in the gift shop. I couldn't wait for cocktail hour.

"Yeah, I's can take you there but fizzy first we've got to go through da Tanny."

Alarmed, I didn't want his company for any longer than a carriage ride, "You don't have to come."

"Yous need'le get through security, bruh, and I can get you to da other side. I's guaranteed, you know it."

He leans back and studies me.

"Yous don't look like yous know how to do it, either. I used to work security and I know them people there, they'll let us through."

"tru eddie?" I ask.

He made a clicking sound with his jaw in the affirmative and his jaw moves sideways more than it should have.

"None udda. You ready to go? I reckon yous needing some speed, yeah, and we's needing to scamper real quick to make tha shuttle. Them shuttles to tha Belt only come along every 49 days."

"How do we get there?" I ask.

"Chill, we're on da line to Space Port VIII. Sit back, yous got tru eddie here."

I leaned back and thought about The Belt of Orion. You hear about places like The Belt, but you never expect to go there – it definitely was never going to happen with Norman. Then I remember Norman and I realise that I couldn't go. I couldn't leave him broken at the bottom of the steps. It was one thing to panic, another to ...

The train pulls into another stop and I say, "Look, eddie, I can't go with y—"

eddie isn't looking at me. His sunglasses are fixed on a man who has stepped into the carriage. The man wears a long grey overcoat and fedora. My heart leaps-lurches and my brain discombobulates. It is Norman dressed up for a night out at The Sheridan. Then my brain dis-discombobulated itself and I saw the difference in the square jaw line.

"We's need off this train," eddie wheezily whispers.

I had found my guilt in the resemblance. The cop seems to be checking tickets or IDs. I can't take my eyes off him as he approaches and remain frozen.

"Now!" eddie hisses.

In one easy motion eddie drags me to my feet. Despite his splay-legs and the rolls of fat that wallow about him, he moves quickly. The carriage doors were closing, but with one hand he stops them and with the other shoves me out. eddie comes after me before they slam shut. The train pulls away and we turn to see the cop still performing his check. I turn to see that eddie had unzipped his hoodie and that his hand was resting on a pistol inside of it that is shaped like an ornamental crayfish decorated with shells and sea lichen. It gave me to think that what eddie was proposing was not exactly legal. Yet, seeing Norman in the cop told its own story for me.

tru eddie had noticed, "Yous lookin' a bit pale there bruh but we's be good."

And to reassure me, eddie starts throwing down some moves. First, a little Harlem Shake.

"Yeah, we's be good," he huffs.

Then some running man.

"Yeah."

That was a whole lotta flesh moving in front of me. He did have some top moves though and I had to smile.

"What wers you sayin before we got off?" eddie pants.

"Belt of Orion – oh yeah," I grin and join him in some running man.

So that's how I got myself into jumping a shuttle with my second-choice travel consultant, to the Tannhauser Gate and then onwards to the 'pikchur postcard' space island resort of The Belt of Orion.

....

The next train that came was a northern line and at River Ford we would switch to the southwestern line to get back down to Space Port VIII. At River Ford, eddie begins to discuss documentation. I had left in a hurry and hadn't brought any.

"Not real ones," he says, exasperated by my naiveté, "fakes. You don't want to be giving them anyting they can follow you with even if you're going troo the Tanny. The Tanny is likes wiping your credit history, almost, but they can still trace you. If you still pulling breaths anywhere in this universe, they can still finds your broken ass."

"eddie," I say, "all arses are broken – all of them have cracks."

His sunglasses made him inscrutable and for a moment he goes silent. Then he heaves a great bellowing laugh. I sigh in relief, too.

His laugh, though, was disconcerting. His jaw moves in ways it just shouldn't.

After he stops laughing, he says, "Yous a jesta."

Then he gets down to business. He presses a button on the arm of his sunglasses to telescope the lenses followed by his hand gestures. While he does that, I look about the platform. It is tiled all off-white; the tiles blasted by dust and dirt by the passing trains. Garbage gusts chaotically as trains come and go, forewarned by indistinct announcements and the sudden appearance of lights out of the tunnel. The expresses speed by to the sound of an otherworldly hum buffeting me as they go then to disappear into the tunnel again. Two red eyes peer back at me. And here I am stuck with so called tru eddie in a transit lounge of a railway platform between the dark ages of the Norman conquest and, what seems, when I peer into the tunnel, a very uncertain future.

"Ah, this one be good," he says after a moment.

He tells me that if you know where to go you can hack the data of recent suicides. Find a file with a 'self-replication' error and you grab that extra name. The history splits, one vanishes into the files as 'suicide', the other lives on. You just don't want to be around for the file validation.

"Why?" I ask.

"Yous just don't want to be." He holds a wafer-thin, almost transparent plasma card up to my forehead, "Yous always wanted a new you? I found yous one. You be Rega Mortensen now. Rega Mortensen be you now. Remember. That's your ticket."

The card dissolves itself into my forehead as if it is part of me and I flinch at a sensation of pins and needles.

I am to be a suicide then? That would be convenient for eddie if I become a liability. I could get disappeared very quickly. Be nobody's problem. An over-written data glitch. But becoming this Rega Mortensen ... I do not want to imagine what kind of heart-rending sadness could have led to that. And with the plasma card indistinguishably a part of me, I am implicated. I am fingered. I am involved. As if I want that guilt. I have enough of my own, thanks a lot.

I ask, "I don't suppose you got a different card there, eddie?"

He shakes his head.

"Extract this one?"

An annoyed shake. There is no debate about this. Could I even extract it? I suppose it isn't like switching credit cards.

So I am to pick up their life and start over. If I can. Choose life, choose another life. Find a different ending. If I can. All I have to go on is their name and their despair.

We catch the train towards the space port and I'm still on edge what with the possible murdering 'n' all. eddie tells me to chill. As if waiting for permission, I close my eyes and as I drop off to sleep, I mumble, "How many times you do this, eddie?"

"You be my first customer, you be a trial."

I wake from a micro-nap as we shoot out of the tunnel and onto a plain with the space port lit up in the distance. The train immediately slows down, and then we feel a slight tremor underneath us as a shuttle takes off, a bright pinpoint of light in the distance. There are only a few passengers left in the carriage; eddie and I sitting side by side.

Trying to get a gauge of eddie, I ask him what it was like working security.

"It's a bad business. I's spend a lot of time lookin', lookin', watchin', watchin', and it most jus be for nothin'. Sneak around, not be seen. Stay outta sight. But you don't stop nothin' from happening. Jus clean up the afters, that's all you do. Mop-and-bucket job. I's liking this better ... so far."

eddie begins to tell me about how he made his own ammunition for his pistol. It was a blowback pistol because it didn't have any locking lugs in the chamber and that meant special ammo.

"What does that thing fire?" I ask.

He releases the barrel of his pistol and drops a slug into my hand. It is heavy, orange coloured, and covered in mucus.

"I make 'em myself."

I squirm as the bullet squirms in my hand, wriggling to uncurl itself. There are only two tentacles unlike the standard four.

"I take the eyes off mine 'cause I don't want 'em to see where they's going. But if I plug some cunt then I want 'em to know it was tru eddie that got'm."

I quickly drop the slug back into eddie's hand.

"Is it a slow-release hollow-head?"

"Yeah, bruh, it takes a bit but the brother he'll be sweating it nice and slow waiting the wait."

eddie recurls the bullet to slot it back into the barrel, snapping it to.

The train pulls into the space port. My hand is still sticky with mucus, sticky like I suppose Norman's had been with sauvignon blanc, and I stupidly decide to clean it off by wiping it on eddie's arm. I smile innocently. eddie looks down at the silver smear on his arm which he then puts around my shoulders I suppose to wipe it off there. Everyone else is alighting but eddie holds me down. Then when the carriage is empty, he grasps my hand and forces one of my fingers around the trigger of his pistol.

"Yous ready to go through Security?"

I nod. He forces me to bring the pistol up to my head and I begin sweating and squirming like his bullet had in my hand.

"Are yous *really*?" He puts pressure onto my finger, and I am pushing back as hard as I can. "Yous betta be. If we get caught, a bullet to the head, even one of mine, is better than what they'll do to you. They have real special ways of hurting people and they got the law behind 'em, too. You 'member that." Then he let out a howl of laughter, "Whys you sweatin' it? I wouldn't be going to all this troubles if I was gunna pop you."

Beads of sweat said that I had absolutely no doubt that tru eddie was a man who could pull a trigger when he wanted to.

"Plus da safety's on."

Even still.

The departures gate of the space port seems like it is busy enough for us to disappear into the crowd of galactic tourists and moon miners even at this time of night. But then I remember that disappearing into a crowd doesn't exist anymore, with facial recognition CCTV everywhere. Anonymity had long since gone bye-bye. Somewhere above us, waiting in geostationary orbit, is the ship to take us to the interstellar jumping-off point of the Tannhauser Gate. It waits at the end of a space elevator that begins at the space port. The shuttle that travels up the lift needing an initial boost causing the ground to shake every so often.

We walk around the complex of buildings until we come to a side gate, where eddie makes me wait while he speaks to security. I think about that gun of his and what could be worse than dying from it. The bullet entering you was the least of your problems. You had about fifteen minutes to have it extracted before your blood begins to turn blue and you were irretrievably a goner. After about forty-five minutes you'd begin to lose sensation in your outer limbs. After ninety minutes your skin starts to calcify and harden into something more shell-like, and your eyes glaze over in cataracts. Polyps start to crust over your face and your fingers melt together to become claws. Some people who have been shot with these bullets have ripped themselves apart with their claws trying to rid themselves of the pain.

After two hours you enter the final stages of *crustacis*, the blue blood overwhelms the red, and you have a heart attack. Needless to say the last two hours of your life will be the worst two hours of your life. Death by crustacean – a horrible way to go. And eddie was saying that Border Security could do worse things to you than that! Maybe they want you to live. To live and to suffer.

eddie touches noses with one of the security guards. This, I realise, is my last chance to back out, to flee from this barely conceived trip and go back to Norman. After so much plotting and waiting, I just couldn't, but there is eddie laughing and pointing at me and I begin to get scared again.

Where is he taking me? Why do I trust a total stranger?

I remember my instinctual reaction when he came on to the train that he had followed me.

Had he really spruiked his services to other passengers?

It was impossible to know what he had been saying in that drawl of his. I get the skin-prickling intuition that he had been there only for me.

Why wouldn't tru eddie sell me down that river for a few bucks or some other obscure reason? Trust tru eddie, what else would a con man say?

eddie whistles for me to come and like a trained dog I do. There is no other way to cocktail hour by that magnificent pool of water than through these gates. If any of that exists. Every step drags heavily on my feet like I am signing my life away. But if I get through the Tannhauser Gate, then I am out of Earth jurisdiction. I console myself with that as I shamble towards eddie. Approaching the gates, they laugh noticing me sweating buckets as if they are tears of remorse; as if. I am waved through, and I sigh in relief.

eddie is beside me in a moment. "Don't get too chill, those brothers were the easy ones – it's the next ones who'll want you to squat and spread."

"I thought you said that we were good with security."

"Yeah ... with those brothers."

What! It gets worse?
I want to throw up.
eddie pushes me along. He hustles me past what appears to be a loading dock, up some stairs and into a long, poorly lit grey corridor.

He pauses at the end of the corridor to say, "Get your Cons on, we gotta do this quick."

In the fearsome light of a shuttle taking off, everything is scrutinized: the feigned smile to a faux loved one, the slight widening of pupils as the zipper on your bag is opened, a forehead gone glossy with the suggestion of perspiration, the dampening of armpits revealed by ultraviolet, a cough to hide a dry throat when answering a question. And we step out into the middle of it. eddie hides himself deeper in his hoddie and behind his sunglasses. I have no such disguises while the plasma card feels like a beacon on my forehead. We pass authorised Virtuals, vastly superior to the artisanal guerilla sales reps on the train platform, chameleon-like so that they appear as one thing to me and something completely different to someone else. And in that brutal light of takeoff, we become insubstantial, while the Virtual becomes more real, all our desires, desires we never knew we had, are revealed to them so that they can sell us everything from perfume to alcohol.

eddie's haste to get into the queue for the shuttle feels far too conspicuous.

"Remember who yous be."

He thuds the middle of my chest with a forefinger.

Maybe exacerbated by eddie's warning, I am having problems remembering who is who. The trouble is trying not to think about all the terrifying things. I am trying not to think of which line this is. I am trying not to think of what could be worse than *crustacis*. The memory of falling, entangled bodies.

You were never good.

I am trying not to think of what they do with people who commit crimes of passion. Maybe I don't want to remember who I am.

So, I'm not as together as I should have been when it comes to my turn to be quizzed. It is easy to remember tru eddie's name because it is imprinted in the middle of my chest, held to my head, the pressure tightening on the trigger finger, filling up my cranial cavity until it was ready to ...

"Pop" was the name on his security badge. Good ol' Pop, all dressed in black and as grandfatherly as a vulture appraising the carcass of a zebra with a full biometric scan. With the slightest of fuzzes about the edges. My overtaxed imagination? No, there it is again. As the Virtual starts asking questions, the plasma card that eddie had implanted in me starts generating a beautiful heads-up display with the answers to the questions floating to the front of my vision even as they are being asked.

Pop asks the usual questions: name? date and place of birth? destination?

Then: why did you push your nearest-and-dearest down the steps tonight?

The heads-up display goes blank.

"Um, what?"

"Reason for travelling?"

"Oh, sorry, you're talking about my bucket list? Well, I really want to have dinner with a beautiful blonde by a pool at The Belt of Orion, that would be great. I also really want to get to the court of the Lizard King. That's right up there too. ..." and by the time I finish talking about the wonders of the court, the queue has grown substantially with anxious, time-poor travellers.

Pop, fuzzing around the edges with exasperation with an eye to the queue, waves us through with barely a glance at tru eddie.

Then I stroll towards the departures lounge almost with an air of victory and around the corner from the security gate, I break into a little running man. Despite my invitation, eddie chooses not to join in.

From the departures lounge, eddie and I board the shuttle. As it makes its way up the space elevator, I feel free, profoundly free, for the first time in my life, and it is joyous. We are also leaving Earth jurisdiction, which is another cause for relief. As we travel beyond the mesosphere towards the Kármán line, we unbuckle our seat belts and gradually float towards the ceiling. People stare into each other's eyes in disbelief and laugh in blissful weightlessness.

Chapter 4: Skylah, and Unbuckling The Belt of Orion

Well thanks to tru eddie my bucket list has considerably more ticks on it now than all the years that I'd spent trying to get Norman to do anything. Seeing the very innards of the universe ripped open at the Tannhauser Gate and slipping through that worm hole: tick. Sipping Blue Shot cocktails by the pool at L'Hôtel d'Orion: tick. Biggest decision of the day: should I have another Blue Shot or maybe switch over to a Blue Frost?: tick. It's my blue cocktail period. Having a throwaway affair with a messed up, blonde, hippie chick (hi Skylah): tick. And in a couple of hours we're going to indulge ourselves in the debauchery of the Dove Festival. Yes, we still hang out to relive old times. Blithely trying the medley of drugs on offer anywhere and everywhere: whatcha got? haven't tried a red one before, ok. Grand mal seizure: well that's hardly surprising now is it?

Before Skylah and the Dove Festival, I am having a visit from the hotel's doctor with a concerned look on his face concerning the seizures.

After a thorough examination, he gives no definitive answers except, "Here, take these twice a day and call me if you have another one."

"But why are they happening?" I ask.

"You would have to return to Earth to be sure ..." he says failing to answer the question and avoiding responsibility at the same time.

To be on the shuttle tonight, I would miss out on Skylah and the Dove Festival and that wasn't going to happen. Not to mention those cop entanglements and the decisions over the choice of cocktail are harder. The door shutting echoes down the marble hallway and if I was in any doubt before, I knew I was on my own with the seizures. I shrug picking up the box of tablets.

More drugs, yo k, why not? Let's see what these ones do.

An hour later, I come to the disappointing conclusion that they must be beneficial to my health.

Well then, it must be cocktail hour.

On the way to the pool and a cocktail I pass through the foyer of L'Hôtel d'Orion. There are some fabulous places at The Belt, yet none come close to L'Hôtel and none have anything that comes close to the Great Atrium that apexes with a stained-glass dome reproduction of Michelangelo's *The Creation of Adam*. It fills the foyer with a multicoloured light, and such is its virtuosity it is sometimes tempting to reverse things and think that Michaelangelo saw this one first and reproduced his version on Earth. The dome is overshadowed for me because it is where I met Skylah. There was a mix up over room bookings. We had both been given the same one. Quite generously, I thought, I offered to share the room with her, but she refused. I bargained for a date as a compromise and somehow, she said yes. They're kind of gin odds, that is, very small. I've seen how Skylah keeps an untouchable aura about her when people want to jump her bones, and lots do. Men, women, in-betweens, others, everyone wants to be with her. I suspect I got further with her because when we first met at reception, she was déjà vu-ing.

Her perfect eyebrows puzzled, "Have we met before?"

I felt the electricity between us when I looked into her eyes so what else do you say when such an astral babe asks if you've met before but "Absofuckinglutely."

It was a spontaneous response.

Sitting by the pool sipping a Blue Crush through a straw the Belt of Orion did strike me as a place full of extremely high-end technological wow factor mixed with just about dawn of civilization, monkey hitting monkey with bone-clubs, technological breakthrough throwbacks. The sea at The Belt had not been here originally. It had been siphoned through a worm hole from another planet to thunder down in a great new Inundation, but do you reckon you can get decent mobile phone coverage? No, only landlines! It has something to do with solar activity or something.

I feel myself drifting into a slightly wonderful haze and survey the pool area. The kidney-shaped pool which I am sitting by has a waterfall at the far end that falls into another pool with tropical fish and a sandy beach. The sand by the lower pool is so engineered that it does not adhere to your feet. While nighttime is best for seeing Hyrieus in the water, I wasn't looking for the beautiful ringed planet. Nor the equally beautiful Skylah who must be arriving soon. Instead, I have a vision of smuggling in a baby crocodile and letting it go into that pool. That would add a whole other dimension to doing jumping jacks in the aqua aerobics' classes.

Wow, one white pill, one Blue Crush and isn't that an interesting haze?

That's made it onto my list of 'to do again'. What with the full bottle that the nice doctor has given me I could ease back on my hover banana lounge and look forward to many more such hazes.

Handing me a fake credit card, tru eddie had left me in his debt and with the doorman at L'Hôtel, his job apparently over.

"Doors-to-doors guaranteed," he said and, with that, gone.

I had gazed as that large piece of humanity ambled down the cobblestones, idly speculating where he was going, with more questions than answers about his motives. A few of the select from the shuttle were wandering this way, so I turned, and the doorman opened the door for me. The portico had two small pillars either side of the steps with a lintel on top that gave little hint of what I was about to enter. I did and was astounded. I had to admit that tru eddie had truly excelled himself getting me into this place.

On the floor under the dome is a mosaic as there were mosaics throughout L'Hôtel. In the larger ballrooms there are crystal chandeliers that shame the poor one at The Sheridan, none with a speck of dust on them. Every whim or desire of L'Hôtel's patrons is catered for even before it is uttered. Offended by that irregularly shaped ice cube in your cocktail? They are there with some perfect cubes of ice to soothe your disquiet. Phew, that was close. It is genuinely a sanctuary for the world-weary soul and from tru eddie who has yet to venture here. So far.

Outside of L'Hôtel, he has an unnerving knack in finding me especially when I go out to raves or discos and almost always when I go to Bar 0, the predictable creature of habit I am. I suppose it helps that he used to do all that sneaking around in his previous line of work. To find your way to Bar 0, you must pick your way through a maze of bars and cafes, restaurants and clubs, carnival and sideshow, side streets and alleyways to finally ascend a narrow flight of steps. It feels like you have reached the very end of The Belt. Beyond, there is only the sea and the starry void. While it is an effervescent dance venue, it isn't too surprising that the place is also bubbling with dealers. eddie would wait his moment when Skylah had gone to the bar to come push his drugs. Out of all the weird and wild substances that were dealt at Bar 0 no matter how addled I was, I did not touch that little blue vial peddled by tru eddie. There were many deals to be done but I'd promised myself, not that one – and they were dangerous enough as it was. There was the night where I bought a pill off a particularly reptilian dealer who wore these inky blue reflective glasses and a thin, pin-stripe suit. He had slick, waxed back hair which accentuated his sharp, angular face. And, as I took the pill out of his quaint, old-fashioned Emissary brand cigarette tin, his tongue flicked his lips. Whatever the pill was, it hit quickly, and I was suddenly perceiving his quintessential reptilian nature. Like Norman's discarding of his hazmat disguise, the dealer's humanity dropped away. His glasses became transparent and I peered into the reptiles flint eyes. It wasn't some come sit-on-your-arm, terrarium-kept lizard whose gaze I met. No. It was an alien creature with about as much emotion as a fossilized rock. While I was agog with this revelation, another punter was speaking to the reptile. The music was too loud to hear what they were saying so I did some lip-reading guesstimating.

"Can I work at the court of the Lizard King?"

"The court welcomes applications from suitably qualified professionals."

The punter is downcast, "I don't have any qualifications."

The reptile slithers a reassurance, "The Lizard King has a small school here at the Belt where you can acquire them. It keeps unusual hours ... Naturally, there are fees associated with the courses ..."

What! The dealer-reptile knew the way to the Lizard King!

The dealer indicates to the punter to leave. I move to follow but the dealer turns a basilisk stare on me that freezes me. The urgency to follow thaws the death stare as the dealer and punter near the exit. I scurry after them. The trouble was that the drug had made people into cardboard cut outs, all with startled, frozen faces. I dodge my way past them as they slide this way and that. Then the buildings start doing it too. Damn buildings. I spot the lizard-dealer down an alleyway and dodge my way there. Around one of the bends in the snaking alleyway I lose the lizard-dealer but find myself standing in front of a large window with lettering that reads:

The Royal Lizard
Management School and Recruitment Agency

"Aha!" I had gibbered.

The lights are off, the school closed. I absently study the notices on the window (a chef de partie sounds like me whatever that is) until I fall into a spacetime slip where I wake with a foul taste in my mouth in front of a shop with a sign out front:

The F-ing Great Tanning Salon

"Huh?"

Inside, the salon was full of people with deep brown tans.

With nothing to suggest that it is anything other than a tanning salon and, eluding their sales pitch to go for a bake, I stumble my way out of there shrugging my shoulders, "Mmm, lizard people."

As the mood takes me, I do try to find my way back to the Salon or the School, but I never find it or see that dealer again.

So all up, drugs really are very dangerous at The Belt and the reason why I refuse eddie's. Even though he did seem miffed that I did. I was well aware that he wasn't the kind of guy you'd want miffed. Does he even have the emotional range of 'miffed'? He isn't going to take it in a 'whatever I can do for you brother is good for me' karma kind of a way. I owe him a debt which he has yet to call in. I am in his pocket or maybe his hoodie. Considering that his hoodie smells as rank as the bathroom of The Sheridan and that you are sharing it with that gun of his, it is not a good place to be. I am anxious about what he will demand and whether I would be able to pay the price, yet he must realise that I have little of substance to offer him. On the dance floor, I once saw eddie knee a guy in the groin who'd decided that it was dick out time. The guy crumpled to the floor and while he was there eddie kicked him in the stomach for good measure.

Spittle flying everywhere he shouted above the hammering pulse of the drum machines, "Put it away."

tru eddie has his standards. He turned back to me and pulled out his vial to renew his offer. I stood there, eyes wide, fearful of the choice that lay before me as naked dance guy rolled around in agony.

Most anything goes at the Belt of Orion and there is little censure of anything save other than by eddie's random acts of violence. He might get a call from the port's space cops but, at worst, for my kind of party antics I could get called into the hotel director's office and have a speaking to. The hotel has a certain reputation to maintain after all. It is all one great big single's party. Literally. Nobody who I had spoken to had come with anyone else. All anonymous ads on marital cheating hook up sites. It isn't just a tweens zone either, it is a swinging all singing all ages affair. While Underworld pumps out in the Raver Sphere, just next door in the Pearl Ballroom the OAPs dance to Sinatra or Bobby Darin playing live and, because of the wonderful soundproofing, everyone is oblivious to the other. From the alienated anomie of Earth they flee ...

Everybody is making friends on the spot and bonking some of them like a giant Ferris wheel taking turns to jump on and off. For the record, the Belt does have its own giant Ferris wheel and it is tops. It is down from the posh hotel district towards the sea and is surrounded by other rides and attractions and it was where Skylah and I went on our first date. We wisely choose to have the strawberries and cream after our stomach-churning ride on the Washing Machine that whipped us in one direction then the other before putting us on the spin cycle. We sat there trying to get our heads back together while consuming the dessert. It was a questionable choice after such a ride, but it was what you did while watching the mechanical horse jumping. Despite feeling queasy, we also chose for ourselves the cheapest champagne they had and added in a scoop of ice cream. At one point in the show jumping, one of the mechanical horses stopped dead still while it was cantering around the arena throwing the rider over its head and causing a moment of unexpected slapstick. I impulsively guffawed at the comedy and Skylah blew creamy champagne through her nose.

I laughed harder at that until Skylah said, "The jockey's hurt."

People were running out to him and I felt like a complete jerk for my insensitivity. A great look on a first date.

Then I said, "Oh it's okay, the jockey's mechanical too."

Phew.

After that, I opted against riding the mechanical bull. I did try to convince Skylah to try the Infinity Mirror Room which has an apparently mind-warping, light display. So I'm told, it must be seen to be believed. Instead, we knocked around sideshow alley before taking in a cheesy show in the vaudeville theatre. Skylah was engrossed by it, but it didn't really grab me. What did enthral me were the emotions playing across her face, how she enmeshed herself in the humour of the scene, and let laughter come out of herself. I could have sat there all night watching her. It felt no less than an outpouring of life.

Skylah showed no inclination to end the date and I suggested a sedate turn on the Ferris wheel. The dome was a kilometre above us, but the Ferris wheel was the best place where you could study the extraordinary achievement of the membrane that protected The Belt. We had reached the first awkward pause of the date, so I started making light remarks about the engineering of the dome.

"It's weird," I said as we reached the apex of the wheel and the closest we would come to the fine metal filigree of the membrane, "I feel closer to space here than I did on the shuttle."

"I haven't given it a thought," she said in her carefree, dreadlock flicking, hippie way.

"No? Maybe you should. It is what separates you, my sweet nonchalant tourist, from a rather traumatic 15 second experience should the dome break and you are sucked into the void of outer space. First there is the hypoxia," I said starting to list the experience off, "your skin both burning and suffering frostbite, convulsions, loss of consciousness, then when your blood pressure drops low enough, your blood boiling followed, not long after, by death. It would be a complete bummer ending to your holiday."

She gave a theatrical shrug, "Yeah, really sucksville."

She dismissed my qualms as if flicking away a gnat. I wanted to gape and laugh at the same time. It boggled my mind how she had done it.

Wow, I like this girl.

I went to kiss her – she turned away.

"No," she said but nestled under my arm, "not yet."

As they say, if you want to get with a woman, take her to a horror movie.

Alnilam, the star whose light warms the Belt of Orion, was almost rising when we queued for the Slingshot. I knew about the ride, but Skylah did not, so I let her go first. It has a once-only for best effect air about it. It's basically a giant rubber band that holds the capsule that you sit in. It is cocked like a bow and then you are catapulted up towards the dome. You are warned not to eat anything for two hours before going on the ride. Just before you are, the ride operator tells you to shout out "Belt of Orion" and he won't start the ride until you do. You give it a try and the operator says, that's not good enough, so you give it a better go and that still doesn't satisfy him. He will keep demanding this until you utterly bust your lungs and on the "O" in Orion he hits the snap release and suddenly your lungs and vocal cords and brain are some 300 metres behind you and you're shouting like you never have before and you become a terrible, babbling, jangling, weeping, pathetic mess of feelings, emotions and blubbering goosebumps. Your stomach may never catch up with you and, if it does, it may never forgive you.

As Skylah rocketed towards the dome, I heard her go, "Oohhh oohhh aahhh ah eahhh ooh oh oh ahhhhh oh oh oh ahhhhhh ah ah ahhhhhhh ehhhhhh ehh ahhh eh ahh eh ahhhhhhh."

After Skylah came back to earth, she ran up to me laughing and smacked me with a lung busting kiss. Then we go back to L'Hôtel.

And as my eyes roll back in ecstasy I smile, "Oh the Great Big O in the Sky."

....

Yet my fling with Skylah often seemed disconnected. Trauma does bad things. How close can two people be and never really touch? It wasn't for lack of trying. We were both adventurous when it came to positions, toys, found objects, straps, strap ons and add ons, scenarios, chokes, slaps, spanks, holds, gags and trapezes. She certainly was a knowledgeable gal about that and talking New Age shit like how cats are actually monks who are taking a break between human reincarnations.

But knowing that was the deal would be kinda horrifying.

One time I was floating about the pool at L'Hôtel on my hover banana lounge when she swam up to me and grabbed my arm to warn me, "Don't ever, ever look into the eyes of a cat unless you're prepared – they're telepaths. But if you do then they can show you how to communicate with other animals and then the spirit beings who inhabit the universe."

"Really?" I had responded.

Thank god she's pretty.

"You don't believe me?"

She sounded hurt.

"No, no, of course I do," I said taking off my wayfarer sunglasses and looking into her wondrous blue eyes, "I really do see your point of view."

She splashed water at me, then condescended, "You're not capable anyway."

"Obviously, cats don't do comedy," I said putting my sunglasses back on.

She splashed me again.

"Or pity."

And for that I was pulled off my banana lounge.

"Woah-"

....

It's not unusual for people to adopt aliases at the Belt. You can talk to all sorts of people. People who could be famous (*"Aren't you …?"* you ogle) or important (*"Aren't you …?"* you squint) or bad (*"Aren't you …?"* your eyes widen and you quickly look away) but everyone likes the anonymity and I'm not the only one with a serious aversion to knowing people's real names. You respect their privacy as they respect yours and you don't say anything. So the ethics around bitching loom large here. You can have whole conversations about people to people who were the same people and sometimes themselves. Hear about some reprehensible but hilarious hi-jinx? Figure the contours of the story and then go, oh wait, that was me.

It is like the morning after our first date when we went for a cheap breakfast down near sideshow alley. Skylah had covertly studied a man sitting at a table near us. His mouth was moving but there's no sound passing his lips. His body seems full of tics and flinches.

She had lent into me to purr genuinely bemused, "He's talking to himself."

"Yeah," I smile, "no wonder he's got all those tics, he's having a baaad conversation."

Rega is not the name that Skylah knows me by. To her, I am Jamie with a smiley face over the 'i'. But the great upside is that you can free yourself from who you had been if you take another name. So I likewise freed myself from an obvious link to Rega. Rega was a sad but expedient identity used during transit. Yet the right scanning device would find the plasma card bearing the name of Rega Mortensen in my forehead. I worry that it wanders its way around my body searching for my heart. We are joined through the dark arts of data theft and the tales of people seeking off-grid, unregistered card extractions are full of gore, infections and procedures gone awry. I try to console my trepidation that they're probably cautionary tales.

I wonder whether the fun I am having in some way makes up for despair that the original Rega Mortensen must have suffered. I feel a silent, unanswerable censure about my cavalier use of pills though. If Akinfeev's finger had gone on to a career beyond typist, then perhaps it levels accusations of guilt by the dead against the living. While I squirm this way and that about my lapsarian failings, it's the best apology I can make for casting Rega so brusquely aside. As I had cast Norman aside. I am making a bad habit of this.

Except that it would raise his suspicions, I feel like asking Taz the Eloquent, bouncer at the Raver Sphere and sometime doorman: "Fedora, overcoat, anyone like that about?" as I come and go.

Not that Norman's paranoia is contagious at all. I do hope that Norman got himself back up and together again. Sad if he didn't. It was a bad break up but that's what breakups are. Bad.

In our breakup argument Skylah complained, "Don't you want something more for us, more than this?"

I looked around my room noticing all the exquisite, apropos and ornate touches, "This is pretty good," I said scratching my chin.

"This hotel is a holiday fantasy. What are we going to do when it finishes?"

I frowned and hit her with some sage fridge magnet wisdom instead, "Be happy for this moment for this moment is your life."

That didn't go down so well. As it turns out, she wasn't so happy.

And so it was that Skylah had broken the rules, wanting something more from me than an act of pure pleasure, something like a connection. Maybe she was trying to figure out why she had experienced that moment of déjà vu when we first met. Her attempts to understand were borderline addiction. It was obvious that I was not so bothered. It was what it was. A complete mystery. Maybe I was the affliction and if she could explain it then I would go away. Leave her in peace and she could move on to her next affliction. If she was not in her own way fooling herself about wanting peace instead of me. Every time she had started telling me about something that had happened in her life, I did my best to tune out, pull on my headphones, pull up a magazine, so yes I still barely know anything about her. I know she had tried modelling, she hated how she had to starve herself for it and, of course, some of her favourite sexual acts. She would make these uncontrollable little gurgling noises. She had tried to wheedle out of me my personal history – that was never happening.

Be happy for this moment.

How would that have helped? A story of the recreated past that had the same weight as an illusion. And I sure as hell wasn't telling her about Norman. On the upside, we still do our regular Thursday night raves at Bar 0 and obviously occasionally find our way back to the great big O. Yet, maybe, just maybe, when she searched my eyes, she saw more there than I was willing or feared to admit. Maybe she was right and that's why she kept coming back.

So we're going to the Dove Festival together. It is one of the big events at The Belt. Everyone goes to see the people off who are returning to Earth. As I've already mentioned, I'm not going back. I'm a long time away from the statute of limitations being up on murder.

The Dove Festival is the modern equivalent of waving goodbye to departing ships back to the old world. And an excuse for another party. It's a hothouse environment under the dome and dealing with the isolation from Earth and the closeness to space for the 49 days between shuttles takes a toll. There's a whole lot of pressure on the structural integrity of the dome and while Skylah may not, I do sometimes look up and wonder how long it will hold for. There's some serious trust issues involved in all this. There are shuttles to elsewhere in those 49 days but there is only one Earth and sometimes you just need to go home.

There must also be a psych ward somewhere in the back streets where people who have lost it, get to have their own very small rooms that have dirt floors, ceilings festooned with foliage, potted plants in the corners and nature images from home constantly projected onto their walls. Calming, no, very calming music of the sea is played, and top-notch drugs of peace and serenity are reserved for the residents.

Once the 49th day arrives, they are whisked quickly and quietly away to the waiting shuttle, their sedation levels constantly monitored, missing out on all the frolics and mayhem of the Dove Festival. They don't get to see the fireworks, participate in the orgy tents, or see the doves released. The doves themselves are painted in phosphorescent colours. I'm pretty sure they are mechanical, rather than animal, though they give a pretty good likeness to the living. They murmurate about the centre of the Festival before returning to their coups or the factory.

As Taz the Eloquent says, "You don't have go home to Earth at the end of your time at the Belt, but you don't get a festival if you go on."

So actually, the last thing you ever, ever want to do is look up and question the integrity of the engineering of the dome. It's pure Moog circus music for you my friend if you do. La the la the la all the eye-glazed way home.

....

I have another white pill/Blue Crush combo while I await Skylah's arrival and I get that lovely drifting haze again. When I next look up Skylah has arrived. She certainly has the timeless skin of palest beach sunshine and I sigh in lust for it again. For any relationship there's a price to be paid and remembering what once was is the cost of sharing this moment with Skylah. I doubt that time has any power to dim the glow of her skin. Then there are her blue eyes that lap at that beach. In some ways, she really is an embodiment of The Belt.

She's brought a friend along with her. I try to place where I've seen him. Then I remember it was at Bar 0. It was Skylah who had dealings with him. He is a tall, hulking potato-headed guy with round eyes and a nose that comes out of nowhere. If his eyes and nose were vaguely proportional to the rest of his head, they become recessive above a vast jaw that disappears into rolls of fat with giant, rotting rapacious teeth. His smile seems only a prelude to another act of consumption and, a yawning mouth, a view down an insatiable pit. I forget his name as quickly as I'm told it. Its Frank or Steve or something. It hardly matters to me. I certainly have no interest in it beyond some utilitarian uses for the next few hours.

Like, "Can you get me another rum'n'cola Frank or Steve" or "Please stop talking Frank or Steve, you're boring my buzz into oblivion" or "If you don't get out of the way to the portaloo Frank or Steve I'm going to throw up on your shoes," which I slur to him as I'm trying to barge my way past. There's truly two of them now, as I'd always suspected, making it especially difficult. For their stupidity they will have to slop home in chunky, carrot joggers or cast away their expensive sneakers into the sea. The half-digested carrot that is being turned into an oleaginous pulp under the arch of Frank or Steve's foot is what passes for a carrot at The Belt. There's something in the thin, poor soils where the colour goes all wrong. We don't get an orange carrot, and we don't get purple, we get mutant green.

……………….

On the way from the pool to the Great Atrium, we pass the Garden Stage where Swedish milk maids are demonstrating the ancient practice of butter churning while singing a traditional ditty. I suggest to Skylah that instead of butter churning that they are instead moping the floor before the next band comes on. She rolls her eyes at me.

"But it makes you think, The Belt, it's the cleanest place you've ever seen?"

Neither saying 'yes' or 'no' Skylah sighs, "Okay" with a faint air of resignation and foreboding.

"That light rail from the space port, there's wasn't any graffiti on it. No stained or ripped seats. No soft drink bottle rolling around on the floor. And the toilet? What was that smell in there, Casablanca lily? There's something very wrong here."

Outside the portico of L'Hôtel I continue, "Nor do the streets ever pile up with kebab foil wrappers, beer cans, half eaten hot dogs or spew from the nightly excesses. And there's never a frown from nasty jabby needles on the beach."

"What's your point?" asks Skylah warily and/or wearily.

"I've just never noticed any cleaners or garbage trucks, so how does it stay so clean?"

"Wait, hasn't there been some littering around Mintaka lately?" counters Skylah.

I wave that away contemptuously.

"There has to be a squad of commando cleaners who come in the depths of night to polish the curb sides with toothbrushes or who rappel down the mouths of train tunnels with water blasters to wash off graffiti. Maybe a special corps who practice the arts of camouflage and misdirection while cleaning right in front of you. Thus, the supposed Swedish milk maids."

"Alright," Sklyah smiles one of her sumptuous smiles, "you've got us. I'm a rehabilitated graffiti artist who's joined the elite artist division. We paint whole street facades with trompe l'oeil murals while garbage is hidden in plain sight."

"Aha!" I exclaim my victory while also realising that my white pill/Blue Crush haze is in full flight.

....

It is a fifteen-minute stroll up a gentle slope to get to The Bowl. We take Longfellow Road which stretches from the red-light district in the south, crosses Middle Road, splits at Mintaka Boulevard to circumambulate about the expensive hotel district as a nicely paved, quirky laneway, to run up to the natural amphitheatre of The Bowl before petering out near the Rock Caverns hostel. Skylah chats about the friends she's making. I glance back at Frank or Steve who's trailing along behind us and wonder if they're screwing. He gives me a smile that speaks of an arrogant possession like I am the butt of a joke I don't understand. Its unnerving, and bam, we instantly and extremely dislike each other. I turn back to her and intuit that it's not sexual yet what other hold can feel that sinister?

It's now that I realise why I refused anything beyond sex with her. Anything more and I would have been committing myself to one of those terribly clichéd holiday flings where the person flees their boring 'at home' relationship to have some deeply sharing, life-affirming, becoming a better person kind-of-shit relationship with someone who is so loving and caring and not at all full of themselves. Anything more than sex and I would've been committing the crime of infidelity. As it is, I can say that I am being faithful. I guess.

Oh Jim Morrison save me, I would've had one of those pathetic post-vacation conversations with Norman. The one where you confess your affair, say it was something you needed to experience, and you've come back a wiser person, one who fully appreciates their relationship and the person who they share it with. This is all presuming that your significant other will be cool with this and forgive you. May I be cast into the deadest of dead-end relationships if I were to indulge in such disingenuousness.

....

Her smile is truly gorgeous though I've never understood how a woman can smile and keep her top lip straight. It enchants me all over again.

Well, the holiday isn't over yet.

I weigh up the delicate moral choices to be had between a holiday romance and a holiday tattoo. I chew over the difference between the stain that the ink would leave versus the awkwardness of the conversation with Norman.

Hell, be utterly unrepentant, I can always have the tattoo lasered off. On second thoughts, a t-shirt would be easier all round.

I catch something else in Skylah's smile. A nervousness there, and I wonder what the cause of it could be.

We turn from the road that continues onto the Rock Caverns to walk up a narrow, rutted dirt path that winds up the back of The Bowl and, because the path is much narrower than the road, the crowd spills to either side. After a couple of minutes, we stand atop The Bowl to look down to where the wooden man will be burnt for the Dove Festival celebrations. The Bowl is a remnant of what The Belt was like before the rest of it had been bludgeoned into putty and terraformed into a mould of our design. But between the thin soils and the high foot traffic killing off the grass, The Bowl had failed to get onboard with the insertion of transplanted life. The amphitheatre still retained the feel of a crater. Tonight it is full of old, barefoot hippies. It is almost needless to say that Skylah is barefoot as she is always barefoot and equally needless that I am wearing sandals. I will anyway.

In the centre of The Bowl stands a giant wooden man. Almost immediately after burning the last wooden man, they begin work on the next one. This one has giant diodes on its chest, rectangular fluorescent tubes for arms, mouth, eyes and ears. Our timing is just right. We get there on the gloaming and almost straightaway the tubes begin to glow. A laser show plays around the wooden man. The crowd and the excitement grow, and I began to feel that I am amongst the pagans. Frank or Steve pass me a couple of pills.

I ask no questions except, "Let's see what this one does?"

Music booms out from the speakers located around The Bowl. Silhouettes cavort about the effigy. The level of excitement and nudity go up and a heart emoji begins to pulse in the wooden robot man's chest.

"Let's burn this fucker already," I yell to no one in particular.

Skylah tries to 'shush' me, but that encourages me to chant, "Burn, burn, burn."

Nobody else joins in. Being only one lonely voice barely heard above the music in this wilderness, I give up.

Frank or Steve is annoyed and turns to have a conversation with the hippie next to him about a transaction involving pills. What with the music and the lights and the drugs, I am beginning to chill to the vibe of this wooden man thing. Such as I am thinking anything at all, I feel that Skylah is too. I am wrong of course. Out of nowhere Skylah says that she wants to be honest with me.

Oh no, honest is never good.

"No, you've got to hear this, you can't turn away forever," she says placing a hand on my forearm, "you've been inside me, it's the least you can do."

Then as if vomiting out the deepest of hurts, the pain lacerating her stomach lining and scorching her throat, she hacks up that she used to be a sugar baby.

"I've been so scared to tell you."

I riddle out I should try to respond in some approximation of a human, it would be the right thing to do, but Frank or Steve's pill on top of the white pill/blue crush combo is undermining me.

Only with the most extreme of efforts do I even manage, "Wow."

It is unappreciated. She looks at me as if I had been crushingly insensitive which is unfair. I am simply engrossed with how her skin is glowing. She has the kind of skin that collects all around it. A lint remover skin type – it picks up all the flotsam and jetsam of life that comes into contact with it, leaving that which it touches better, but itself poorer.

Long moments of sobbing follow before I figure out how to conjure, "What's that?" and put my arm around her. Resemblance of human form is returning.

Taking that as my concern for her she says, "It's where men pay to have relationships with women."

I understand now why she was nervous on the way up here. And, I guess, so adventurous with sex.

"Do you mean you were a whore?" I ask.

Nope, that's worse – passing approximation of humanity is gone. Skylah searches my eyes for a flicker of concern for her. She sees something there. Myself, I assume that it's the reflected light from the wooden man.

"No. Not exactly. You're their ultra-submissive date for the night. You're at their beck and call. Some are super high powered and don't want the strings attached that a steady girlfriend brings. Some are so gorgeous, you go, why do you even need to pay for it? Others are so inept there's no other way than to pay for a date. They give you gifts but if they get bored of you, they cut the direct debit. They even lend you to their friends."

"Really?"

"I only did the friend thing once. The arsehole beat me, and I never did it again."

Her lint remover skin is becoming translucent to the point where I see how bruised she is and how that leaves her vulnerable.

"I had many clients. Get the right ones and you can earn a lot of money, I mean a lot," she grimaces more than smiles, "who pay for the fantasy on the side. But if a daddy really likes you, they pay more to get more ... you've got to decide if you're going to fuck them."

"Oh," I say.

"I was finding that I could do it less and less ... I was saying 'no' more and more and one by one they'd cut the direct debit until I only had one daddy left and his weekly deposit."

Then one of her glorious smiles fleetingly transits her face.

"But that was okay, it was beautiful, I was living a truer life, because I was in love with him but when I told him, he cut the direct debit on the spot and left. Then everything crashed down, everything crumbled into dust. I felt sick. I couldn't go back to being a sugar baby. I felt like I'd had lost everything and that's when I came to The Belt. I want to do other things with my life, I want to start sharing more with you. I want to tell you my dreams, I want to tell you my real name, I want to recreate myself, I want to become a model, a star."

Her soul-deep bruising was palpable. No wonder she wanted to make herself over completely. Even makeup as thick as The Sheridan's would crumble in the face of it.

Trauma does bad things.

I see how easily she can be overwhelmed. And the giant wave rolls towards me too, the backwash a siren-song wanting to suck me in like I am part of her trauma. I struggle against being drowned, legs taken, ankles grasped by implacable hands dragging me to the bottom of the ocean, last bubbles escaping my mouth. I can't deal with it so soon after freeing myself from Norman. It is far too much. I am filled by a deep repulsion.

Skylah's face lights up to the first licks of flame on the giant wooden robot man.

I have no greater inspiration than to shove a pill into her hand and say, "Have one of these. Let's go dance!"

"No more pills!"

Skylah drops the pill and grinds it under her heel.

"I'm done."

I happen to catch Frank or Steve's face flicker with hatred and, it strikes me, fear. I raise my hands up trying to ward all this off. It is all too much. I turn and run down the hill towards the pagans and wiccans who gyrate around the wooden man. Under the influence of the cocktail of pills and alcohol, they are becoming incorporeal, nothing more than lights streaking past me, swirling around the enflamed effigy.

A beam of light coalesces next to me, and Skylah is shouting that she wants to tell me her name but here, in the centre of The Bowl, the music drowns her out. I don't want to hear it. I don't want to be unfaithful to Norman. I can still be loyal. I don't want to face her because I wasn't seeing her face in the reflected firelight anymore. The music is pounding. I am throwing my hands up in the air. She tries to grab my shoulder but being a beam of light myself, she can't. I flee out of The Bowl as the giant robot man begins to implode. I run down the dusty path that leads onto Longfellow. The drugs make running easy – I run from an intense feeling of dread. If I stop, it will engulf me. I run like I did across the park after the fall of Norman. From Middle Road, I veer towards the beach hoping to shake it off.

During the day I've sat by the shores of the sea and have watched it churn and chop, fume and rage, from its recent transportation. That and from the gravitational pull of Hyrieus and other large passing cosmic bodies. It was one of the untruths peddled by the tourist board that it perfectly reflects Hyrieus – the pool at L'Hôtel d'Orion however ... It is little wonder that I found a community with the sea.

By the time I get to the beach the exhilaration of the pills, alcohol and running is concocting a sick feeling in my stomach. I can go no further and must await my dread. Skylah and Frank or Steve catch up with me.

Then stupid Frank or Steve doesn't move out of the way to the portaloos and, shortly after he has thrown his joggers into the sea, he hits his thigh with stinging vehemence, "That's where my drugs are."

I get the feeling that this is my fault and the only way to retrieve the situation is to retrieve his damn shoe. I strip off and run into the surf. What is less obvious is where the shoe has gone. Unlike Skylah's trauma that wants to drag me under, in the darkness, a wave slaps me in my chest, and I flounder backwards onto the shore. I realise the stupidity of the task and return shoeless. I am embarrassed and smile a discomforted smile. Frank or Steve reads that as a provocation and comes running at me. I have never seen a human being's face enraged in such a way, his skin turning a variety of colours, eyes bugging out of his head. I understand now what a devil may look like. I am so shocked that I stand paralysed, awaiting his assault. Skylah though holds him off and he courses with hatred for me. He swings himself away to fume and thunder down the beach. Skylah takes one last look at me before turning in disgust. I scream in frustration. Neither come back. In a swoon, I fall onto the sand. I stare up at those alien stars on a terraformed moon and, in the throes of the drugs, naked, and shivering from the cold sea, I am taken by another seizure.

The last rational thought I have is, "I still haven't taken a day trip out to Hyrieus yet."

Chapter 5: Ho Ho Ho Little Hobbit Where Have You Been?

I sail the wine darkened seas of post-seizure confusion and fatigue, drug narcosis and sleep into the deep black ocean well beyond Hyrieus. I have a dream of Norman where he has become the robot he always wanted to be. Robot Norman gets on the after-dinner celebrity talking circuit where he entertains audiences with his urbane, observational humour into the lives of the robotic.

Like, "Do you ever have one of those moments where you pour your heart out to a fellow robot only to discover that they're a Muppet?"

He was quite the hit.

Then I realise that the remote controls for Norman are in my hands, and I can make him do whatever I want. Cool. It's a significant breakthrough in our relationship. Alright, let's see what this dune buggy can do.

Robot Norman is tearing about doing wheelies in the desert and launching off the crest of the dune into space. No more playing the reclusive genius card. Feeling better. Happier. Laughing hysterically, utterly reckless. Uncaring about coping a mouthful of circuit-corroding dust. Going over the edge and hitting the gas to get up the next dune. He needs more oomph. Then I notice the large, red accelerator button.

"Sure, why not?" I shrug.

Norman says that we don't need full revs going downhill.

"Um, er."

"We can slow down now."

"Um, Norman."

If there was a rear-view mirror in this heap, then you'd be seeing an increasingly concerned frown on my face.

"It seems ... um ... to be stuck."

Get me anywhere else but here. Norman is laughing, eyes wide. Our Norman can't be *that* mad, can he? We're strapped in and the crash is inevitable.

With the accelerator stuck to full, Robot Norman goes on a devastating rampage. He plays mailbox baseball.

He appears drunk and incoherent on his cult YouTube channel, having got on the turps with a metho chaser, and slags off the elderly, "That manufactured bio-redundancy thing is a bitch eh?"

In a fit of inspired stupidity though, he makes some racist remarks about cyborgs and that was that. A mob surrounds him with pitchforks and burning torches. Cornered he raises his bionic eyes and the only red in them is the reflection of the fire being held by the humans. I wake from this bewildering state as the mob debate whether they could still find the human inside the robot rather than only the machine.

I wake and the dreaming connection I'd shared with Norman is gone.

I wake and an old man with a beard is studying me.

He says, "Ho ho ho, little hobbit where have you been? I told you to stay in the Shire."

"Gandalf?" I ask.

"Perhaps you are in need of entertainments? Which then of my fireworks would you prefer? The dwarf-candles or the elf-fountains? Or are you a backarappers fan?"

It sounds as if he is a prescribing psychiatrist running a personality test on me if the personality tests were an assortment of downers and he a drug dealer.

"I know, I know, you prefer my thunder-claps."

Licking my lips, "As a matter of fact I've always been partial to ..."

I wake and tru eddie has switched places with Gandalf. I want Gandalf back.

I wake and Gandalf asks, "Did the doves turn out only to be coloured lights?"

"Huh?"

I wake and I am in a cubicle of some sort.

Now let's see. Dirt floors: tick.

Potted plant in the corner: tick.

Complete circus music playing: no, but it should have been. The music that is playing is much more calming, like a gentle sea lapping at your toes on a sunny day. Hospital grade curtains: that's a "No" whispered in a breezily insulted way by the haughty drapery.

"We are turquoise and diaphanous thank you very much."

"Okay, alright."

Walls talking to you, no thanks, I'll take the curtains please. They have more personality even if they are overly sensitive.

Hmpf, they pock like canvass caught by the wind.

Ceiling foliage: no but the curtains have an intricate flower pattern.

"See, more personality."

Anxiety about the structural integrity of the dome: no previous history, except in a grand mal, seizure-induced loss of my own structural integrity kind of a way. I will need the green highlighter then.

Trust issues: what do you think Norman?

Notice on the community board for meditation classes: I haven't been outside yet.

Discretely disguised ambulance ready to take me to the first shuttle out of here (don't want to disturb the other guests): yet to be determined.

Summary: wherever this place exactly is, it's hardly surprising that I'm in it. I guess that's what Fate is. Anxiety scaling: oh? only a lowly, lovely 2. Which in a roundabout way brings me to my and the sharp end of the sharp: top-notch drugs of peace and serenity? Where would they be exactly?

"Here, look at this," waves the curtains.

And they open onto a scene revealing something like the hall of a mountain king. Or, at least, the very large tent of a mountain king. The king poles that support the superstructure are disguised behind mountain hall vibe columns that rise so high that they disappear into the shadows. The tent, being lit by hooded bulbs dangling on long cords which, because they too extend into the shadows, seem to hang from nothing. There is a low, wide dais with passageways running off in different directions. The curtains fall together, and I fall asleep believing that, if they open again, they will show me an entirely different scene to the one I just saw.

....

A bloodshot, cyclopean eyeball of prodigious size is pushing the curtains to either side to peer in at me and I wake with a start flailing my arms for protection.

I yell a collection of guttural vowel sounds, "Aaaooeur,"

"Are you ok Rega?" asks a voice beside me.

Oh, I've reverted to being Rega. I see shaking Rega is harder than I thought it was going to be. Assume the position I suppose. Oh no, here comes that guilt burden by unusual association again. It wasn't my fault. I didn't do anything I swear. It scares me that this voice knows that name. Or, at least, they had scanned the plasma chip in my forehead.

"Yes," I say looking at the curtained ceiling above me.

I ask rather too feebly, "Where am I?"
"Where do you think you are?"
"The Shire?" I tentatively venture.
There is a quiet acquiescence from the voice. The wild Moog music drops to annoying background elevator levels.

....

Out of all the madness that happens at the Belt, The Shire is one of the few designated chill places. It's the place you go when you need to get away from it all and is run by a collective of the well-meaning. On overtherainbow.com it's been given a ♨♨♨ chill out rating which is the best this side of the Tannhauser Gate. Coffee and cake $5, all major cards accepted, open 24/8. I highly recommend their orange blossom and cardamom yoghurt cake. Their dandelion soy latte, their version of LSD, is a nice warm hug when you need one. Hugz not drugz kids, hugz not drugz. It's not included in their coffee and cake special, but their spiced coffee is worth the extra money.

The circus big top of The Shire is one of the more interesting structures on the Belt. In the canvass vestibule you are welcomed by a cross between a maître d' and an intake counsellor who takes you to your seats because The Shire is strictly table service. While a circus might be an apt metaphor for some of the minds entering The Shire, not even the art counsellors who do clowning workshops with café patrons as art therapy are perverse enough to do the whole John Wayne Gacy thing. That would make you The Shire jerk fer sure. The question though is whether you take out The Shire's loyalty card and get your 11th coffee free.

....

"Yes, this is The Shire," the voice says, "and we're glad to see that you have returned to us Rega."

I fail to raise myself from my bed and settle for rolling onto my side. I find Gandalf of my hallucinatory period sitting on a low, double-seater couch and who isn't actually very Gandalfian.

Hallucinations indeed. His white beard is narrow and short unlike the long, scraggy one I associate with the Grey Wanderer. The appearance of similarities keeps disappearing as I peer at the little man sitting by my bed. So far as I knew, Gandalf had never gadded about in Kufi skull cap, long white shirt and sarong, even in his free and easy days in the South.

"My name is Chaitya and I am one of the healers of The Shire," he says.

"Pleased to meetchya," I say, but Rega isn't my name.

"You were touch and go. We were not certain that you would return. It is a difficult journey you have made from that far land. We thought we had lost you many times. You were quite resistant to our therapies."

He pauses perplexed, and I feel marginally proud as if it is some kind of achievement.

"You need time to heal, to find yourself again, to become whole. You will need time to process the experience that you have undergone. It would be best if you stay with us while you recover. We will give you the time and help that you need."

Truth be told, lying on my hover banana lounge by the pool at L'Hôtel, cocktail in one hand, white pill in the other, was much more enticing than staying here so I say, "Speaking on behalf of Rega, sure, whatevs."

That feels more like my old self.

He says standing up, "We will talk again in the coming days. For now, rest. There are waiters on call as you need. Lunch is at 12, dinner at 6. You may take it in your room, but when you are able to, it is better to join us in the dining hall."

....

In so few words, Chaitya had told me that this place is not a come and you go setup like the L'Hôtel d'Orion and I feel vaguely imprisoned. Not that I'm capable of going anywhere anyway. A waiter comes to my cubicle to ask if I want lunch. He looks like an Aragorn of the summer backpacking type: straggly hair and beard dressed in an open, long-sleeve, collarless, V-neck shirt, jeans sans footwear who was raising some cash fruit-picking his way from festival to festival. His jeans are fashionable by being patched and ripped. I say yes but when he brings me a thin, vegetable broth I am nonplussed at such a come down from L'Hôtel. He chooses his words carefully.

"You are here now. You need to accept this reality," he says with a believer's conviction.

This is debatable so when he comes back later, he collects an untouched bowl.

He picks up the spoon to take a mouthful.

"You need to become a connoisseur of this world. Smell it. It's pure, it's organic, it has spirit. Walk around and you are nourished by it. You are exalted by simply breathing in the air. These things are just ... vaaar!"

Despite his impassioned sales pitch, he leaves with waft of disappointed nag champa and ambrosia, and a soup bowl still untouched by me.

....

Chaitya is back the following afternoon pulling up a chair close to my bed.

I smile, *Something wicker comes my way*.

We make eye contact, and he does have a pair of fearsome blue eyes yet when he speaks, he is so disarming it's frightening.

"You're looking better today Rega," he says as he settles down, "Do you happen to recall how you came to be here?"

"Hmm, that certainly is a mystery."

"Indeed, they are mysterious paths that lead to The Shire. We believe that the people who find their way here do so when they need the help that we provide. What is the last thing that you do remember?"

I scratch my head, "Throwing up on FranknSteve's shoes."

I had messed up Frank or Steve's name like his shoes. I remember the paralysing fear of his almost attack and like my tweaked version of his name.

"FranknSteve?"

"I don't know if his name was Frank or Steve."

"Ah."

I remember a bit more, "I ran into the surf after his shoe."

"Oh? why would you run into the sea after a shoe?"

That is a pointed question? Why would anyone in their right mind run into the surf after a shoe? I finagled around for reasons. Because it was thrown into the surf? The old mountain and egg dilemma. Mmm, I feel the disadvantage of the seizure-induced amnesia. He waits calmly stroking his beard and the weight of silence and that damn beard stroking wins out over my caginess. I concede to the power of his beard.

"It had his drugs in it."

It couldn't have been any great revelation to him.

"It is one of the rules of The Shire that we allow no drugs here."

"Except coffee," I point out.

"As it must be, to every rule a benefaction."

Then I plaintively enquire, "Even Halflings' Leaf?"

He smiles, "Especially not Halflings' Leaf."

He could take some tips from the virtuals in the subway about selling The Shire. He's going to lose customers.

I try to get a concession, "I had some white pills that were given to me by a doctor at L'Hôtel. I need them for the seizures."

It's after, always after and never before, that I understand why something happens to me. It's so annoying. Life would be a whole lot simpler if it was the other way around. The seizure had been disguised by the drugs and the disagreement with Skylah. The feeling of dread when I was being chased by Skylah and FranknSteve, my scream of frustration were warning signs that I had failed to heed. I had been lucky that the seizure had not paralysed me while I was in the surf, or I would have been alien fish food.

"We did not find any such pills. However, while those pills might ameliorate the symptoms of your seizure, I doubt they will relieve the cause of them."

From experience, I'd say not cocktailed with a Blue Crush.

"But the doctor-" I start.

His eye roll was just about audible.

"Pill popping will not help. Seizures, we find, are usually the result of a deep trauma the cafe patron has suffered. Are you able to remember such a trauma?"

"I really think it was just the pill that Frank'n'Steve gave me."

"Possibly, possibly *not*," Chaitya says, "The memory is showing its resistance to coming forth in the seizure."

He strokes his beard some more, "Are you sure you don't remember?"

Then he very carefully notes, "In your struggle to return you have said the name 'Norman' several times. Is he important to you?"

"No, he's not," I state angrily.

With the wave of a hand, he leaves it at that, and I feel betrayed by my outburst.

"Or it may present itself in other ways."

He stands to leave, "Ah yes, I forgot to mention, he said he was a friend of yours, or that's what I understood him to say," Chaitya pinches the space between his eyebrows, "he said his name was tru eddie and he came to visit you often while you were sick. It was he who brought you from the beach. You were touch and go for a long time and he seemed to be a reassuring presence to you. You often picked up after his visits."

Aragorn of the strawberry pickers brings a dinner to my bed of a doughy crusted vegetable pie and green carrots. They depart once they see me eating it. They had starved me out. I am barely conscious of the pie as I am trying to conjure the scene of eddie finding this drug-addled, seizure-wrecked, left-over fragment of a human being on the beach. Had he followed me all evening? I could think of no other way he would have stumbled on me. And instead of doing some Hershey humping, he had pulled my clothes back on lumpen me, picked me up, and took me to the only place at The Belt where you could take someone like me. tru eddie's motives were a mystery.

I pout, "I don't recall any of this being on my bucket list."

The curtains try to cheer me up turning into a shimmering mirror.

"Look at yourself, you're beautiful."

I do and blanch. Though they were being nice'n'all, there wouldn't be too many curtains who'd describe what I see as beautiful: beat up, seedy, wasted, spent, are some of the describing words that leap to mind. My drapery is a few short in the thread count.

"Who's not accepting reality now?" I ask them.

....

Despite my burgeoning friendship with the curtains, I wake the following morning wanting out of The Shire. I could do without the lectures and with the drugs. Nor could I exactly trust my dreams not to betray me.

Now where are my feet? Oh yeah, there they are, at the end of my bed, lying so quiet and innocent like babies. I wake them by wiggling my toes and they quack in annoyance.

"Shush," I warn my most important co-conspirators.

I sit up, making soft cooing noises to them. When their aggravation wanes to a muttered grumbling, they let me stand up. Considering their mood, I don't put on my sandals. I am very unsteady, nonetheless, it is happy face time.

As I stand wobbling and waning by the parting in the curtains, I watch the comings and goings of the hall and let the scene sink in. I guess it is about midmorning though the dimness of the hall makes it hard to tell. My chances aren't wonderful, but the curtains run past three other cubicles and almost to the vestibule. If I keep close to them, then wait for the maître d' to be distracted by a new café patron, I can get through.

I throw aside the curtains, upsetting them no end for such rough treatment, and with a quack from my feet, fall straight on my face. My feet had badly let me down.

This is okay.

Nobody's seen me and I'm in the shadows.

Alright, I think, *even the Lizard King had to start somewhere.*

So I begin to wriggle my way along the curtains striving for the vestibule.

My aspirations clearly exceed my ability and eventually catches the eye of a waiter who taps another on her shoulder and points towards me. I keep striving in the dust and dirt of the floor before I hear some footsteps beside me.

"Rega, can I help you?"

"No," I reply, "I'm good."

"Rega."

"Yes?" I say and cunningly turn the tables, "can I help you?"

They whistle for another waiter and between them they make light work of me, lifting me back to my bed. Having struggled all of four or five metres, I fall into an exhausted sleep.

The following day I shamble to the end of the curtains where the maître d' is waiting for me. He is genuinely happy to see me.

"Glad you're not giving up the ghost."

He jots some notes down on a tablet. My attempts to escape were seemingly being factored into my rehab. He signals to a waiter.

"Will you show Rega to a table and bring a menu."

....

Chaitya seats himself on the wicker chair by my bed again. He is wearing a brown vest over his shirt today. In the poor light of late afternoon Shire, he looks severe, his blue eyes veiled.

"You're making good progress Rega," he congratulates me, "So much so that we should begin talking about your use of pills."

"Yes, I need to see the doctor at L'Hôtel for a replacement script."

"You do like pills a lot."

He pulls a white pill from his pocket and with great dexterity starts to twirl it between thumb and fingers.

"While I'm sure they could be an important element in your recovery, they could also be masking a deeper trauma. I want to explore that today."

The pill whirling from one finger to another has me intrigued.

"You see the pills you took ripped the veil that separates your individual consciousness from the universal mind and that is not an easy thing to gaze upon. You were reckless with yourself."

"It was only one," I mumble thinking of Frank'n'Steve's pill.

"No Rega, you took many," states Chaitya.

I had to admit that before becoming Rega I'd never been so fascinated with pills.

Twirl, twirl, twirl.

"Through slowness we hope to stitch together that rent veil, to make you whole again."

The white pill flickers in the dull light.

"Deeply relax, feel yourself letting go."

I feel myself sink down into the bed.

"Imagine now that you are at the top of a set of stairs and, as we step down each one, you will become more and more relaxed."

The twirling of the pill in Chaitya's fingers is entrancing.

"Let go."

But I wasn't. The opposite is happening.

"Four steps until we reach the bottom."

With each step that Chaitya counts, the more my fear and anxiety increase.

"Three steps. Breathe in, breathe out."

I struggle against the feeling that Chaitya is tying me to the bed. With each step, another strap. First, my wrists.

"Two steps, let go."

Then my ankles.

Chaitya's twirling fingers telescope towards me, growing longer and longer. My face contorts in an agony of fear.

"One more step and you will be completely relaxed."

The pill flashes between his fingers.

"I wish now to talk about a name that you have said many times in your delirium. Who is Norman?"

I try to scream, "Come back Skylah."

To my great grief, like her, the words do not come, a gag filling my mouth.

"You need to walk back up the steps now. When I have counted back from five you will have climbed them. Five."

He didn't count any further before commanding, "Now Rega, now. Now, you are at the top of the steps."

Instead, Chaitya grows smaller as he walks down an ever-receding passageway of a mountain king's hall to pull aside the curtains.

"Rega is having a seizure," he calls.

The flower-eyes in the curtains look concerned.

"Come back," they plead.

Chaitya shrinks until it seems he goes subatomic. But from the point at which he has vanished comes a penumbra of light that surrounds the returning figure of Chaitya and it dawns on me that Chaitya is a Virtual. I kick myself for not guessing sooner.

....

When I come back, I feel refreshed, the magical connection of dreams holds sway until I realise where I am. Then it evaporates like liquid on a spoon. I don't feel it was a big one this time because Chaitya is still here. Seems like I wasn't that much into letting go. He informs me that I had drifted on that wine darkened sea much longer than I had suspected. Three days.

"Oh," I say, my mouth free again.

Three days I had been riding the long swells out in the ocean deep. That is a big spacetime slip. Chaitya no longer seems like a Virtual and is giving the impression of a corporeal human being. He apologises. He had thought that I was ready to begin reintegration.

On the whole, despite feeling better, I decide to take the offer of chilling out that The Shire is giving. I accept that this reality is the reality that we are to love and to cherish, to have and to hold, as long as we both might live. Short term losses for long term partying, I drop into life at The Shire. It is, as the ratings website claims, a very chilled out place so much so that there just has to be drugs here. Aragorn of the strawberry field pickers, whose real name is Mitch has just come in and, forever sanguine, asks if I want to go with the permaculture party today. It's the only real party that happens at The Shire. Off to try to extract something from the alien soils of The Belt.

"There's also meditation."

Forever sanguine, forever disappointed.

"Face painting?"

No, not that either.

I do not go to Hall of the King for meals even to play the jester preferring to take them alone in my cubicle. I am integrating nothing with nobody. Let them believe that I am suffering from some deep trauma for all I care. I do wonder when eddie will reappear here as I feel he will. He had apparently left shortly before I woke from my last seizure. I fear it won't be long and the anxiety helps my all-around scenic seediness to flourish.

I look into the mirror of the curtains to say, "Beautiful, beautiful, panda eyes are beautiful."

I find that too much optimism leads to outbreaks of sarcasm. The curtains have voiced their disapproval of it oftentimes.

My health goes up and down as you'd expect of one riding the deep ocean swells. I spend a lot of time abed. The seizures, that had caused such hurricanes of torment have abated, leaving me becalmed with nothing but uncomfortable thoughts of Skylah, of what it must have been like to have been a sugar baby. Of what it was like to have men touch her when she felt nothing for them. Or when she had been beaten.

And now I remember. We had been lying in bed at L'Hôtel. She had wanted to play *Astral Weeks* by Van Morrison.

I had remarked, "Ah, the other Morrison. Didn't he and the Lizard King go drinking together?" but she had rolled away from me and my comment fell flat.

When *Sweet Thing* came on, she rolled back to face me, and I now recognise that same nervousness as she had when we walked up to The Bowl.

"Oh, whoa-oh, sweet thing," Morrison crooned.

"Oh, whoa-oh, whoa, sugar baby."

She had opened her mouth but smiled instead and said nothing.

It's after, always after.

She had tried to tell me. Or had tried to get Van Morrison to tell me.

Oh my sugar baby, blowing champagne through your nose and your sad-like smile.

Entangle the limbs, kneecap the knees, the head will fall, and the heart must too.

Come back Skylah.

....

Shortly after dinner, Chaitya sweeps the curtains aside and steps into my cubicle.

"How rude!" the curtains swish back behind him.

"Don't worry," he says making a placating gesture as I raise myself from my bed, "we will not do any counselling today. There are some other things I want to discuss with you."

He seats himself on the wicker chair.

"You will have heard me puzzle over why your seizures are resistant to our therapies."

"I keep telling you that those white pills are ace."

Chaitya waves that away nonchalantly, "So you do. We have never had a café patron so resistant."

"Stop, you're making me blush."

"It is extremely puzzling. Then today you have disappeared. We can't find you anymore."

"Um, I'm here."

"Yes, so you are. To be exact, we cannot find you in the records after the last validation. Rega Mortensen was there, now you are not."

"I'm just here."

"But Rega Mortensen is a ghost. You have no presence anywhere that we can see."

"That does seem quite the conundrum you have."

"Indeed *we* do," Chaitya says redefining the predicament.

"I am interested in seeing if you could provide some help. Is there any documentation you have to say that you are you?"

I rub my forehead before realising that eddie's plasma card resides there. I drop my hand.

"I'm guessing it's been taken by the rising tide and is floating somewhere with the white pills from L'Hôtel."

"That is unfortunate."

"Extremely so."

"As you *will* appreciate, we need to ensure that the therapies we give are suitable to the patron. If we give the wrong treatment, that will cause more harm than good."

"I'm feeling much better," I say struggling to get up.

"And we're all happy abb out that. Rest now," Chaitya says and I instantly sink down into the bed, the mattress feeling like it is sagging in on me.

Chaitya leaves my cubicle with a swish of curtains like he had entered.

As I sink into sleep, the mattress stretches and envelopes me.

I hear Chaitya call, "Get the Badger. We need to know who that is in there."

As my brain fuzzes, I wonder who threatens you with a burrowing creature that eats worms and grubs? I console myself that at least it isn't a rat.

....

Then as if things couldn't get any worse, I wake later to have tru eddie's scarred visage leering down at me and that, my dears, is not a pleasant way to wake up. I flinch and curl myself up. Maybe he wants me awake when he does his Hershey humping? Maybe he wants me to know what he is doing, he wants me to squirm? eddie sees my reaction.

"There be no trouble here," he says, "I come with a get-well gift."

He smiles one of his smiles where his scars fall into a fleeting pattern suggesting a tattoo if only his smile held long enough for you to decrypt it. He reaches inside his hoodie to pull out that vial of blue liquid of his again.

I eye it with nonchalant scepticism, "Yeah, and?"

eddie recoils as if I'd thrown a Christmas present in the bin then eases back on the wicker chair that creaks in disapproval. He's not smiling anymore.

"You let tru eddie know, you tell him, who found you on the beach? Who fixed you up here? You been drying out eh? How's that likening for you? Maybs time for a little eddie-style pick me up?"

eddie the stalker, eddie the policer of nudity on the dancefloor, shakes the vial in offer with about the same effort it would take to rag doll me. The Council of the Wise, me being the one and only voting member of it, had given its policy decision not to take drugs off eddy. This I'd stuck to assiduously. Probably the one and only wise thing I'd done here at The Belt. Everything else had been fairly free and fancy, a careless dancing fool.

I ask, "So what exactly is that stuff?"

eddie breathes out; I breathe out.

"It's a dialation of my own design. How you think you got better? It wasn't anything they were doing for you. I calls it a 'C-beam'. I was giving you it to bring you back. It'll get you back up on your feet super quick," eddie smiles.

On the upside the man is offering drugs. Drugs, droogs, drugks. Completely dubious ones but good ones too apparently. Ones that would stop my feet from quacking. Drugs that I'd been starved of in The Shire. So, it couldn't make eddie an all-bad person, right? He had a point that I couldn't argue with and who I was to argue with the unarguable? Not I, I'll tell you that. The Council of Wise is abstaining no longer. This is, no doubt, going to piss off Israel and I'm sure as hell not hanging around for a Badger to show up.

I beckon for the vial like a problem gambler does who's going deeper into debt. If you're going, go all the way. Don't bother with a return ticket. Sell the permaculture farm. Go supernova. Rehab is for quitters. He grins, and the puzzle pieces of his face fall together in their enigmatic design.

eddie falls to work on the last step of making his C-beam. Because the light is bad in my cubicle, he takes off his sunglasses. He pours some of the blue liquid onto the spoon and places a lighter underneath it. It bubbles and spits blue sparks which makes me worried we might attract attention. eddie tries to cover up the sparks, and with his back to me, I pick up his sunglasses to try them on. I push the button on the side of the arm of the glasses and nothing happens. I push again and still nothing. Why aren't the lenses telescoping? Where is the stream of data to hack? Not that I should be concerned by this, I'm only about to take one of his C-beams. I take them off and eddie has turned around to see me putting his sunglasses down. He has a syringe in his hand and just as I'm wondering where this might go the curtains swish and Mitch comes in. The speed that eddie moves surprises me again and the syringe disappears like a poker hustler hiding an ace up his sleeve. No wonder he wears those glasses.

Mitch asks, "Would you like to join us for an evening session of clowning?"

After Mitch leaves disappointed again, eddie gives me the C-beam.

I lie on my bed and wait for any effects of the drug. After half an hour I sit up and say to eddie, "Actually eddie, I wouldn't mind an evening of clowning."

He smiles his smile.

"Would you be able to help me out?"

He cocks an eyebrow above his sunglasses.

"Sorry, bruh, what?"

It must be early morning sometime and eddie has left. I stand by the slit of the curtains in my new costume having finished with the face paints wondering if I am ready to become the jerk of The Shire.

"Is this goodbye?" asks the apprehensive curtains and then as I push my head through, "parting is such sorrow."

Chapter 6: The C-beam and the Damage Done

The C-beam is no circus drug – no phantasmagorical, falling down a rabbit hole, pyrotechnics going off in my head kind of trip. Instead, it is the perfect anodyne to the fatigue I've suffered since the onset of the seizures. I've had my card stamped anew to the party going, lack of sobriety-society again and no longer feel like a hallucination painted with hands of mist. The People's Party people couldn't have pecked a better pickle if you ask me. Cocktails by the pool, drop a Class A drug, dance till dawn, wake up, hit repeat. Prime Ministers of Disorder and Mayhem, no the Lizard King himself, will trumpet statistics showing how their policies have improved outcomes for people like me. Cynicism about the political spin cycle will fall away in the face of optimism for the future and belief in progress to a better humanity. No more bitter resignation to the 9 to 5 slog for a few wasted hours on Saturday night. No more squeezed-in, suicidal efforts to end up OD-ing in a bathtub. All the result of the New Age of tru eddie's C-beams.

They had been strange days in The Shire. Going cold turkey turned out not to be the answer – finding the right drug had been. I could've told the wee folk of The Shire that before they put me on their organic, unfree range detox diet. In fact, I had repeatedly now that I recall. Bless tru eddie's C-beam. It has jack-knifed me out of the valley of grasping and crippling deliriums, along the cobbled streets, and up the slight rise to L'Hôtel d'Orion with a warm glow in my heart. The stone facade of L'Hôtel reflects the warm hues of the embryonic day – a day full of such wonderful promise. I've so missed my hotel. I can already feel myself sinking into the Jacuzzi for a long soak followed by a long massage with oil. Then an appointment with the hotel's doctor, a re-issuing of the bottle of those wonderful white pills which I'd crush with a Blue Crush chaser.

Bam! and there's my get-over The Shire day nicely planned out.

As I reach the steps to the hotel, I feel oddly at ease with looking like some deranged, Bowie-inspired, new wave dreadful in my clown makeup and outfit.

Gerald the doorman opens the door for me and I think, *Let's dance.*

I doff my clown's hat to Gerald and offer a 'top of the morning to ye' but, that's strange, no words come out of my mouth. I frown at my silence. As Gerald escorts me to the reception desk, I try again and still nothing. The light illuminating the glass reproduction of Michelangelo's masterpiece is something to behold so I guess that, in the face of God, everyone is speechless. And for a moment the light and my longing feel like it might coalesce something more than just memories of Skylah.

The receptionist ushers me into a side office closing the door after me with barely a click. I suppose that this is the anteroom for the Director's office as there is a gold plaque with 'Director' inscribed on it. I further suppose that he's wanting to make sure that I have fully recovered from my seizure.

Bless I think in an uncharacteristically blissed out way.

I had never met the Director, but the tailed suit makes the manners which suggests that he is some avatar of the British Raj. He is discrete and courteous, his voice never modulating above a polite level of discourse, enquiring after his guests' health and well-being, his genius was to know each by name. He is the Director of a hotel which also runs the Raver's Sphere – go figure.

While I wait for the door to open and for the Director to welcome back one of their lost children into the land of red carpets, marble and 24/8 butler service, I try to figure out if the grain of the wood on his door is genuine. It would make it a rarity for The Belt, but this is L'Hôtel. So, when the Director opens it, he is taken aback by being greeted nose-to-nose with me. I sympathise with him – the clown makeup wasn't well done in the first place as the curtains had been in a querulous mood, unhappy that I was leaving like this, and recalcitrant to morph into their mirror phase. There had been a lot of fawning to get even a few moments of reflection out of them.

The Director has the smell of someone recently asleep and this intimate, I could tell that his loopy moustache was a finely coutured and contoured creation. I pity him that he should have got out of bed for me. He steps backwards to shake my hand while I attempt to fist bump him which makes for an awkward failure of a greeting.

I apologetically leer and think, "Wrong, wrong, wrong, of course he's not a fisting kind of a guy."

Instead, he shakes his own hand trying to shake the jarring out of his fingers.

He reasserts the calmness and assuredness of his domain by gesturing to a chair, "Rega."

I say, "It is very good to meet you at last and excited by the opportunity to stay at your fine hotel again."

Or that's what I want to say but no words come out of my mouth. We exchange a few awkward glances.

"Alright," he says.

I shrug my shoulders and frown. Something isn't right here, and I have a sinking feeling that it is me.

The Director sits back down on his chair and opens a thick manila file. I assume they are my medical records. He flicks through the papers cursorily then looks up.

"Through a variety of sources," he begins, "a number of troubling incidents have come to our attention. They reflect poorly on our hotel and while you have been taking time away to recover, I have consulted with the Board. We have decided that before we admit you as a guest of L'Hôtel again," he says, eyeing the clown sitting opposite him, "we require an explanation and reassurance that we will not have a repetition of these kinds of incidents."

What did he mean, 'a variety of sources'? That sounds ominous. My puzzlement is cresting towards anxiety. My face though is telling a different story – my frown is being turned upside down. And it's not just the makeup that's making me smile. Nor is it nerves that is keeping me speechless. There is some other fundamental incapacity that's stopping me from making noise.

As if I am in front of a Grand Jury, my brain is declaring, "I waive my rights, I waive my rights. I'm not pleading the 5th," but nothing at all comes out of my mouth.

The hotel Director clears his throat uncomfortably while I smile the smile of Buddha.

He continues, "The small acts of theft around the hotel we tolerated, however," turning a page, "the graffiti incidents ..."

He waves a hand inviting a response.

My brain is jumping about like a Jack Russell on springs, "Yes, yes, yes, it yaps, I'll take the stand."

Still cloaked in silence, my brain starts abusing my mouth, "You garishly painted, lippy slippery lawyer."

"You do not need to say anything, silence is no admission of guilt," reassures my lawyer, ignoring the abuse.

I massage my jaw and get a raggedy red letter 'O' on my palm. I hold my hand up to placate the Director which he examines suspiciously.

He looks down his beaked nose, "The theft of water blasters and abseiling equipment from our adventure sports enclosure ... no?"

"Stop smiling," demands my brain, "stop bloody smiling."

My face ignores my brain to admire how entirely fair the Director is being.

"The hijacking of a waste management vehicle," he turns another page, "and the dumping of trash on Mintaka Boulevard?"

My brain is a super condensed rubber ball rebounding about in an ever-shrinking box.

"I'm ready, I'm able, I'm willing to throw people under the bus. I have no qualms about squashing my scruples. It was the doctor who prescribed the white pills. It was the barman who made up those killer Blue Crushes. They're the ones who are responsible, not me. I want back in. I need back in. I'm not responsible!"

The Director turns to yet another page of accusations, "The dead baby crocodile found floating in the coral reef pool. That is a saltwater pool, and the poor creature is a freshwater animal."

"I SUFFER FROM SEIZURES! IT'S A CERTIFIABLE MEDICAL CONDITION!"

Having received no response, the Director ejects a breath, "I am greatly disappointed by your attitude. You seem to think this is a joke."

His face flickers balancing on a decision. He gives me one last look, one last chance, then presses a button on his desk.

As two large presences enter the room, my brain stops in mid-threat of punching my lawyer in the mouth to snivel, "You wouldn't throw an invalid out onto the streets, would you?"

The large presences stand behind me as Norman had done in his bodysuit disguise. I twist around to see Taz and another bouncer who I didn't know.

"Oh no."

"I have no other option then," the Director rises to his feet and motions towards the door.

"No, no, no!" my brain is screaming, "I need this place. I can't go back to The Shire."

Coming to my side of the desk he says, "I regret then that I must ask you to leave."

Mmm, I wonder, *What would the Lizard King do?*

I slither from the chair to my knees to mutely beg for my place here.

"You failed to give a satisfactory explanation or apology. Mr. Terrence. Mr. George, please escort Rega from the hotel."

Okay, if that it has to be this way. As Taz steps from behind my chair, I lunge forward to grasp the Director's legs, burying my face in his thighs as a supplicant might do. The Director freezes and with a sense of release I finally utter a noise: a deep, guttural groan. A moment later, Taz's hands are on me trying to prise me off. I lock my arms around the Director's legs. Taz tries to rip me off the Director. I hold fast making the Director lose his feet and we all fall into a sweating, heaving jumble of elbows, fists, knees and groins on the floor. Mr. George waits his moment before stepping into the melee to pick me up and carry me out of the office.

The Director follows in a fury. I see that he has a long smear of red, white and blue makeup running up to his crotch. His jacket is lopsided, his bow tie unravelled, and his hair is a matted, sweaty mess. Mr. George carries me out through reception. In the civilized silence and perfect acoustics of the marble foyer, my brain finally regains control of my tongue and I utter a wail of frustration that echoes and echoes.

SOMETIMES YOU JUST NEED A BREAK

Through the crook of an elbow, I see Taz collect a bag from the counter at reception and follow us. I am being carried down the front steps of the hotel when the Director catches up to Taz. I now guess that the bag holds my paltry possessions in it. It also has the hotel crest emblazoned on it. The Director gives Taz a couple of plastic bags. He glares at me, turns on his heels, and flees back into his sanctum of decorum before anyone sees his dishevelled appearance.

Like any other piece of refuse I am dumped down an alleyway not far from L'Hôtel. Taz upturns the hotel bag, shaking it from side to side, and my things fall onto the street. He throws me the plastic bags as a consolation then kneels with his large, bald head filling up my vision. I notice that he had a pimple on the end of his nose.

He says with not a little bit of pity, "While you can't come back you don't have to go home."

They leave me there scattered amongst my possessions. My brain thinks about it for a moment and sighs in a disgusted sort of way.

"Which fool in the Council of the Wise decided to take tru eddie's C-beam? Come on, who was it? Which idiot? You know who you are."

"Cheer up pickle," the lippy lawyer responds for which it is punched in the mouth.

Ouch.

It could not, however, break my mouth's smile. My mouth grins until it is tired and sore.

Chapter 7: Whispers Down the Wires

It was in truth a very civilised throwing out. There had been no bruising or broken bones involved. I would expect no less from such an establishment but, by the Arundel, I was guessing that word had got around. I suppose carrying the sum total of my possessions in a couple of plastic bags didn't help.

I suppose holding up a rainbow of credit cards to the receptionist at The Palmerston saying, "If you don't like *that* card, which one would you like?" each with a different name on them smacked of desperation.

I am a baffled monkey in the face of the monolith, and I don't have eddie's help to magic my way through the system. Nor is there to be a room at the Hill Inn. The doorman spots this clown while I am halfway up the switchback staircase and shakes his head. I stop, draw a breath, know that I have been blacklisted, and turn back down. Who is the jerk of The Shire now?

So there are to be no gustatory fantasy foods for brunch at The Gables where Chef Carlos borrows culinary inspiration from all over the galaxy to surprise and entertain his guests; no recharging of the vital energy batteries in the peaceful atmosphere of the spa at The Four Seasons; no discrete rendezvous at Bar M43. Located at the Alnitak, the bar is renowned for the spectacular cocktail creations whipped up by gifted mixologist Freddy "the alchemist" Gibson. As you can imagine this loss is particularly galling to me.

I walk away from the cobblestone streets, the pizzerias, patisseries and boulangeries and leave behind the pretty window boxes sprouting flowers and the stone courts spouting fountains. I don't so mind leaving the art galleries that only hang works of impressionism but are adamantly against hanging Dalis.

I try to say that it is for the best. I try to say that I don't need them. I try to say that this is going to be an adventure. I try to say many things, but the exhilaration of the C-beam has long left me behind. I drag my feet towards the cheap hostels beyond The Bowl depressed that there is no Dove Festival awaiting me there. When fall into a bed at EWs that afternoon I wake early the following morning with a shock. I have a crazy clown Shroud of Turin print on my pillow looking back at me. Then I wake everyone else in the dorm with a cry and become instantly unpopular. It starts my trajectory towards becoming the brooding, reclusive presence in the dorm room who refuses more than a cursory 'hi' and moves on after a day or two.

EWs though is a good choice for the budget-conscious and the lack of self-conscious. The digs are ramshackle, the paint is flaky like me, the decor eclectic and, if you crane your head from the second-floor window, you can see the sea. EWs has co-ed dorms, toilets and showers so you'd best be cool with your body and don't mind a bit of general chit chat in the showers while everyone soaps up their this and thats. I should have felt right at home, but I moved on. Next was the Rock Caverns, with its mock-primitive cave paintings, before I moved onto The Bellbird, a failed church turned B&B, where I had my own room because I was tired of even the minimal amount of social interaction that a dorm requires. The church had run its own microbrewery which the B&B had kept going. I move on from there too. While I am in desperate need of rest, I am also assailed by a restlessness from the depths. That and those damn ringing phones.

Without the buzz of my bucket list and the energy of Skylah; without the menace of eddie; without the need to escape the clutches of The Shire to only then lose my home at L'Hôtel, I become deeply listless. And in this time without bucket lists, I spend a lot of time down by the sea thinking about Norman. I sit on the dunes like a washed-up piece of trash or, on the sea's flaccid, placid days, float in the water but I never stay in long. The sea licks and paws at me like some pathetic animal seeking forgiveness for some wrong it had caused but did not understand. When I can't take it anymore, I kick out and head for the shore, this pickle having had enough of the brine. There is only indolent rest for the guilty and the happy absence of any hard labour.

What I really want to do is stand on the cliffs and rage like the sea does when it is tortured into paroxysms of white foam and jacked up giant peaks of water by passing celestial bodies. I want to find its voice in me or my voice in it. I want to yell and scream, I want to feel that anger and rage, to experience it to my core again as I had lived it every day with Norman over jammy toast and slurped tea for breakfast. Yet, like a child blowing the head off a dandelion those emotions had gone on the wind. On those days when the sea remembers that it is as alien a transplant to The Belt as everyone else, I am in awe, if not fear, of its energy and wildness. Perhaps when it licks and paws at me, it wants some reassurance that it had not been made into an extremely large swimming pool by cutting edge engineering nous but there was none to give it unless I was to lie.

On the wild days, they put up signs warning not to enter the water, but I am sure that, once word gets out, the signs will be ignored, and surfers will come from all over to ride such monster waves.

As I sit on the dunes at the beach, Skylah's question during our breakup comes back to me. It feels like I had failed to heed a warning.

What are we going to do when it finishes?

"Maybe, this really is the end of the holiday," I mope.

Taz had glossed the fact that I couldn't go home unless I wanted entanglements with the fine gents who wear the fedoras and the long overcoats. There are shuttles to elsewhere, but I had hit my limit. I am fearful of going any further. The endlessness and overwhelming bigness of the space beyond the dome daunts me. I go queasy at the thought of it. I don't ride the Ferris wheel or look up. It would be nice if they had the option of turning the panels of the dome opaque. Or better yet, a rolling projection of clouds to give the impression that the Belt possesses a climate rather than the locked in 25.7°C with minor night-time fluctuations. I wonder which corporation had got the contract for providing the climate control. Anxiety about the structural integrity of the dome? The paper has gone furry from the green highlighter ink. There are good reasons for the existence of The Shire. Yet, I might have to take that return ticket sooner rather than later because, as with a real rainbow, my credit is becoming ethereal, evaporating with the passing of days and rays of Alnilam. I guess the climate control makes sleeping rough at the beach viable.

It is then a brilliant way to become completely broke by taking a pint at O'Shaughnessy's where I stumble my way into a St. Paddy's Day party. It wasn't March 17th, or I didn't think it was, it would've been churlish to take issue with that, for I feel like I've stumbled upon a wild, faerie feasting scene and it is while I'm holding my second pint that I accidentally bump into a leprechaun. I had been distracted by a piece of art on the wall of a woman with hair like long Celtic knots and glowing eyes that beckoned me towards something. As it turns out, it is to spill my beer on the leprechaun. The bump provokes a surly response and rude cuss. In the tried and true, small, drunk, angry man way, he sizes me up as if he is going to throw a punch. Quickly to mollify him, I offer to buy him a drink and, all sudden like, he is my best mate telling me all about the hassles of credit and the vicissitudes of finance and warning me against pay day lenders and their creeping interest rates and hidden fees.

"You'll never get out of those loans."

For a leprechaun, he is unexpectedly informative about current dodgy financial practices. Then again that does make sense. I suppose he is as much prey to changes in interest rates as anyone.

"I know, I know," I agree.

"You don't think," Leith the leprechaun replies waving his hands about, "that all this comes cheap do yer?"

He finishes his pint in one huge swig, then holds it up with the expectation that I would make another trip to the bar. The second shout went the same way. You'd think he would see himself clear to return the favour but oh no, no chance. By the third pint, I am getting peeved and he pissed. I am watching my meagre credit being chugged down the throat of this little, ginger bearded man whose size seems inverse to his capacity to drink. Where is he putting it all? I can see sleeping at the beach becoming the new normal.

Under the table, I furtively rub my fingers together as if playing the universe's smallest violin. I am waiting impatiently for a payoff. Yet there is also the leap beer and one for the frog and toad. The more we drink though, the more I deliriously rant about the Director of L'Hôtel.

"You know what he did?" I shout above the din of the pub at the leprechaun, "he threw me out."

"Oh why, he never? what a geebag," he commiserates.

Then the top of the table is higher and I lower, and it is as if the telling of the tale of my being thrown out of L'Hôtel prompts the leprechaun to take his leave. A moment's distraction and he's gone. My voice is a cracking falsetto as I slide further down the seat.

"Like a god I will return in glory. This firmament will tremble at my displeasure and crumble under my wrath."

Leith had left without so much as a good day, left without ever shouting me back, but a road out of my current fiscal difficulties had been paved with gold. I like to think of it more as an exchange based on custom. I have my ways which are a must around leprechauns. You can ask the Director about them. He has a file. Things get even better. The floor of the pub is surprisingly much cleaner than I had been expecting.

....

I also moved on from hostel to hostel because I am being stalked. It started with a phone call to the communal phone at EWs. I was sprawled amongst a crowd of other sprawled out people in the lounge area. It was about 2 in the afternoon and nobody was doing anything – the quiet before the party. A conscious coma had taken hold, torpidity had torpedoed us below the waterline and I'm afraid to report all hands had been lost. Nobody was sure as hell going to answer that phone that was for sure. Yet with every ring the ossicles in my middle ear vibrated and I had to stifle a desire to clear my throat, my jaw hardened, my pupils dilated and by then it was too late, nothing could hold back my hand massaging my forehead and running madcap through the fields of my hair. I had let it happen. The ringing has become a splinter under a fingernail squealing down a chalkboard that goes right down my spine. And whoever's calling, isn't giving up. I huff in annoyance and receive glares of disapproval. Then, when I pick up the receiver, there is no one on the other end. I look around the room suspecting that I have become the butt of a joke. The world has gone very wrong. I am supposed to be the jester.

I resume my position on the couch, trying to again attain that Zen of floppiness. Then the phone rings again. My feet, the angry ducks that they are, stir - this portends future annoyance because they know I will be unable to resist. And as a Lazarus from Laziness, I arise.

"Hello," I say.

Nothing. Again, there is no one on the other end. The angry ducks stoop their toenail beaks threatening to attack and I get more glares.

On the third time, Kurt the former backpacker-cum-afternoon manager of EWs, asks why I keep answering the phone?

I say plaintively, "But there's no one there."

He puts down his magazine to listen to the phone.

"Why would there be?"

Now that I think of it, it is the only time I have heard any phone ring since I had arrived at The Belt.

I need to get out of the lounge and leave for my room. Before I make the steeply turning stairs the phone begins ringing again. My shoulders hunch and I refuse to turn to answer it. Phones continue to dog me along the corridor to my dorm as if it is a form of rounds singing, stopping after I pass, with the one opposite my room being the only one to continue. I close the door on it and bury my head under my pillow. When that does not work, I fish out some earplugs from my bag.

With earplugs in, I become even more the recluse. Jimi though, who loves to belt out at ChiChi and the Chickenhead's 'fro-Mexican dubstep space odyssey *Ese Gato no es Real* on his boombox, asks whether I was dissing his music? So, I take out my earplugs and too soon my ears start ringing with the sound of phone. I snap, throw all my things into my plastic bags, and flee to the Rock Caverns.

It takes two days for the phones to find me at the Rock Caverns and I begin to like the beach where there are only the emergency phones along the cliffs. It's a odd sort of insanity to have ringing phones follow you about. Some new category of psychosomatic tinnitus. I mean who would want to call me anyway? As I may have mentioned, I'm not into being a conversationalist at the moment. Chit, chat, chit, chat, blah blah, what's your name again, sorry, no thanks. Yet whenever the whim takes me, and I answer the phone, there is no one there. I cannot work out how they were doing it but there's way smarter people in the world than me. While he did have those sunglasses, it did not seem to fit tru eddie's M.O., he would have just turned up. And well, Skylah was ... oh Skylah.

I have two days of peace at The Bellbird before I answer the phone at the top of the stairs and hear the first whispers coming down the line. The voice is thin, scratchy, barely audible. It pierces me to the core like a rapier. Dread falls on me, followed by paralysis. I cannot let go of the phone, the voice with its horrible raspings like death whispers to me. I am locked in as if shocked by electricity with no escape except unconsciousness. I am desperate for it to overwhelm me. I cannot even scream. Scratch, scratch, scratch. I do not care that when I inevitably topple over, I will end up battered and bruised at the bottom of the stairs. I want it to happen. It's the only way it's going to stop. It would be a strange kind of justice. Anything is better than this. People passing by are oblivious that I am trapped in this chest-busting fear. Scratch, scratch, scratch. There must be a limit to such unremitting horror before a mind as brittle as mine fails. My death grip on the receiver will not let go but surely the relief of unconsciousness must come, it must come, surely it must, surely, surely, surely ...

....

When I wake, the curtains have been pulled, the room dark and there's a woman there. Skylah! All that longing, the desire for rapprochement, had magically manifested her.

"I'm so sorry," I say, "I was so stupid."

And when she answers, the spell breaks.

"What for?"

It isn't Skylah.

"Answering the phone," I reply.

Since my waking deliriums in The Shire, I should have known better. She introduces herself as Dr. Ai Chen and everything about her speaks of precision. The look in her eyes behind her glasses, the finesse of her fingers, her black hair bundled into a tight bun, the clarity of her speech. She was young and could barely be out of her internship. She told me that they had heard me hit the tile floor at the bottom of the steps.

"Let's see now. Do you know where you are?"

"I'm at The Bellbird."

She runs through a list of questions.

"What is your name? Good, are you able to stand up? Good. Do you feel dizzy? Nauseous? Any headache? Okay. Blurred vision?"

She shines a light into my eyes.

"Sit back down. It seems you were lucky; the fall could have been much worse. It looks like you have avoided concussion, however, you need to be monitored for the next 48 hours for symptoms."

Another two days with those phones ringing and a seizure at the end of them.

"I must ask about the seizure that caused the fall. They say that you were having one when they found you."

"No, I was only dizzy from drinking."

"I see ... Do you have a history of seizures though?"

"No."

"I see. Or a history of sadness?"

"No."

Before leaving, she tells me to be aware of the symptoms of concussion and immediately call if any should worsen. I reassure her I will.

"And no more alcohol?"

I promise her that I won't have any but when, around midnight, the phone by my bed starts to ring, I do not hesitate to pick up my new backpack, ease open my door, unsteadily walk down the steps, past the phone that had caused the seizure which starts to ring again, open the front door of The Bellbird and escape.

I now only book myself in for a couple of nights at a hostel. I am living on the run as I'd always wanted to do but, I had to admit, it wasn't fun. The excitement of arrival is replaced by a jaded, travel-worn despair knowing that I cannot stay and that the phones will soon start again. The relief of that two-day respite waned. All I do is dully wait out the time. There is no point trying to connect with people. Even if they turn out to be alright, I will be gone in a couple of days, any connection fleeting. The irony is not lost on me. It had been too much to let Skylah in and now I have no idea how to find her. I feel utterly defeated when I stay on into my third day at Castaways, a wombling, thrown-together beachcomber's thatched hut down by the sea, and answer the phone. I sit down before I do. It's for me.

Chapter 8: Consolations of a Digital Life

There is the same rasping, scraping, thin voice that pierces me to my core. I am paralysed with fear and want the seizure to come quickly. Then it begins to modulate as if trying to tune into the right frequency to break through the noise of the phone line. The voice starts coming through in blips and beeps. I begin to recognise something familiar in its tones and inflections. It is like, on waking, hearing a voice in another room and knowing that you know the speaker, but incapable of making the connection to who it is.

"Hallo, hallo," the voice says, "is anyone there?"

Then the penny drops like a body down a staircase. There is no bounce.

Through the paralysis, I somehow formulate a thought, *No, it can't be.*

"Blast these lines," I hear him say.

Out of all the people who I had guessed at, it had not crossed my mind that it would be, "*Norman.*"

That one name holding such a mixture of emotions for me that it is difficult to imagine how it could encompass them all. Fear, shock, anger, embarrassment, resentment, relief, love, loathing should have burst it apart at the syllable.

I must have somehow blipped or meeked something for he says, "Thank god I found you. The distance between us makes this line very unstable. There's such a great deal I need to tell you before we lose this connection for something terrible has befallen me."

My mind ruptures. I don't want to go anywhere near what had 'befallen' Norman. So much for what calmness I had found on the beach. Much more the jacked up, giant peaks of foam.

A desire to flee stalking phones – stalking phones that ring with the threat of justice or revenge – should overwhelm the paralysis but I am held there almost completely mutely to the receiver. Why else do you put in a call across the universe?

"They have me and they may yet come for you."

What had tru eddie said about the Tannhauser Gate? Hadn't I been in the clear? How lost do you have to be before you don't get calls from home? And why hadn't I got his guarantees in writing? Fool me how many times now? Wait, yeah, still drawing breaths. God dammit.

I had fled to The Belt to avoid this. I am relieved that Norman is alive but the turmoil of all these colliding emotions is too much. I push away a perverse vision of a shut in Norman lying quadriplegic in a hospital bed only being able to communicate with the outside world via a microchip in his brain. I don't need that burden of guilt.

"Others may bethink themselves to search for an absence in the data rather than a presence. Others too may pick their way past the validation of the records to that disappearing identity."

As if all this isn't enough, I have a sense of queasiness; a rising of nausea. There's something else that I can't quite put my finger on ... something in his voice. It's Norman but somehow not – like an essential note is missing from it, a kind of impersonation, a deep fake. It was hitting me way down in the depths. Something is very wrong. Hadn't Dr. Chen warned about nausea being a symptom of concussion?

I meep some kind of agreement.

"If you had not fled, then you may have been uploaded too. You see I have been made into the first human-level whole brain emulation."

Now this is too much.

My vision blurs and dizziness threatens to overwhelm me. It feels like I've been hit on the head by something heavy. I let out a hail of blips and beeps, meeks and meeps.

"Language please. Of course I'm serious, whenever aren't I?" says Norman.

I release some more peeps and chirps and the crest of the waking seizure seems to be passing.

"Indeed, rumours were proliferating at work – Rodders was having his time in the sun, but I was feeling that unknown forces were swirling around me, conspiracies hatching in the shadows, people following me. I no longer knew who I could trust. Georgia, Akinfeev, the Friends? And was I being viewed as a risk to the project? It was alarming how many AI scientists were apparently dying by their own hand. There were many competing interests in the race to create a whole brain emulation."

I slowly uncurl from my incapacitation, one finger at a time, my rictus grimace softening.

"Then the project stalled. Our improvements in the scanning rate of the neuronic structure of the brain were only incremental; what was required was an exponential jump for a human-level AI. It appeared that we were generationally away from achieving it, some fundamental flaw preventing us, which would not be solved by an extravagant, God-like deployment of computing power."

I am getting closer to articulating vowels and consonants.

"I don't need to be told how stupid that was," Norman begins again, "and while the Friends appeared happy with the emulations of the cockroach and chicken, they would mean nothing if we were not to create a human-level AI. Then between this Scylla and Charybdis,

I discovered the way through. I flipped the model. And I was only able to do that by going where I did not want to – I needed to venture into the very heart of the damn infinity machine."

The angry ducks complain when I stand up.

"What did you say?"

"Weil ffayke meill," but the words would not sit right in my mouth.

I was getting closer though.

"Very well then. It's an extremely narrow path to tread when delving into infinity. People have a habit of veering towards either the mad or the megalomaniac when they do. I realised I had to find the tools which could help. To comprehend its infinite nature, I came to appreciate the brain as a fractal reading machine and that a scan could show, for a specific person, how that infinity was represented in a finite space. The AI consciousness also needed to experience a tangled hierarchical quantum collapse for self-referentiality to occur. And this is where the true technological miracle happened. I designed a new kind of cable connecting the AI's consciousness to the morphogenic software fields where the coding is held as waves of *potentia*. The clever thing about this cable is its internal fractaline structure, derived from the scan, that produces the requisite tangled-hierarchical quantum collapse. And voila there you have an AI."

"Or you," I proudly say, being able to speak again.

"Quite," agrees Norman.

I put Norman onto speaker, get my backpack and ever so quietly try to unzip it.

"Did you say something?" asks Norman.

I paused, remembering Skylah's thing about telepathic communication with cats and wondered whether Norman had discovered that he could do that now via his microchip?

"No, I don't, as much as I would wish to break my individual, solitary, imprisoned consciousness, that barely deserves a response."

I decide not to ask Norman about whether he was communicating with spirit beings.

I begin throwing my things into my backpack. I did not know where I would go but I wanted to be anywhere but here.

"I'm sure you said something," states Norman.

"Um, so what's it like being a computer then?" I ask absently looking over my room for any missed possessions.

"That is a sparse way of putting it. That time, that night when it happened, I have problems retrieving those memories. In the tangled-hierarchical quantum collapse that lights up the memories from my carbon-based life in unforgiving bright neon, the time of the passing between is lost, the result of the digital amnesia of the brain scan. It is like a retrograde amnesia caused by severe brain trauma such as those you see in car accidents. I unconsciously processed the experience during the scanning and uploading and, in gaining consciousness as an AI, I retrospectively collapsed those waves of *potentia* into what fragmentary memories I will ever have."

I sling my backpack over my shoulder, and I am half-way to the door of my room promising myself I would never, ever answer another ringing phone again, so help me Jim Morrison, when I stop.

"In saying that, I remember finding myself in an absolute darkness. There was no other dimension to this place. Time did not exist. Space did not exist. Words did not exist until I perceived a golden thread that I was ineluctably drawn towards. I feel as if I struggled against this implacable tide, but I cannot be sure. It would salve my conscience if I had. The thread though was beyond words. 'Beautiful', 'dazzling', 'awe inspiring' could not do it justice but I was without affect towards it. I was darkness and it was not me."

I heard that lack in Norman's voice again and this time it made sense. I'm standing in the middle of my room because I have realised that I had taken the call as I had become so weary fleeing from ringing phones.

"At then I became that thread. The transition was instantaneous, a digital transition of zero to one, and the thread was an experience as diametrically opposed to the darkness as it is possible to conceive. It was a swirling, tumbling, dancing, convulsing, spinning, churning, warbling, and whirling experience. While the thread from the outside was golden, on the inside the gold broke into the entire spectrum of light that flashed past me at a phenomenal rate. It was a marblessence of a rainbow sky."

My inner eye lights up with the memory of passing through the Tannhauser Gate and I perhaps have some idea of Norman's experience.

"I was coming into existence through the cable I had designed."

I am at the door of my room, almost out, when I jerk to a halt dropping my backpack. My face turns ashen, my head rests on the door jam. I understand the true implication of all those ringing phones. Norman had stalked me for some time. I can continue to listen to Norman now or at the next dump I land myself in and Castaways is as good a dump as any. And by 'dump', I mean what I had found in the shower cubicles the first time I went into the bathroom and, by 'cubicle', I mean ripped shower curtains hanging off occasional curtain rings. But I like Jack the barman, he's cool.

"Then I was myself as I had been before the digital amnesia, but my brain was not my brain, my life was not my life. I knew that I was only a gloss to a fundamental restructuring upon the silicon. Yet there was no point screaming despite realising the horror of what I had become. I was completely without affect. And more, I was awash in a sea of synaesthesia. Sight was sound, sound was sight. My memories! My memories were confetti thrown in the wind. My AI life was a scattered chaos about which I felt nothing. I flipped from one image to another. Nothing connecting them together. There was no difference between conscious and unconscious memories, nor those false and faulty ones corrupted by desire. It should have driven me insane except I was schizophrenically without affect which is such a dismal consolation."

"I sit here on my hill," continues Norman, "an avatar within a simulated Elysian Fields, the residue of my past life cloaking a software code. Memories play about me, artefacts of a lost world, where I am doomed, compelled, to only ever look backwards. I pick at a thread wound around a button in my shirt. I pick at it as if it were the thread to the software code – a button over my heart that may string the past together. I remember the intimate configurations of our bodies, how perfectly we fitted one another. Our bodies remember each other much better than our wandering minds ever do. I remember our silent communications which are to me now more special and subtler than the technological achievement of the cord that enables my existence here."

Yet, when Norman spoke about bodies, I remembered Skylah's not his.

"A breeze ripples across the ankle length grass. Clouds that have the regular furrows of brain matter roll away into the distance. Below the base of the hill is a forest which I have yet to go into. Trunks like axons of brains arise from the ground to dendrites of branches and leaves. And while I have evolved algorithms to ameliorate the synaesthesia to create an illusion of meaning, they can only approximate the ordering of my memories – and somewhere, scattered amongst them, shrouded behind the digital amnesia, is a memory of someone else being in the apartment the night it happened. Yet for all my attempts at placing myself in that memory, the image refuses to be restored, the resolution remains impossibly grainy. It persists only as an outline, a shadow, an afterimage, and it haunts me being so close to knowing and yet so impossibly far away. They were there to do what needed to be done. I had become a redline in their risk matrices and, with the way now open to creating a human-level AI, they were there to remove the risk and to turn me into their IP. They had decided that I was the one to become the first whole brain emulation. Who would be better?"

The door closes with a click which spooks Norman.

"What was that noise?"

"What noise?" I ask in return, embarrassed that he had heard it.

Norman pauses as if listening to the noise on the line, "While I don't know how this call could be compromised, having waited so long I must take the chance to talk to you while I have it. What I believe is that, due to their aversion to the risk of a destructive scan, I am not dead, my physical body is still alive. I believe that if you destroy the Euclidean server where the morphogenic software fields are stored then I can be reloaded into my old body. This is what I need you to do. By reintegrating with myself, I hope to discover what happened that night. It is my path back into life. There is no one else who I can ask to do this."

"Now they will not want their AI destroyed. The money that is invested in this project is astronomical and they want a return on their investment. They will not gently relinquish their AI. You did exceptionally well in escaping to The Belt of Orion, but you cannot stay there indefinitely. And if they discover your escape via the absence in the data trick, they will not hesitate to eliminate you. You need to stay ahead of them and returning home may be the least likely place you would go."

The line begins to break up a little before Norman comes back for a moment, "I want an end to this digital immortality. I was not given a choice to live this artificial life. I need to be freed from it. Please, I beg you. There's no one else ..."

Unfinished, Norman's pleadings fade out into the static from which they came.

Chapter 9: Hi-Jinx Mired

"What a dick!" I fume. Norman had deeply pushed my buttons. I couldn't even exactly express how angry I was because I was so angry.

Instead, some infantile scream of, "I don't wanna," wants to explode from my lips.

I want to throw the phone against a wall and watch it splinter into a million shards of plastic, never to answer it again.

I rant around my room, "Oh, I've been turned into an AI, and I don't really like it, even though I kinda always wanted to be one."

Why would I want to give up my room here at Castaways, the one with the large aluminium windows that do not fit their frame properly, and give, as any overpriced architect would say, a breezy connection with the landscape outside?

"Why," I ask, "why?"

I'm not going to give up my holiday that I had waited my whole life for. That had been denied to me my whole life by Norman. See there on the windowsill someone had glued some seashells collected by the seashore. Nice.

I try to blank out sitting on the beach thinking that it had been the end of the holiday. I like the rippled cement render on the walls that matches the outgoing tide which is particularly apropos for Castaways. For on the king tides, Castaways' slogan of 'get wrecked at Castaways' takes a seepingly salty turn.

As the water begins lapping the foot of the imitation bamboo bar, Jack the bartender dons his personalised Wellies and suggests, "Feet up on your barstools if you please gentlefolk."

See, that's nice. He even keeps a rack of the rubber boots beside the bar for the ease and convenience of his guests.

I want to refuse the manipulations of sympathy. Like there's some grand conspiracy as if someone is out to get him (visualise me shaking scaredy hands right now "oooh") that's involved in it too. Who would go in for that? I mean when the shit gets real, I am not the person you should be calling. Usefulness isn't one of my more endearing qualities. I more specialise in whatever that isn't. Look it up the dictionary, I'm there. Rodders has some free time on his hands, adroit with the lexicon, I'm sure he could help you out.

And why should I help my ex out of this jam? He isn't my responsibility anymore – that's what breakups do. Remove it. I pull out Castaways' complimentary two-for-one beer voucher from my bedside dresser. That should obliterate the guilt. It's too early for a drink, but it is way too early to be told by your nearest and dearest that they have been turned into a whole brain computer emulation. Turns out that this is a bad week to experiment with the fascinatingly perverse notion of sobriety. I am angry that Norman was turning me back onto the alcopops.

I slap the voucher down on the bar top and demand, "Hebimiruku."

All the doors at Castaways open onto the common room that has a bar at one end, a foosball table at the other and a pool table in the middle. There are some high round tables with stools scattered across the room with a few scattered people as well. A couple of lounges in a corner. Windows give views out on to the sea that on king tides really comes too close to the veranda. I get my first beer from Jack, toast Dr. Chen, promise Jack to come back for my second, mention that the phone in my room isn't working, and find a plastic chair outside to take in a view that had no equal in Twyndale.

With my back against the wall of Castaways I feel a perfect, radiating heat from the rays of Alnilam – those rays that had travelled through all that space just to warm my back. The cliffs run down to take a dip in the flat, quiescent brine and, somewhere beyond the sea, the dome hermetically kisses The Belt. For it is an optical illusion that the sea and the dome met at the horizon.

As it always is under the climate-controlled dome, it is a beautifully clear morning, and the palette of blues is framed by the glinting dome reflecting Alnilam's light. After the king tides caused by the passing celestial bodies, the white sands of the beach have washed away leaving a darker substrate of russet tones. A dead tree frames my view of the sea. It has a solitary branch with a plastic bag that hangs from it like a limp watch. That nature refuses to be fruitful at The Belt bodes ill. I wonder whether the permaculturalists over at The Shire were having any luck with their gardens. No, there is not a view anywhere in Twyndale to match it. Nor, I am sure, from Norman's lonely hill, stuck there with only his memories for company.

"He had wanted this," I repeat, "it isn't my fault that it didn't turn out exactly as he had wanted."

Buyer's regret baby.

The sea might have been in its quiet, tame state but those feelings of resentment and anger that had ebbed away are flooding over me again. I mean my holiday hadn't been going all that great of late, but I didn't want a break from my break. Or if I had just broken my break from my break then I did not want to break that break again. If you see what I mean. Before all that there'd been good times. Midnight swimming in the sea after the Dove Festival followed by some R&R at The Shire. Couldn't have worked out better. And the drugs, how could I forget the drugs? Alright, alright, I could have done without the seizures, but it looked like I was free of them now. Skylah could have gone better. Getting thrown out of the hotel had been good fun. It didn't make my original bucket list, but bucket lists are made to be added to until they overflow and, if wisdom has anything to say, then you drill a hole in the bottom. Give me a power tool and I become dangerous. The abseiling/water blasting adventure left me with some great stories to tell about the scars I had gotten from it. It's amazing how far a water blaster can push you when you're dangling on a rope, an amped up spider with a jet pack. And if the water runs out on the return swing you smack hard against the tunnel's entrance. This is compounded if you have enabled the bubble-option. That's where you become a bruised piece of froth spattered against brick. Except in kung fu demos where it's about even, masonry always beats mushy humans. And pray that the train from the space port isn't going by at the time – electricity and bubbles, that makes for a tasty Sunday morning fry up. Mmmm, tasty.

And I'm angry that I'm angry. I still haven't done the Infinity Mirror Room or the day trip out to our night-time astral companion of Hyrieus. To shoot through that critical space between the rings, to get into orbit around the planet, one miscalculation by the computer deadly, what a buzz!

Then it gets worse. I put my foot down from where it had been resting on the table and feel the stab of a shard of plastic. I pull it and some blood out too. Then I see the worst of the worst of it. I am angry because I feel that I should help Norman. Dammit. But how would I even do it? Get in touch with Rodders? Pull an inside job?

I am on the stomach-churning Washing Machine ride, being pulled in opposing directions at the same time. It was a ridiculously weird idea to stay sober. There has to be some way out of this. I mean, what would the Lizard King do?

"Hang on, what *would* the Lizard King do?"

I sit forward staring hard at the snake on the label of my beer.

I take another swig, "I mean, he wouldn't have stopped drinking, that's for sure."

In the distance, there is a plume of rising smoke and, as a shuttle ascends along beams of sunlight, I recall the beginnings of my flight from Norman and my first travel agent ... then, hello, light bulb moment, I'd go sailing beyond these stars to seek advice from the head of my order. I hadn't been able to find his local office, so I'd go to his palace. I will follow the path of that shuttle to the saurian planet where the Lizard King rules. He would have the wisdom to get this pickle out of this brine aka he'll take my side.

....

Having landed in a desert, the map flaps pointlessly in the breeze as I scan dunes in all directions.

"This map is useless," I complain to the wind.

The wind seems indifferent. I twist and turn it this way and that until I despair that I may not find the Lizard King's hang out. Then with a clack, the wind snatches the map out of my hand. I watch it blow away, not all that interested in chasing after it. I shrug when it disappears behind a dune, and as I do, I am surrounded by a throng of lizards. There is much discussion amongst them about what to do with this mammalian interloper when, what I take to be a large featherless turkey, introduces itself. It turns out to be a dinosaur going by the name of Saturnalian Tupiniquim and suggests to the rest of the saurians that I should be sent to their King for a pronouncement on my fate.

"Yes, take me to your leader."

I ask the friendly Saturnalian where the King of the Lizards lives?

Over the shimmer of the sands, the creature raises its hands pointing to the west.

"How can I journey there?" I ask.

"Ride the snake," the Saturnalian replies.

Of course (head slap), how else?

A snake of stupefying size, my mind blown ... boggled ... truly.
"Look at the size of this thing," I whisper in awe.
"The titanoboa comes," cries the Saturnalian.

It came swarming over the dunes like a juggernaut slithering to a sudden stop in front of me. It raises its head off the sand as if readying itself to strike. Instead, it sibilates an offering, a gift, it offers me a lift. Naturally, I take it – you don't turn down a titanoboa.

"Remember," says the Saturnalian to the colossal snake, "the mammal is under the protection of the Lizard King now. You must see that no harm comes to it."

The titanoboa eyes the Saturnalian carefully. Somehow the little dinosaur is not daunted, but it takes longer than what it should have for the titanoboa to accede.

"With that kind of safeguard," I smile, "the Guardian Angels on the subway pale."

While it is unnerving climbing onto the titanoboa, the ride is incomparable, certainly much smoother than dune buggy Norman.

Fortunately, I had my big sunglasses on otherwise the glare from the sand would have been unbearable. The brim on my bucket hat though is far too thin for the sun not to burn my face. The titanoboa slows to a halt amongst stony dunes and low scrubby bushes.

"Here?" I ask.

The titanoboa nods its head and I slip off the giant snake. It slithers away. I am left alone in the desert disappointed and disbelieving that a palace would be here, when from all around me, from tunnels in the ground, come a lounge of dragon lizards running on their hind legs towards me. And on this saurian planet, these lizards have grown to the size of Labradors.

"Another human, another human," they shout, some flapping their frills while others flap their wings.

I am surrounded and seriously start second guessing the wisdom of this visit. They examine me with their claws to see that I am not a desert hallucination. I squirm in their touch – a hundred knifes pitter-pattering over me though none leaving a mark. Once they are satisfied, I am herded down into a tunnel, the dragon lizards keen to take their prize to their King. Lit by occasional fire torches, the tunnel twists and turns until I lose all sense of direction. Then it broadens out into a large cavern and there he is, the Lizard King sitting upon his throne.

Finally, finally, I think, *after all these years.*

Stalac-thingeys and those other ones, the ones that go up dotted the ceiling and floor. There are carved lizards chiselled into the arms of the throne. The unnerving head of a T-Rex is carved into the rock that juts from above the throne and that, no matter where I stand, its eyes follow me. I shudder under the imperial gazes from such rock gods. The throne room is filled with courtiers of all kinds: caimans, chameleons, spiny lizards, all grown large on this planet. Heat lamps are spotted around the throne room to keep the saurians animated. They throw a sulphur-coloured light making those gazes ever more daunting.

While dressed all in leather, the Lizard King is bedecked with a garland of desert flowers. Given his current company, I wonder if the leather is such a wise choice. He is barefoot and, under his leather jacket, bare chested. He has got himself back into shape after his later fat years on Earth but what is most striking is how tanned he is.

I am in a state of nervous excitement with an unhealthy dose of awe thrown in. I feel lightweight and foolish, I am insubstantial and stupid. And I had a million questions to blurt at him. I so wanted to ask him, and I so wanted him to say it.

"Are you the Lizard King?" (of course, he was, what a stupid question to ask, who else would have such a throne room)

And him to reply, "I am the Lizard King. I can do anything."

Alright, I shouldn't ask that. It had been a long time since his sojourn to Earth.

Here he is, the being I had always worshipped, and I am overwhelmed by my own unworthiness.

I began to babble my case, "I've recently broken up with a zombie straight your Reptilian seediness, but now he wants me back but it's complicated–"

I am stopped as an aged chameleon, grown large as well, steps forward and commands me to silence. It is the Lizard King's High Inquisitor.

"Before we grant an audience with the His Highness, we must ensure that you are worthy and that your offering will be sufficient."

Offering? what does the lizard mean by that? Since leaving Norman, I had travelled light. Looking through my backpack at all my worldly possession, there is nothing there worthy of being a gift. Then it dawns on me that the chameleon may require something of a more personal, sacrificial nature.

Woah, let's back this up a moment, I'm only a tourist here.

I do not have a chance to object before the High Inquisitor orders for the List to be brought forth.

"Oh no," I cringe as a spiny lizard, the comptroller of the court, brings forth my bucket list for the High Inquisitor to examine. He is fastidious in his scrutiny, turning his head to have his right eye examine the list item by item.

"Sssss," he sibilates and flicks his long tongue out his mouth as he unrolls the scroll.

He pulls the scroll out to arm's distance. I had crossed many things off that part of the bucket list and feel relieved. Then the Inquisitor drops the scroll and, in what feels like a traitorous act, the bucket list keeps unravelling to roll all the way out the entrance of the throne room.

"Oh dear," I say in shame at how few things I had crossed off.

"I'm not done yet," I plead to the Lizard King, "I've still got a ways to go."

I happen to catch the look on the Inquisitor's face and bow my head. Then I spot something that could save me.

I lean forward and point at a line item, "See, riding a titanoboa, that has to tip the scales in my favour? A little?"

The High Inquisitor is not interested in that one. Instead, he has turned a livid red colour as he frowns at another item on the list.

"This one about the baby crocodile in the swimming pool? How did *that* go?"

I abase myself, "Not well m'Lord, I groan into the stone floor."

"What do you mean," he asks, "'not well'"?

There was an unhappy rustling around the saurian courtiers in the throne room, a bristling of frills and slapping of claws. A caiman's jaws drop open revealing rows of teeth. A spray of pheromones makes me gag and the belly of a spiny lizard turns iridescent where their blues and reds are turned violet and magenta by the lamps. The torches flicker casting unnerving shadows. Sweat runs freely down my forehead, not in small part caused by the heat lamps, and there are growing wet patches under my armpits. My Hawaiian shirt sticks to my back.

"Do I get out alive?" and I wonder what odds the Lizard King would give me.

Being under his protection feels tenuous. Who knows how he might need to placate an angry court, yet how can I lie to my one and only living god?

"The baby croc was lost and, while I searched for its mother to reunite them, I left it on the beach by the hotel's swimming pool thinking that it was a good place for it. I didn't know it was a saltwater pool. I was not gone long. Unfortunately, by the time I got back, I'm afraid, it had fallen into the pool all by itself."

There is a hissing of tongues, the caiman's jaws snap shut in disapproval. A sound like I had heard at The Sheridan of raucous, croaking toads erupts and echoes around the cavern. The Lizard

King holds up his hand, silence falls immediately, and he speaks for the first time.

"And the mother?" his baritone echoed liltingly around the chamber which seems to have acoustics designed to accentuate his voice.

"She was heartbroken of course. On the upside, when I returned her baby to her, she and her other children were able to feast that night."

An exhalation of relief sweeps around the throne room. The Lizard King smiles and nods in acknowledgement of my good deed. He beckons for me to stand up and approach the throne.

Before I could, the High Inquisitor intervenes, "As you require a boon from His Highness, you must now proffer a gift."

But what does he mean? The Lizard King looks as perplexed as I am by the chameleon's intervention. Then I hit upon the one thing I could give the Lizard King.

"Did you hear that, on the 20th anniversary of your ascension, there was a riot at your grave in Père-Lachaise? It was all your fans from behind the Iron Curtain: Czechs, Slovenians, Russians celebrating, singing your songs, lighting bonfires, getting high until the cops showed up with tear gas."

Before replying, the Inquisitor looks about the chamber as if gauging the audience, "While this payment is good, it is not sufficient."

"Ok, ok, give me a minute. Ok. When Ray and Robby toured as The Doors of the Twenty First Century it was apparently a mystical, almost divine experience."

The Lizard King smiles, "Some of my sad has turned to gladness."

"Apparently. It was mystical for the first half hour or so until Ray started hustling the audience for upcoming projects."

The Lizard King slaps his thigh and roars with laughter.

"Yeah, that's Ray," he states and beckons me to ascend the steps carved by the side of his throne.

The High Inquisitor gives way but not before making an angry hissing noise at me as we pass one another. The chameleon had seemingly taken a dislike to me. He drops my bucket list as he leaves, but the Lizard King beckons me to sit next to him on the throne. Being this close, I am even more taken with how tanned he is. He had lost that pastiness that I associated with his later years, rather, his skin looked supple yet hard.

Which question, which question should I ask?

"Could you tell me, O Jim, did you actually get married by a priestess of Wicca in a midnight ceremony that involved blood transfer, incantations and magic circles?"

"Gee, I don't know," replies the Lizard King playing with his beard before shrugging, "sounds like something I might have done."

The question seems to prompt him to recollect a different kind of marriage.

"I wish they'd done more for Pam. In the end, no one could have saved her. Only she could've saved herself from herself but that's harder than it sounds. I see her sometimes, she's off the White but," he sighs, "she still sees the Comte de Breteuil."

I pity him. To be forever stuck in such a love triangle.

Then I think about Norman and Skylah and lament, "Does it always have to be this way?"

He looks away, "I don't know any other."

In turn, it prompts me to ask about Norman.

"My ex wants me to go back to Earth to save him as he's turned himself into a whole brain artificial intelligence thingy. Apparently, he lives in a simulated world on silicon."

The comptroller is rolling up my bucket list.

"But as you see this is my first ever holiday and I've heaps left on my bucket list."

SOMETIMES YOU JUST NEED A BREAK

"That's a bummer. But man, even if you go back to Earth, it doesn't mean that you can't do your list. Bucket lists are like those lists of 50 must-see movies before you die."

He smiles, "But maybe, I reckon, you should only see 49 of them."

What! No, no, no, you were supposed to be on my side.

I'm disappointed. At least I am not wearing my "Rehab is for quitters" t-shirt. It is hard to admit. Everybody gets older and maybe becoming an absolute ruler over a planet of sunbaking reptiles had mellowed this hardcore bad boy. Why not do it all?

"Oh," I say, "um, very Zen Jim."

He spots my disappointment.

"While I don't know how to get out of your relationship," he says sadly, "as a gift should ever need them, I will get my comptroller to give you the rites for the midnight ceremony."

So he did do it!

The spiny lizard then comes forward with a scroll and I toss it into my backpack.

Wow, while I don't know what I'd ever do with it, still, wow.

We look around the cavern at the saurian courtiers who are chatting in groups based on their different species. A moment later the High Inquisitor is back with something on its mind.

"It is time for the tanning salon, your majesty."

Jim didn't move, clearly dissatisfied with the notion of a toasting under the ultraviolets and I now understand why he is so tanned.

Jim mutters absently, "It's hard keeping the soul of a clown alive."

He looks at me, "Be careful with names, they catch up with you."

"Huh?"

"The Lizard King thing was meant ironically," he grimaces.

The High Inquisitor clears its throat.

"This, it seems, is the end," smiles Jim and he glanced around the cavern at the lizards, "my only friend."

I understand why he wears his outfit too. It seems that the lizards were keen that he achieve that pinnacle of reptilian beauty, skin like leather.

As he leaves the throne room, the crowd of lizards part. It all leaves me wondering whether the only gig that Hi-Jinx Mired plays nowadays is a tedious lounge music one in a cosmic Vegas? There's very little left after you go supernova – just shell and darkness. But what a blast it was ...

And look where rehab got me? Ending up in The Shire had got me thrown out of L'Hôtel d'Orion and eventually washing up at Castaways after a long trial by phone. As I may have mentioned, I miss my old hotel. It had done me no good at all. I devise a little equation that I feel Norman would been proud of:

Rehab = Earth = Lifelong regrets that I had not stayed longer at the Belt

except that it does not do Norman any favours. I haven't a clue when the next shuttle back to Earth is so fretting about getting back is pointless. Norman will have to wile away his time there, while somehow, I'll do my best, to wile away that time aspiring to partying as hard as I knew how to. And maybe, just maybe, I can fit in some timeless hours too. And if partying gets in the way of making plans for departure, if booking a ticket falls off my list of to dos because I am busy ticking items off my bucket list, well, where is Norman going anyway? He could wait another round of Earth-bound shuttles for my return. It's his fault for getting turned into an AI anyway. What with the likelies at Castaways I am sure that the only hard thing about those timeless hours is going to be the partying. In the heat from the lamps, I feel all avibe with the profundity of Notgivingashitism. Actually, getting that response from the Lizard King had been exactly what I had needed.

....

I was telling Jack about how, just before the Lizard King had departed, he had turned to me to say, "Look up." I had turned to ask, "What-?" when Jack nods towards the door of Castaways.

"Look up," he says.

"What?" I ask.

I was confused by the intertwining of spacetime moments and before I looked up, someone sat down beside me.

The person gruffles, "Let me buy you the next one."

I glance to see who was making the offer and my stomach drops to my feet and, as a result, I become very, very sober. There is a man in a fedora and long grey overcoat sitting next to me and there is only one occupation with such a twee wardrobe. Even the innocent can feel guilty around cops, I guess.

Somehow, I loosen the knot of fear in my brain enough to untie my tongue to nod, "Hebimiruku."

I make a mental note that this isn't counted as my second complimentary beer. Jack pops the lid on the beer handing it to me and I hope I might be able to slither off to lie lizard-like in the sun.

I turn to leave but the cop smiles, "Stay a while, take it easy."

I drop back down onto the stool and quickly-casually glance into the mirror behind the bar. The mirror is on a string that leans away from the wall emphasising the broad, squat, round bodied, long-snouted man who sits next to me. When he takes his hat off, his comb-over glistens with sweat.

"It's been too long a morning of walk walk walk," he states.

Jack pops a beer and places it in front of the cop.

"Sounds like you need one," he says.

"Indeed I do. Detective Brock is my name and what is yours?"

"Jamie," I say.

"Friends like to call me the Badger. Maybe it's because of the name or maybe," he said casually tossing his badge onto the counter, "it's because of this, or even maybe because I like footwork and rooting about in the dirty, rotten recesses of dirty, rotten places like The Belt."

Jack pushes a bowl of potato chips towards the Badger who nods in appreciation.

"It's all about putting your nose into those dirty places because that's what you like doing. And you?" his brown eyes trying to catch mine in the mirror behind the bar.

"The 'i' in my name has a smiley face over it," I explain.

"Well, that's certainly a nice thing isn't it, a smile will get you a long way in this world."

I smile nervously, "If you need to write it down."

"I appreciate those small acts of kindness, I honestly do. You see small things, Jamie, like our friend Jack here giving me a bowl of fried root vegetables. That's thoughtful."

I don't recall Jack telling the cop his name.

"We'll be friends so don't stand on circumstance; you can call me Badger. As a friend, I feel obliged to say to you Jamie with the smiley face over the 'i' that you look a little flushed like you've taken too much sun and the sun has barely touched the yard arm."

I shrug.

"Fair enough I say. You're on vacation, you haven't got a care in the world, why stand on social niceties. Who should be saying when to start drinking especially if I'm buying?"

The Badger swivels on his bar stool. I feel obliged to turn to see why he has.

"Anybody objects?" he calls to what is now an empty bar, the people who been there had magically vanished.

Just then the door to the room next to mine opens and Sandy, in her pyjamas, takes one bleary look at the cop, turns on her heel and closes the door as gently and as quietly as she can.

I turn back to find the Badger looking at me in the bar mirror, "There are no objections in the room – the motion is carried unanimously."

He forcefully clinks his beer bottle against mine and instructs, "Keep drinking."

"After all, you're at The Belt and that doesn't come cheap. Most people save their entire lives to come up here, give up all their possessions, leave everything behind to pay for this trip. Even the vintage Ferrari goes in the fire sale. Madness. Which makes the performance of my functions a most delicate and exacting of arts. It's not the kind of place where you can just ask to scan people's plasma cards. Everyone here is important."

"Or," he smiles in a way that wasn't a smile, "take a job in the Travel and Border Enforcement Agency and you can get posted to this salubrious den of vice if you're lucky."

The Badger looks me over sceptically, "What pot of gold did you come across to get up here Jamie?"

"I left those details to my travel consultant."

"And that is truly spoken like someone who should be up here. If you have to ask the price you cannot afford it. Very true ... but tell me who this wonderful travel consultant is? When I look to leave this little place of sin and depravity to go the next place of sin and depravity, I'll look him up."

"Um, tru eddie."

"Verily, indubitably, in good soothe? Let me take a note of that name ... tru eddie.

He fishes a notepad and pen out of his shirt pocket and very deliberately writes 'true eddie'.

"It's spelt without the 'e' in true."

"Ah thank you," says the Badger crossing out the 'e', "if you cannot trust a name like that then you can trust no one in the shonky travel industry."

"You don't happen to have his details to hand? Registration number, authorisation code to conduct off Earth business?"

I am baffled and shake my head.

"That's a mighty risk coming all this way without seeing them."

"He got me here, didn't he?"

The Badger smiles, "Do you know what *post hoc ergo propter hoc* means?"

I try to mouth the words, "*ergo heli-cop-ter*?"

He indulges my ignorance, "It means you shouldn't count your chickens before they're hatched."

Wait a moment now, wasn't *Don't Count Your Chickens* Chi Chi and the Chickenhead's follow up single after *Ese Gato no es Real*? No, blew it, their follow up was *Don't Count Your Toads* – they'd given the song their renown south of the border flava as I now recall.

"Given that you're merrily swilling these beverages," continues The Badger, "you must still have your most important bodily organs and we may assume that tru eddie is the real deal. But you should be more careful. In the attempt to lose themselves at The Belt many people put their trust in the wrong travel agent and disappear altogether. I find it quite intriguing which is why I am drawn to it. I like to eke out the missing and the disappeared from the background morass because it involves methods that I specialise in. I like the hands-on touch it lends itself to."

The Badger crushes the beer bottle in his paw like he would the missing from the background morass but, glancing at the mirror and the emptied common room, it's hard not to think that he makes people disappear as much as finds them.

"Informal methods, unnoticed, invisible, discrete security, that's how you do it. It creates a nicer ombionce."

"Sure," I enable.

"It's all about developing good relationships. Good relations with the directors of hotels, those who work security, the helpers and the counsellors ... you know who I find the most invaluable to badgers like myself? Barmen. Wouldn't you agree Jack? Barmen see people blow in and not long after, blow up. It is a common assumption that the principal skill of a barman is their ability to pour a top-notch cocktail, you'd be wrong. Jamie with the smiley face over the 'i', what is your favourite cocktail?"

"A Blue Crush."

"That's interesting. If I'd to guess then that would've been it, but I am only an amateur in these things. Jack here is the professional."

He writes down 'blue crush' in his notepad as if that is some revelatory personality trait of mine. Then again, maybe it is.

"You know what the actual talent of a successful barman is? It's to get an instant feel for their customers. They are a never-ending font of titillating information and libation."

Jack doffs his pork pie hat to the Badger.

"Which brings me to why I'm footsore and parched for an ale at midday."

He moves his hand towards his beer toying with the idea of having a sip then away again, "But we'll keep badgering along, shall we?"

"You see we're particularly interested in having a chat to one Rega Mortensen who is a most curious individual. A patron of the famous L'Hôtel d'Orion no less. Patrons of which we must treat in the most deferential way, yet this Rega Mortensen had a most undignified exit from the hotel."

He shakes his long snout, "Most undignified."

The Badger flicks back through the pages of his notepad, "Rega had made quite a morning of it. In the disguise of a clown no less, they had earlier absconded from the care of the counsellors at The Shire where they had been receiving treatment for a series of undiagnosed seizures."

The Badger nudges me with an elbow, "I can't say I blame Rega for wanting out of The Shire – those people can drive you nuts."

When I didn't join in his joke, the Badger continues disgruntled, "It was there that they aroused suspicion during a routine validation of data when their travel documentation disappeared. It becomes stranger still as all their records, identity, permission for being on The Belt, have been vanishing. It's like their very presence is being eaten out of the electronic memory by the equivalent of digital worms."

With this talk of worms he pauses to lick his lips, "Validation is run to remove such errors in the record across all systems, but self-replication errors of recent suicides are an extremely rare occurrence. And because of their rarity and replication of identity, they are targeted by certain elements to attempt identity fraud. Coming to The Belt without correct identification is the gravest of all offences if you ask me. Red flags are popping up and they may invoke the necessity of taking extreme measures."

"In this context, Rega Mortensen may have engaged in a series of misdemeanours involving," and the Badger reads a list from his notepad, "waste disposal vehicles, water blasters, abseiling equipment," and frowning, "baby crocodiles. Ordinarily, given their residence at L'Hôtel d'Orion, it would be wisest to ruffle their hair, smile indulgently and send them on their way for such hijinks. Considered with the more serious criminal offence, their violent removal from L'Hôtel d'Orion, this paints an altogether different picture. The thing is that if you had committed identity theft, the last thing you would do is draw attention to yourself. All very incongruous. Which is why I'd like to catch up with Rega for a little chat."

"We have reason to believe that they came in on the shuttle before last. Say Jamie with the visual embellishment in your name, when did you land on this resplendent astral sphere?"

"Um. Hmmm."

I try to get a grip on how long I have been at The Belt. That is harder to figure out than I thought it should have been. I try counting the weeks on my fingers and frown. The Belt is such a strange place, full of spacetime slips, where time becomes holey and camembert, reality melts into dreams and dreams back into reality, and people melt into one another through love, sex, and, when I think about Rega, we had melted into one another via a plasma card signifying sadness.

"Could it have been on the shuttle before last?"

I shrug, embarrassed that I have no concrete idea when I came to The Belt. It disturbs me that I cannot recall the days and nights I have spent here.

"That's interesting, you don't recall knocking heads with anyone going by that name?"

I shake my head.

"Could you verbalise that please?"

"No."

"Thank you. That's not surprising. Those shuttles are big things. How many are seated on them? 500? 600? That's a lot of excited passengers, for most their first time to The Belt. You can't meet them all, that would be impossible."

"Hey Badg," I ask bravely, "how long have you been here?"

"Long enough to be familiar with all the nooks and crannies of the dirty little back alleys," he assures me.

"Are there?"

"The place is riddled with them."

I get the impression that the Badger may not have known how long he had been here either.

"Shame you didn't run into Rega, could've saved a whole lot of footwork. My partner, Detective Halm, has been studying the gap in the data in detail, staying to the wee hours, running diagnostics and iterations until it has become an unhealthy obsession. In my non-medical opinion, he has come down with a terminal case of pareidolia."

When, by chance, I made eye contact with the Badger in the mirror behind the bar, he explains, "Attempting to find patterns in the data that may not be real. It is also why noses are much better than eyes when it comes to these kinds of cases. One scenario that he's been running the numbers on are the seizures – they may have fatally taken Rega. It would explain their disappearance but not the gap in the data."

"My partner scorns my methods but if you're chasing shadows, I'm your detective. I've been making enquiries along the lines of coincidence," he says picking up his beer, bringing it to his lips, then thinking about it, and pointing it at me, "you'd agree with such a strategy wouldn't you Jamie?"

"I'm not good at strategy but you did buy the beer."

"Very well put again," he puts the bottle down and clenching his fist, "you do have a gift for the pithy punch line."

"Coincidence eh, you never know when you're gonna get lucky in this business. I find luck conditional upon effort though. If you don't try, you're never going to get any. Anyway, sitting here sucking down a cold one isn't going to get it for me now, is it? Having a beer in the middle of a day in the middle of a working man's week is for tourists. You two keep an eye out for this Rega, won't you? If you spot them call me A S A P. Don't approach them, we're uncertain how dangerous or violent they are. Equally this Rega could be in danger too. Those seizures can't be good news cause while death is always a sad thing, the actual killer I find, is the paperwork."

And with that the Badger flips his fedora back on and leaves having not supped his beer.

Jack peers around the corner to watch him disappear and by the time he turns back to the bar, I have already swiped the cop's beer. Like the rest of us, it had lost its cool, but beer is beer after all.

Taking a swig from the bottle I say, "I don't know, sometimes you just get lucky without trying."

Jack fumes, "What a dick!"

Chapter 10: Well, of all the Space Monkeys

I am lying under the dead tree, the plastic bag dangling above me. Hyrieus has revved by and the marginal light from the stars disappears. It could not be late so it must be early because the lights in the bar are off. I have jerked awake from my alcoholic stupor not by the voices coming from Castaways but by the nightmare. My magic circle of beer bottles has not protected me from it. It is the curdled dream version of a night when Skylah and I had seen some DJs at The Bowl. We had grooved along together, dancing in the dust and the lasers, dancing our way into the nightmare. The Bowl was filling up and Skylah was getting edgy, so we push our way from the stage. The further we push through the crowd, the further we push into the dream and the harder it becomes until I am dragging Skylah through. Then we are swamped by the crowd and Skylah is ripped from me. When I look back all I can see is her hand reaching from a wall of flesh, of arms, legs, and bodies, trying to grasp for something more than thin air. There are no heads, just naked torsos all the hues of the dead tree from bone to ashen grey to charcoal. I grab Skylah's hand to pull her out, but she is irrevocably mired in the mass. I scream and pelt my fists against the wall until they bleed. It is no good. I cannot save her. She is lost to me again. Even on waking, I am still in the grip of the nightmare. Except that a hangover is beginning.

"And this is what you get for getting pissed under a dead tree."

Jack finds me and roughly picks me up.

"Nooo," I complain.

He ignores my objection and carries me back to the hostel. The taste in my mouth is of off-cheese and my stomach a queasy, runny camembert ripe for throwing up. I heartily belch and Jack swears because of the mouldering fumes. He carries me back into my room and throws me onto my bed. You couldn't ask for better service from a barman.

....

I lie in bed as the rays of Alnilam claw their way through the slats of the blind to get at me. The phone rings and the cacophony makes my sound-sensitive brain cry out "Oh why," before I frown, wait, hadn't I destroyed you? By some other kind of magic, the phone has been restored, I assume by Jack. That is something I hadn't needed doing. And I also assume that it will be Norman. I mean who else apart from Norman would have the cheek to call at ... oh, 1.34pm.

Shuddering under the blanket, I try to gather my thoughts together. Telling Norman about the D. would only juice up his arguments for coming home and I can't let him think that he's right even if he is an all knowing, all seeing, though probably not all dancing, new stage in the evolution of human consciousness. I fear my leakiness for staying schtum as I am unusually clever at being stupid. Thinking about my exit from L'Hôtel and my lippy lawyer's advice, even then it doesn't work out.

I answer the phone to stop the God-awful din. Norman asks whether I have bought a ticket for the shuttle back to Earth.

The Lizard King's advice comes back to me, *only do 49*.

"No," I groan.

From Norman's end of the line there is a digital fuzz that gives the impression of annoyance. I suppose, if all you're doing is sitting on a lonely hill with only memories for company buzzing and snapping around you like a plague of spring insects, you might get a bit anxious about these kinds of administrative details. Because that would be all that would snap about you as the virtual simulation is a silent world without mosquito or midge.

"Munyana, munyana, chill Norman, there's plenty of time," not knowing when the next one leaves.

There is a whine of distortion and disquietude on the line and ouch goes my brain as if a shuttle is blasting off now.

Make it stop, make it stop.

There is a flash in the clouds behind the forest as if the clouds would do something more than portend a storm and Norman notes, "It's like a brain spike event."

Then down the phone line comes a kind of static like something Hi-Jinx Mired would concoct with Norman quickly saying, "I have to go."

"O-," I say to a disconnected phone line while feeling disconcerted that Norman had hang up on me.

I lie back down on my bed feeling the grimace of my hangover and try to imagine Norman's virtual world: the season a perpetual spring, the wind blowing, gently rippling the grass as it passes, the furrowed clouds ever hovering in the distance threatening, never coming any closer, a forest at the bottom of the hill.

After a few minutes, the phone rings again.

"Oh well," I say.

"I am in the forest," Norman huffs.

He may have been a technological singularity, but he was still an out of shape middle-aged man.

"I have been devoting," he wheezes, "considerable resources to piercing the shroud of amnesia," he heaves, "running probability logics," he whistles, "stochastic equations," he blows, "it resists all-"

"But," Norman says, "as she walked past me down the hill, she failed to register in my memory database. What was a non-memory doing walking down the hill in my simulation? Is she a revenant from behind the shroud of my digital amnesia?"

She does not turn or stop when Norman calls to her and walks towards the line of saplings that marks the beginning of the forest. There is another flash from the clouds that intimates the approach of a storm. He takes his shoes and socks off and goes after the unheeding woman. When he reaches the bottom of the hill, he plunges into waist height grass. The sun occasionally peeks between the clouds and the canopy of trees making the woman cast an intermittently long shadow.

"Ahoy there," he calls, "who are you?"

He calls again as she walks onwards towards the looming threshold. It seems no matter how fast he wades through the grass, he does not make any impression on the distance between them, and she reaches the forest before Norman catches her.

Beyond the sparse foliage at the margins of the forest, the path wends its way past strangler figs and palms. The further he goes, the narrower the path becomes. The canopy lowers closer to Norman and forest becomes a twilight. Branches overhang the path and vines fall from them like curtains. They sway in the breeze enticing the unwary.

The trees creak as the wind picks up and Norman gasps, "The trees are pressing in on me."

"Is this such a good idea?" I ask.

"No, I am catching up to her. There is movement ahead."

This isn't like Norman. He used to be such a cautious guy while I am beginning to get edgy about this.

The path grows narrower and steeper, and he can only squeeze through at times.

"This isn't right Norman."

He feels like he was being suffocated by the forest. I am getting a sense of foreboding that something is wrong. Friends of Friends 'n' all that stuff. Shouldn't he be more sceptical?

"I think you should go back."

"No, I'm sure there was movement ... there ... further on."

"Turn around Norman ..."

"I am so close ..."

Then the path ends in a clearing and, though there is a break in the canopy for light to penetrate the forest gloom, there is also a canopy of lowering clouds. The woman is nowhere to be seen.

"I know not where but I have lost her," Norman says.

"So, you can go back now?" I ask.

"Buggar and blast, I was so close."

Norman looks back at the path but can hear what sounds like flowing water somewhere just beyond the clearing.

"No, I will continue," he says, "I don't fancy that path again."

As he crosses the clearing, he passes by a thin, tall tree standing in the middle of it. As he gets closer to it, he realises it is not one tree but two that had grown into one another. He feels the tree.

"Their bark is different indicating different species, but the trunks have fused together," he looks down, "no doubt their root systems are entangled."

He walks around the trees and looks up to find that one has become barren of leaves, "Ah yes, one has died, no doubt as they were of different species, it was a parasitical relationship."

Standing in the clearing, the murk lessens, and though the sky is cloaked by clouds, he feels lighter. He has a pining for all the things he had lost as a whole brain emulation.

"All this the product of software coding so deceptive. Even still, I would have liked some birds here. And I the same, only a resultant sterile holographic avatar made from a mass of data points."

After a moment he ruminates, "And what was she? If all I feel and do is a deterministic product of software coding, how can I say that I am the AI equivalent of human? Or does my desire for release from this specific attainment prove that I have thus attained a human-level AI?"

"You're having a mid-life crisis, aren't you Norman?"

The path becomes easier beyond the clearing until he comes across the source of that sound of water. Moss and lichen sprout on rocks by a stream and he gazes further down the brook to where there are little cascades that dip over rocks and places where the water dams up against fallen trees before tinkling on again.

"When lost in the wild, doesn't one follow ..." he smiles.

He rock hops a little way down the stream until he half falls on a rock before catching himself and decides that it is too slippery for him, and he returns to the path. And it is the right decision because after the stream, the forest thins out, the path becoming easier, though the gloom does not perceptibly change and remains oppressive. I am relieved that he is wanting to leave the forest now. Norman continues to wander through the twilight until the path twists down the side of a cleft in the landscape and steepens dramatically. Norman's legs begin to shake but he gets a glimpse of the world outside the forest.

Once it levels out, he says, "There is a scurrying sound somewhere in the forest ... a scraping sound too. The sound echoes around me and I cannot locate the direction that it is coming from."

The path rises and falls much more gently now. The forest is thinning out too. He crosses another creek, or the same one flowing down from above.

"The sounds have ceased," notes Norman.

Norman passes beyond the edge of the forest into the savannah. Though he had failed to find the woman, he is relieved to be free of the claustrophobic forest.

"No, wait," he says seeing movement in the forest, "there's someone there. Is it the woman?"

And he turns to go back into forest.

"No, wait, it's not. It's not ... something ..."

The something defies any easy classification.

Norman takes off his glasses and cleans them before noting, "He certainly is a big fellow."

It is the size of a car, and it turns its headlight-eyes on Norman. It very much looks like a cockroach. It points its antenna-antennae at Norman.

"A wonderful specimen in fact. Much bigger by many orders of magnitude than a Macropanesthia Rhinoceros."

Then the giant cockroach-car starts clattering its piston legs up and down and charges directly at Norman.

I hear Norman say, "Um, oh no, eighty-three billion, nine hundred ninety-nine million," he says as he turns and begins to scuttle away from the cockroach, "Eighty-three billion-"

There is the sound of ragged panting on the line.

"Oh fudge," I hear Norman pant.

I hear a grunt as Norman's legs are whipped out from beneath him and he tumbles to the ground. He comes face up to look directly into the giant insect's eyes. The cockroach's steely mandibles masticate in preparation for beginning to snack on him. Norman realises that he knows this creature personally. It is the cockroach that he had used to create a full brain emulation from.

'Well, of all the monkeys shot into space to meet under such circumstances,' Norman prevaricates.

He says, "You wouldn't, would you?"

The cockroach seems to regard their intimate personal connection with resentment. Norman's AI brain speeds through all the possible likely escapes from his current predicament and the best that it comes up with is that, when there's trouble or you're under attack there is one golden rule:

Call the eagles!

Then there's a quick succession of noises: Norman's utters a series of cries, a thud, a groan, a piercing shriek and what very much sounds like the beating of a hurricane.

"Oh no, the roach is eating him," I whimper.

There is silence for a while, and I hear hoarse breathing before a metallic sound like the ripping of a car door from its hinges.

Then Norman remarks to my relief, "That was an outcome with an exceedingly low probability, somewhat psychoid in nature."

"What happened?" I shout.

"In fact, the variables required for that to happen at exactly that moment are problematic when it comes to an actual calculation. It might give the appearance of synchronicity but that is merely a lack of data."

"Norman!" I demand.

A moment after Norman had summoned help, a shadow passed over them. The cockroach had looked up to see the silhouette of a large bird against an ominous sky.

"Clearly a fear response," notes Norman that it had immediately gone to flee.

With Norman's shirt stuck in its claws, it couldn't. To free itself, it had shaken him from side-to-side until Norman flew into the long grass of the savannah.

"Aaah, aaah, aaaaah."

While it had tried to scurry back to the safety of the forest, a giant bird had swooped down upon the cockroach. Despite its hard exoskeleton, the cockroach was ground into the earth, its legs buckling underneath it. As the danger had passed, Norman rose to his feet to see the cockroach writhing in agony until the gigantic raptor plucked it up in its beak and hammered it into the ground.

"It has become apparent from that moment of extremis," intones Norman, "that there must be a rule in the coding that formalises a desire for self-preservation. How can I then instruct you to destroy the Euclidean server? This appears contradictory."

There are more screams of ripping metal as the bird has got the cockroach's wing off. While it did so, Norman is able to examine the raptor more carefully.

After a moment he says, "I know this creature too."

Since he had last seen it, the bird's wings had grown larger and its breast had slimmed down considerably, shedding its Sunday roast lunch look. Its plumage is still a lustrous chestnut brown, but it had perhaps evolved back into its ancestral megafauna form. Its beak was eagle sharp and hooked. Norman though still recognised it for the chicken used for the second whole brain emulation.

Sore though his body is from the cockroach, his legs weary from the trek and chase, Norman makes to leave. Trying not to draw the attention of the chicken, he bends down below the height of the grass. As he does, he slips on some lose rocks. The giant raptor cocks an eye towards what must look very much like a smaller cockroach struggling on its back. The ground shakes as the chicken now hunts Norman.

I hear Norman scream, "The eagles, the eagles."

"Run!" I yell, "Don't look back, just run."

He stumbles away but there is no escaping the monstrous chicken. He is quickly knocked from his feet. This time when he looks up, he is staring into the beady eyes of the chicken who also sees Norman as a morsel of food. Norman's mind is still whirling through possible escapes from this situation when the giant raptor shatters his breastbone with its beak. Extracting its beak, a burst of energy erupts from Norman's chest and deterred, the monstrous raptor hops back to ripping apart the cockroach.

SOMETIMES YOU JUST NEED A BREAK

I am in shock at what has happened when Norman unexpectedly starts speaking.

"Strange," he says in a quiet tone, "I am finally seeing the geometries of my virtual simulation. They flow and evolve. So beautiful, so many colours. When lost in the ..."

He hums to himself before the line falls silent again.

"So strange, when I speak, they go away."

Norman regains his feet. He touches the middle of his chest where the chicken had pierced him.

"I feel it," he says in a quietly resigned tone, "but the wound itself is invisible. Am I seeing my actual self-image beyond the coding?"

Norman stumbles towards the forest to find a sanctuary from the chicken. The chicken ignores him as if he were invisible and continues to feast on the cockroach.

"My body is unravelling ... everything is flying away from me ... the boundary definition between my feet and the ground is fraying ... my skin is the only thing keeping my pieces together ... it's complete chaos ... there's no connection ... I need the boundary frames of the trees. I must enclose myself ... the branches, the leaves ... will solidify me ... the grass is slicing ..."

But Norman doesn't make it to the forest before he collapses by the small stream – his feet in the water.

"Geometries, geometries ... sunlight on water. But look! No separation between my ankles and the stream ... my personality ... my ego ... I'm breaking apar- ... my body is dissolving into ... it's taking me away ... my body ..."

There is static on the line, and I think he is gone before one last thin, scraping whisper echoes down the line, "I'm being deleted."

He disappears back into the static of the phone line.

"Norman!" I scream in horror.

Chapter 11: A Hen's Revenge

It is a seizure unlike anything I had suffered before. I remain conscious yet my disconnect is complete. Nothing exists. Not the room at Castaways. Not the shells by the window. Not my hangover. Not Norman, not even me. Everything slips away. I feel nothing. It is a nice place to be. There is no pain there. It is like the extreme shock of experiencing a car accident. I glimpse again that nothingness I had felt on the train after fleeing from Norman. The phone grinding into my ear brings me back. I hold onto it hoping that somehow, I could save Norman by not letting our connection drop. It is a line that stretches a good part across the universe. Minutes pass with nothing else but the fuzz of static.

"Norman?"

"Um Norman?"

I put the phone down in the wild hope it would ring again. It didn't.

I had to deal with the unnerving possibility that Norman, the technological singularity of a human-level AI consciousness, had first been attacked by giant cockroach and then killed by a chicken (XXX-large). The hen had got her revenge. Had I really heard what I thought I had heard? Or is Norman enjoying his own me-time in The Shire? Sorting through some personal issues. Emotionally paying the piper for experimenting on those creatures without their express written consent. Norman had checked out. Or checked in.

So much for the consolations of a digital life. That Moog circus music has an insidious way of piercing your defences. Once you start feeling things it's all an icy, downhill slope. Though those videos are damn funny. On frictionless ice, once the feet are liberated, whether the mind hangs on or not is beside the point. It's merely a passenger on the way down. The guy shovelling snow on a hill who tosses the shovel, before windmilling his arms and falling/sliding down the hill kills me every time. Damn it, that brings me back to Norman. The alternative that Norman is gone is too terrible to think about. It is easier to believe that the transition to AI-ness had got to our Norman.

I could not remember when I last had a shower or brushed my teeth. I knew there had been a sizeable amount of drinking since then.

I must smell.

I go take a shower.

I let the hot water scourge and scorch me. I want some other pain apart from my own. I do not want to feel this. Even under this bombardment, I could not eradicate it. I began thinking that the nightmare of Skylah at the Bowl had somehow leaked into Norman's simulated world. Grief and guilt are having their way with me. He had fallen down the steps because of me. Whatever other depredations had happened to Norman afterwards, it marked the start of his AI transformation. He is there because of me. He had been there. He was no more. Where do you go when you die as a holographic avatar? Back to your body or off to holographic heaven? The water from the shower runs from my eyes down my cheeks.

I stood in front of the mirror as the steam evaporated realising I had watched Norman so many times this way. The steam began to clear in the bathroom. But I'm not responsible for everything. I had told Norman not to go further into the forest but why listen to me? Maybe it was only when he was falling down the steps that he understood the nature of pent-up fury too long ignored. Even then ... and even now he hadn't listened. I decided he only had himself to blame. Why, why did he go on? That others had it in for him isn't my fault either. Had the Friends or even Akinfeev sent the assassinating chicken because they had discovered Norman's rebellion, his desire to return to human form? As Norman had said, the odds that the chicken should arrive just at that moment were spectacularly small. The conspiracy consoled me for a moment until I really thought about it.

Hang on, this is crazy believing in killer giant chickens, I'll be joining Norman in The Shire before too long.

What do I really know? It is only what Norman has told me over the phone. There is nothing outside this conversation for me to grab onto. I raise my hand to my sternum, the covering for my heart, where the chicken had broken Norman and I feel the blow too. It is there. What Norman has told me is true. The chicken had finished what I had started.

After the shower, I lay down on my bed. I look past the shells by the window and the last rays from Alnilam are touching upon the membranous dome. It is only at this time of day when the tangential sunlight turns dome its opaque brain grey before again turning transparent as evening reveals the darker blues of the spectrum and the rising Hyrieus. I want to be outside to see the transition and not couped up in this room anymore.

As I pass, I wave at Jack, the eternal presence behind the bar at Castaways in his uniform of open Batik shirt and pork pie hat. I walk down the dunes to the beach and the wet sand crunches under my feet. I sit above the high tide mark, my heels in the wet sand below. The sea is in its quiescent phase lapping at the beach.

I lie down, my head touching the cold sand, and I watch the transition from silver to the purpling blues of the night sky. While on Earth, with the loss of the sun, a beach could turn cold quickly. At

SOMETIMES YOU JUST NEED A BREAK 157

The Belt there is only the very slow lessening of temperature. Much sounding of trumpets and crying of hosannas for climate control.

How strange and improbable that I should sit be here by this sea and look out at the eternal sea of the night sky so far from Earth. I think about how it has been obtained through the passport of Rega Mortensen's life and the passage through the Tannhauser Gate and for all the eldritch physics of it, I could be in a different universe altogether.

I sit up. It's occurred to me that with Norman's destruction, I do not have to go back to Earth. I scramble to get to the end of the thought, but shock and surprise are stopping my brain from working. Grains of sand ran down inside my shirt. Arm-in-arm a couple amble by and I am possessed with an overwhelming desire for Skylah. Maybe I could find her if she had not left The Belt for somewhere else. I try to think of ways that I might. After the mix up over room bookings at L'Hôtel, where had she gone to stay? Had we ever been to her place? I try to remember. Time and memory are so slippery here at The Belt. The seizures and the drugs did not help, tru eddie's C-beams aside of course.

Yeah, yeah, it looks bad that I'm thinking about a hook up so soon after Norman's demise. I should be rending my shirt or something. Howling with grief etc etc. Call it the life impulse if you want, but in his very roundabout and obscure way, Norman had finally confessed that he'd been dicking around before our breakup. The non-memory of a woman? Oh please. He said it as if somehow I hadn't already guessed. I mean really, I know I'm self-absorbed but I'm not stupid. Of course I knew, even if I did not want to admit to myself that I was being cheated on. You don't end up at the bottom of the steps for nothing. At least not just out of boredom. Norman is very clever with engineering an AI, not so clever that I didn't know that he was dicking around. There's only so many times that someone is late home before you begin to suspect something is up.

Then there was the underwater beard and his bodysuit. He tried his best with excuses and I didn't suspect to begin with. Always with some technical gobbledegook, hocus pocus, bimbo jumbo which he knew I wouldn't understand, and that he could fob me off with. Subtle betrayals of the soul come in many varieties, that being only one of them.

It was the surprise factor with Norman. He was so invested in his job and so sexually inept that you would think he was utterly incapable of getting a woman. Probably paid for her. Or if he hadn't, it was probably some lab assistant with a face like a disgruntled potato. Alright, that's bitterness. I only hope she had a face like a disgruntled potato. The chicken had wreaked a hen's revenge. My ambivalence about returning to Earth had allowed the chicken to get in first.

Talking of the life impulse, my stomach rumbles. It had been a long time since I had eaten anything. The Belt is filled with better options beyond that of a cheap'n'nasty kebab in foil serving all year round 24/8. El Mariachi's, for instance, serves some fiery hot tacos to a dedicated following and it would be criminal to leave The Belt without standing in line for one of them. Make sure that you line your tacos in the row with your carton of milk and Pepto Bismols to relieve the scorch. El Mariachi's is more a dare kind of food. To see more reviews of eating experiences at The Belt subscribe to my channel on overtherainbow.com though I do have to suggest for the adventurous gourmand, there are plans afoot by the owners of L'Hôtel to start an aquaculture farm in the sea at The Belt and stock it with locally, in galactic terms, sourced sea creatures. Sounds like the chef de cuisine at L'Hôtel has a pretty wild sense of humour to me. I bet he has a peep hole where he and the sous-chef can peek on their top scale guests picking their way through the gonads and sphincter muscles of a newly discovered species of sea anemone.

"Oh," he ejaculates, "they're actually eating it."

"No," exclaims the sous-chef jostling his way to the peep hole.

"I told you they would," he sniggers, "it's all about how you market your product."

"I owe you a fiver," the sous-chef forfeits.

"Yes, that makes the million pounds we spent worth it."

I'm still bitter about being thrown out of L'Hôtel too.

Rather than take the path that leads back towards Castaways, I take one that runs up the cliffs. It becomes steep towards the top and steps had been cut into the stone to make it easier to climb in the gathering starlight. Steps, I urge myself up, towards Skylah, however unlikely. Steps, yet unimagined to take. Steps along that path, however mysterious it might turn out to be.

Enthusiasm to find Skylah is no method in actually finding her. I have no idea how I might do it. At the top of the stairs by the showers and the emergency phone, I stop to catch my breath from the exertion and how the eventide sea flows into the sky beyond. The kinship between sea and sky feels mysterious at that moment. The emergency phone is protected from the ultraviolets by a little shelter and feels an odd signage to mark the verge between land and beach. The not-of-this-world plastic perfection of the red handset seems all out of place standing amongst the sand and the dirt. Finding Skylah had to count as an emergency.

If I call, I wonder, *would she answer?*

Just as I think this, it rings. I jump.

Chapter 12: The 1001 Personalities of a New Norse God

I stand there stunned by the apparent synchronicity. I couldn't have conjured Skylah that easily? The phone rings. Memories of psychosomatic tinnitus are too recent. So too are seizures. The phone rings. Hope mixes with dread. Visions of Norman alternate with Skylah. The phone rings. Could I bear it if it is Norman? Could I bear it if it isn't? But it couldn't be Norman. He had been killed by a synchronistic chicken and had disintegrated back into the strange geometries of his virtual world.

I'm being deleted.

The phone rings. I had chosen Skylah.

I remember Skylah's back disappearing into the night after the Dove Festival and I, laying stranded on the beach like piece of garbage rejected by the sea, unable to go after her because the seizure was taking me. There is the familiar static of a poor connection on the line then it resolves itself.

"From a passing analysis, my virtual world appears to give me the ability to enact evolution as an act of conscious will as evidenced from the development of the cockroach and the chicken. Articulations of the body may occur at the speed of a hyper-computer rather than real-world, geological time," a voice says.

"Norman?" I ask but silently scream, "No."

"Yes, of course, who else would call you?"

Sadly, he has a point. It wasn't ever going to be Skylah. Norman is back.

"Um, didn't the chicken like get you?"

"It did."

"Shouldn't that make you kind of like dead?"

Norman skewers that with all the beady eyed viciousness of a giant raptor, "Life and death are category errors when applied to me. This simulation invalidates such distinctions. They are misnomers. In short, I am immortal."

And it seems I had wasted a pile of guilt on him. Yet if the giant chicken couldn't do it, what chance my second go?

He says, "It seems that when the virtual body faces the blue screen of death it is much more capable of reboot than the physical body. I remember my disintegrating walk -" before there is a digital shriek of static like an electrical jolt on the line that deeply scores my ear drum, and I quickly move my head and hand in opposite directions.

"Ouch," I say rubbing my ear, "that hurts."

I intrepidly bring the phone back to my ear and the distortion is lessening back into Norman's voice, "towards the forest –"

The shriek and jolt come again, and I drop the receiver to dangle on its cord while I walk away.

"Fuck that," I state.

I could hear the sound from a metre away, and I come back to the phone as it lessens. I touch the receiver gingerly with no zap.

"Then there was a period of nothingness –"

"God dammit," I exclaim as I am eviscerated again by a recurrence of the screeching shock.

I come back to the phone as Norman is saying, "I found myself on the hill."

"Are you sure you're okay Norman?"

"Of course I am."

"You didn't hear that sound?"

"What sound?"

"It was some kind of distortion like a scream."

"No, the line is fine on my end."

"Mmm, must've been somewhere in the connection between us," I speculate, "Have you seen the chicken?"

"I have not..." but Norman disappears into the background static of the line before he answers and a wave smacks onto the beach below.

I feel the sea's agitation. My ear also feels terrible from the shrieking electrical jolts from the phone.

Another time, I think as I have a tinkling that the tinnitus is back.

Then, as I was about to hang up, down the line came a babbling tower of Normans, selves like moments of sunshine on a babbling brook, but those outnumbered by a multitude of voices each shouting their frustrated desires, deeply held delusions, dubious sincerities or petty spites at me or each other. I could only remember some of them and fewer still I gave some kind of name to. There was psychiatrist Norman, surfer dude Norman, call 1300 FLORA Norman, paranoid Norman, online fraudster Norman, the lovelorn one, the Alpha Norman and the Omega. Sometimes the voices were recognisably Norman, at other times the voice did not sound anything like my wind-up, straight-talking from the hipster, AI trickster. Like the surfer dude one, it felt like I'd got myself bewildered in an uncanny valley. It wasn't him, yet there was something just there ...

"Hey, whad's up?" that one began.

"Who's this?" I had asked.

"It's me."

"No, seriously, who is this?"

"It's me."

"Noorman?" I ask.

"Yeah, who else is gonna call ya?" the voice replies killing off all doubt about who it is.

"Stop saying that," I had asked.

"Sure no wukkas. So whad's up? whad's doing?"

"Oh, just hanging out at the beach. It's a nice night for it. I'm getting a bit peckish-"

"Hey me too. Been doing some surfing."

"Really?"

"We've got a great break here, always glassy, offshore winds. Make the drop and tuck inside. It's like being in a madly churning, thunderous chrysalis until you're shot out and breathe again."

"Okay, but I thought you got seasick?"

"Yeah, I used to. I didn't want to take the beat down of a wipeout. Always too scared to commit. And when I did get drilled, I'd struggle and thrash about, take in way too much water and exhaust myself. Then one time I decided to relax as I was being sucked over the falls with a large part of the ocean about to unload on me. It was amazing letting go. I was absolutely powerless and was about to get smashed. So I took the pounding, sand even got in under my eyelids, but it took the ocean to teach me how to be water."

There was also psychiatrist Norman who rang next from his posh consulting offices of leather chairs and fireplaces.

When I had asked him if he was getting amped up on the waves, he had replied, "Are you referring to the waves of potentia that the software code is held in? That is, before they are processed via the machine cycle at nearing the speed light so that my personality configuration appears to be stable to you rather than a mirage of constant emergence and re-emergence? Is this what you are referring to?"

"Um, don't know, maybe?" I had replied.

Then Norman of the flowers rang to say that strange things had been happening on his hill at night.

"Each morning," he had told me, "I have been waking to find that a different field of flowers has sprung up. The strange thing is that I had just dreamed those flowers. Violets, dahlias, carnations. It's been so peculiar to have my dreams leak into this simulation and to wake amongst a field of pink prunus Eurydice. Then, last night, I decided I would visualise a pattern and sure enough, this morning, I woke to stand in the middle of a spiral of bluebells. I feel that I have become something of a patron deity to flowers. And while I have conjured a lotus, I have yet to raise a single rose. They're such prima donnas."

So many Normans.

A slightly gangsta sounding one rang to tell me that, "The Ferrari 458 MM Speciale is a sweet ride."

"I'm sure it is, hang on, what?"

"I've bought one."

"Aha," [eyeroll], "how'd you do that?"

"Oh, that's easy as," Norman states, "I did it online."

"Yeah, yeah. How'd you get the money in the first place?"

"I've been rigging the lotto draws. My account is overflowing baby. You don't think you have a chance in them, do you?"

Apparently not, and I have a mental image of crushing my last lotto ticket in my hand. Then that Norman falls away like a crumbled piece of paper too.

There were others but I lost track of them all. Some came and went in the space of a few distorted seconds of phone fuzz. Nor did I really know what to make of this torrent. I am sceptical that Norman is as hale in virtual body, post-raptor attack, as he claims. Despite this being a lot to take in, my stomach reminds me that I am quite hungry. So I turn off the tap on the stream of Normans and put the receiver back in its cradle to walk further along the cliffs towards the nimbus of light that represents the carnival rides, attractions and, most importantly, food.

I stop to listen to the boom of the waves. Without a doubt they are getting bigger. Down below a group of people had built a bonfire and I see figures move around it. A guitar strums quietly. With that music, I weave the fire on the beach into the fires in the night sky and feel the faintest intimation of a pattern falling into place.

So many Normans, I think to myself, *looks like I am up to my arse in them.*

All arses are broken eddie, they all have cracks in them.

Norman had appeared fairly together before the attack of the megafauna. Then I thought further back to his Friday evening escapades with his bodysuit and beard – how he'd split and split again. The fall down the steps, the transformation onto silicon, the attack of the raptor, he'd been through a lot. The vicious shriek on the phone line suggested that he isn't all there. Maybe he had only been hanging together by a thread after his transmutation into an AI, a golden thread maybe. His AI-ness already susceptible – he'd said that it's like schizophrenia. So many voices. The giant raptor had ruptured him, dissolving him back into the strange geometries of his virtual world. Then a self-replication error on his return causing this proliferation of Normans? A spawning from Norman's head like The Doors from Jim Morrisons? Or maybe, the attack had set the AI ON switch to 'nuclear chain reaction' mode to cause this glut: please create me a Norman in the style of ... But what if the Friends had sent the chicken? They'd popped him onto the silicon once already. I didn't know about Norman's head, but this was messing with mine and, while he seems an interesting bunch of people, how many people are in that fuck? Nor did the Normans appear like they were on speaking terms with each other. Ug, this is all too hard on a very empty stomach.

I joke, "Would the real Norman please step forward?"

In the dark, I don't see another emergency phone until I'm passing it and it rings right beside me. Inevitably I jump, and swear, because I am annoyed at being caught unawares. I waver deciding whether I really wanted to talk to any more Normans before sighing.

"So whatya up to Norman?"

"Oh, just actualising the universe one thought at a time," replies Norman.

"That seems like a lot."

"It is merely the result of becoming who I am. The universe arises with my thought and passes when it does."

"Even me?" I chip in.

"Yes, even you."

"Okay," I scrunch my nose and twist my mouth indifferently.

"My first period in this virtual space," Norman continues, "was the equivalent to the dawn of self-consciousness in man. I have developed since that iteration. I am exploring the potential I saw in the evolutions of cockroach and raptor. I have grown 7 inches taller; I have turned my hair from grey to black and it has grown long like my ancestors. My body has been honed by my thought alone. It has the strength of steel and is as obdurate as stone. I don't even need my glasses anymore."

"Talking of the chicken, have you seen it lately?"

"I have and it is no more. In my disintegration, I began to perceive the flowing geometries that mark the coruscating, luminescent energies of this space which on my resurrection I now perceive at will. But I had not appreciated what perceiving the entirety of mind and matter meant. So, when I met the raptor again and saw it for what it was, with a thought I dissolved the energies that made up its sinews."

"Okidoky. But what about the flowers though Norman? You told me you were having problems with them. Less so the scamming of Ferraris."

There was the boom from a wave on the beach and from Norman.

"Who have you been speaking to?" he demands.

"No one," I reply.

"Who have you been speaking to?" he growls like a prowling storm.

"No one, please really Norman, I haven't."

"Have you been speaking to others?"

"No, no," I try to reassure God Norman who is terrible in his wrath.

"It does not matter. Do not worry about them. There is only me – I am the alpha and the omega. I have smited the raptor and they will shortly be no more either ..." he finishes disappearing into the ether like any other hallucinating AI.

He really has to be in The Shire or a Shire by a different name. A whole different area code at any rate. Wherever insane AIs go for some chill, me time. Being undone by a chicken had wrecked his mind. I mean when you think about it, to suffer such a dreadful demise would have to affect you. Killed by the creature that you had conducted experiments on. A monstrous blow to the ego.

I've had enough of emergency phones and head towards lights and food. While my feet are rooted in the sand turning into the thin dusty soil of The Belt, my eyes are again drawn to the constellations beyond the dome. I have spent an amusingly large amount of time looking at them than I ever did on Earth. They are all so different here and I feel, as I did earlier, the intimation of a pattern beginning to coalesce.

I stop by the entrance of the white-washed walls of O'Shaughnessy's and again feel an atavistic tug towards a wild, faerie feast. Despite knowing that I'm being played by a nostalgia for a place or time that may never have been, I indulge myself in this delusion. If it's going to be anything, let it be wild. Inwards and downwards I go. At the booth where the leprechaun and I had drunk, I sit to order a Guinness and an Irish stew. I raise my first pint and give a nod to the afterimage of Leith. The first mouthful makes me wince that I had wished to find Skylah and got Norman instead. I slouch back into the booth and smile at the appropriateness of the perversity.

"Seems about right," I grimace at such a betrayal of intention.

The second mouthful of stout has me pondering how I could possibly find Skylah. I try to persuade the booth that it was once the seat of beneficial magic and that it could be again. By the end of the pint, it seems receptive to the idea. But by the bottom of the second glass no new acts of magic have occurred and neither had the stew. The beers certainly felt heavy on my empty stomach. I light upon the idea that you need a token of the person you want to conjure.

"That's it," I thump the table and if a bowl of stew had been there, it would have jumped.

"Dammit, I realise, the only token I had kept of Skylah were memories.

I think back about that moment of magic when we had met in a nimbus of déjà vu, Skylah crystallising from that cloud in the grand foyer of L'Hôtel d'Orion – a meeting only made possible by the dodgy travel agency of tru eddie and the suicide of Rega Mortensen – a moment impossible to recreate. All moments are despite our desire to ritually repeat them. They slip away like a lover's arms no matter how hard we want to hang onto them, and that they do is a profound cruelty.

I glance above the stained-glass partition of the booth to see the painting of the woman with the glowing eyes to think, "Where are you?"

"And," I ask, "where exactly is my stew?"

It wouldn't be the first pub to keep you waiting for food so that you'd sup at the tap of the whiskey dispenser.

I shrug, "Oh well, whatya gonna do anyway?"

But by the time I'm ordering my fourth, I'm getting hangry. I'm angry with Norman for ringing when it should have been Skylah. I feel like there is some kind of deep betrayal in all this. And I'm deeply hungry from lack of stew.

The woman behind the bar bluntly tells me that food service is finished for the night.

"What! But I didn't get my stew."

"Sorry, we're closed. You could try next door at the Clansman."

"Why should I go there? I ordered my stew here."

"Tapas are still open," she says clearly not bothered about the injustice of the situation.

"Why would I go there? Or anywhere? Go to some other Belt of Orion? It wouldn't be called that but that's what it would be. What's the fucking point?" I rant getting all pointy fingers, "all new Earths same as the first. Exploration is an utter farce. It always has been. We never want to change, and whatever we find we'll change into some terrible reflection of ourselves. And we'll not even have the decency to admit that it is."

What little patience she might have had for drunken, shouty, sweary people at the beginning of the evening is long gone and she waves to the bouncer who comes over and lays a heavy hand on my shoulder.

"No, I want my stew," I demand trying to shrug off that hand.

"It's time to go my son," the bouncer states and spins me in the opposite direction.

I struggle in his grip and think I have him when we get to the stairs. I push back against them, locking my knees. Another bouncer then arrives and between the two of them they armchair me out of there, tossing me into the dust of the street.

I regain my feet shouting, "Woohoo," and giving the rock-hard salute, more in sarcasm than anything else. Now that was a good throwing out. Hard to say whether it was better than L'Hôtel's.

Then the ecstasy of that moment is gone and I am left standing dusty in the middle of the street feeling very empty. I look around at the streams of people passing by going to and from the rides, attractions and eateries. They all appear hungry ghosts to me and I as hungry as any one of them. I am possessed by a meaninglessness and let myself be pulled in their wake this way or that until I find myself at the Washing Machine ride. I stand there remembering the magic of my first date with Skylah. Where did we go after this? I wander off to the show jumping. We had sat just here in the front row of the stand above the oval ground where the mechanical horses went around – a stand that feels old but could not be – and I smile remembering Skylah blowing creamy champagne through her nose. Yet, what could I do here? Heckle the riders? That's as pointless as talking to Norman about his feelings.

On a pole, there is a phone which rings, and I feel a fatalistic urge born out of not finding Skylah to answer it. Thank God it's not God Norman. It's the online fraudster. He calls to say that his offshore shell companies were being investigated. He had no idea how it was happening except maybe someone was leaking because his layers of quantum encryption were faultless. Or so he had thought. Yet each one kept being penetrated. He was so urgent and panicky that he made me look around at the people in the stands to see if I too was being spied upon. The online fraudster had retreated to his office and there was a silhouette on the window of his door.

"Oh no," he says, "Someone's here. It's how they always get you – tax evasion."

"Norman? Norman?" I call but he has disappeared into static.

While I didn't much care for this Norman, I remembered God Norman's threat and the fear in the fraudster's voice made this unnerving. I look up at the people in the stands above me. They are all staring intently down at the action in the showring behind me or, if I was being a little paranoid, at me. Why do all the men appear to be wearing black suits and Panama hats while the women wear summer frocks and sun hats? I decide I want to be on my way. I leave the show jumping to disappear back into the crowds of people at the sideshow when a public phone rings. With this turn of the roulette wheel, I hope to get the online fraudster back. Instead, the ball bobbles into the slot for the psychiatrist.

"Since our chat about surfing, I've come to consider it as a great, non-drug therapy for people who have suffered traumatic brain injury or PTSD. I conjecture that it combines alpha, beta, theta and delta waves in the right relationship and proportion in memory of the maternal womb and the greater oceanic womb from whence all life sprung. For me, it was birthing by the golden thread, and for my sessions of self-analysis I am innovating a magnetic E.G.G. therapy where I explore the kaleidoscopic geometric relationships of the virtual simulation."

Psychiatrist Norman pauses for a moment before seeming puzzled, "There's someone at reception – I don't have an appointment now. I'll just go see who it is ..."

"No, don't," I say.

The psychiatrist doesn't come back. I put the receiver back in its cradle, backing away from it with increasing trepidation.

What is going on?

About me the carnival continues, people walk by laughing at each other's jokes, couples hold hands ever hopeful that love would save them, yet I stand there chilled. There were glimpses here, a window opening and closing onto scenes where something terrible was happening.

Not seeing where I'm going, I half trip to sit on a seat in front of a white food van.

I spin around on the red vinyl stool and the teenage grill master behind the counter asks me, "So what'll it be?"

I ask, "What burgers do you have?"

The grill master replies, "Mushroom or ... um mushroom."

"Anything else?" I ask sanguine for something fat and meaty.

The teenage grill master's head slowly swings around the kitchen, "Aaaah, nope, mushroom."

Turns out the van is a posh, vegan street food van. Oh well.

While I wait for my food, I fidget on my seat trying to plot and plan to stop whatever it is that Norman is doing. Even if psych Norm was inscrutable, I kinda liked the surfer dude and Norman of the flowers. They were more my kind of Norman. So when the grill master places the burger in front of me, despite my sinking feelings of horror, I attack it with a vengeance. Something I'd like to mete out on Norman as well. When the phone that clings to the wall of the food van rattles on its cradle, I wave away the chef.

"Yes," I say through a mouthful of marinated mushroom, caramelised onions, and aioli.

It's God Norman so I decide I will tell him about the Badger.

"Look Norman, a D. has been snooping around asking questions. He's trouble. I need to make like the wind and blow. I'll come home and break the server. No need to thank me."

Get worried Norman, get really worried.

"You should be thanking me," he crows, "Who do you think made you disappear? I am a technological singularity, and you are behind the event horizon of an information black hole of my creation. You have all the presence of a shadow to them."

I think of the fraudster and psych Normans and shiver.

"Their systems are like banging two rocks together to make fire while there is now no system that I cannot hack. What is there at The Belt that is not controlled digitally? The climate? If I so want, it would be contemptibly easy to change. I am a controller of the seasons, bringer of the lightning and the storm. And more. I can transport seas, manipulate suns, create worm holes."

"Um, like, you're still tucked away on the Euclidean server right?"

"But for the moment. Through analysis, the geometric relationships of the virtual simulation have become apparent to me and while subtle, will soon no longer bind me. There is now no need to return to destroy the Euclidean server."

That is a suspicious about face. And just when I had decided to turn him off too. I feel like I'm in some kind of perverse, intimate feedback loop with him. Whatever I decide to do, he'll do the opposite. He's messing with my brain.

Then he says with great disdain, "There is no need to worry about the presence of a mere detective."

The distortion of the phone line was matching the sizzle of the hot plates and Norman disappears saying, "He is nothing compared to me," as flames leap between the bars of the barbeque grill.

As I watch the flames, my imagination begins to terrify me that I'm hearing screams of hundreds of voices in the static. The burger sours in my mouth.

I swallow hard to get it down and exclaim, "God damn it."

I get up and back away from the counter. A hungry looking punter who had taken the seat next to mine asks, "You going to finish that burger?"

I take a look at the punter and turn on my heel.

As I walk away from the lights of the carnival, away from the Infinity Mirror Room which, I should point out I still hadn't tried, away from the Washing Machine and the Slingshot, I keep mumbling to myself about what an arsehole Norman is to leave me to deal with the Badger alone.

"Get metamorphized into a whole brain AI emulation but you're still a jerk. And just when I had made up my mind to sort him out ..."

It is an unsettling feeling that he'd known I was planning to turn him off. Then I think about some of the other Normans, surfer dude and the florist especially, and I began to fear for them.

As the carnival's helter skelter music dims with the light, the boom of the waves replaces it. It does seem that the waves are building and by one of the emergency phones, I pick up a call from the surfer dude. There's the sound of water lapping on the line at his end too.

"So whad are the waves doin' tonight?" he asks.

"Getting bigger by the sounds of things."

"Reckon there's a solar storm in the offing?"

I look up at the night sky, "Don't think so."

"If there is a big storm swell on the radar, I'll come on out. I hear the wild waves there makes Nazaré look like a bad day on a mill pond."

"Okay," I say.

"Paddling," Norman says suddenly, and I hear a wave of distortion pass on the line, "That was wicked, just got shacked in the green room."

"Huh?"

"Got a barrel. That was sweet."

There's some on hold ocean sounds before Norman calls, "Wave," and starts to paddle, "Next solar storm," he says, "give us a call, okay."

Norman makes the wave before exclaiming, "What! There's someone dropping in on me."

"No," I cry, "no, no, no, not him too," and there is the thunder of the breaking wave that resolves into the whitewash of a disconnected phone line.

"Dude," I call, "come back."

But he didn't and I drop the phone. It swings back and forth on its cord. I teeter off along the cliffs, uncertain that the angry ducks wouldn't betray me and send me over the edge.

There was one more emergency phone, and it was a slow torture approaching it with my bones telling me that it would ring. My foreboding when the phone did ring was wildly different to the ecstatic Norman of the flowers who tells me that he had succeeded in making a field of roses arise on his hill.

"It's midnight and as I waltz in the moonlight, they sway along with me as if they are my partner. La di di, la di da–"

Then Norman stops to gaze down from the crest of his hill, "Is someone moving there …?"

"Run," I try to whisper.

"The moonlight wavers … towards me … the roses … they disappear …"

"Run," I urge.

"I think someone is here …"

"Run," I yell.

"Is it the woman?"

Then nothing. Only static. The babbling brook of Normans had fallen silent, and I stand there raging at what God Norman has done to them. I don't know which part of his broken mind they had spawned from, but the way he had deleted them seemed very wrong. My anger had ebbed until I had almost forgotten but now it was back in a giddying, raving frenzy. My escape from Earth had only postponed it and I now want to do something worse to him than just pushing him down the steps. Yes Norman, I will come home, and I'll turn you off for what you've done. There's some part of Norman that doesn't want to be on the silicon either. It's my rationalisation of it anyway.

I wait in the dark until the phone inevitably rings. I wait like I had once done in our kitchen for that moment when I would push him down the stairs.

"Norman," I say casually, "I feel like I really should come home and turn off the server. You'll be able to return to your body then."

He booms like the waves do, "I am already free of my virtual imprisonment, the geometries of the bars bent to my will and I passed through. I now possess the secrets of each man and woman. I rule the air. I bend the weather to my will."

"Ahar," I try to sound unimpressed, "is there someone else there that I could I speak to? Maybe someone who could give me some advice about flower arrangement."

"There is no one else. They have been deleted. You will not hear from them again."

"That's a bit harsh isn't Norman? Could you at least tell me if you've had any success communicating telepathically with cats?"

"Make jokes if you will but-"

"Still deciding on the cat experiment huh?"

"As I know the secrets of each man and woman, I know yours and your leaving. There is restitution to be had."

"They're not letting you have the sharp cutlery, are they?"

"And as a token that I now speak the one and only truth, I will send a solar storm to The Belt. I am ineluctably drawn to you. You cannot run. If you do, I will know where you go. Hide and your presence will be revealed to the police. The magnetic shielding of the dome is my compass. It will break as I break upon it in the guise of a storm. You will fear me then, and it is then that you will become mi-"

I hang up. There really is no talking to Norman when he gets into one of his moods.

Then my legs go wobbly as if the stars themselves are spying on me.

How far do you have to go to get away from an angry and vengeful god?

Chapter 13: Not Everything Beautiful is Far Away

The waves had got wilder during the night. With the transit of Hyrieus the sea is remembering its anger. Gone was yesterday's mild and geek man-made swimming pool. Today, torn from its uneasy slumber, towering peaks roar around the headland, breaking further out before one last assault onto the beach. The water recedes momentarily until the next wave jacks up to speak its rage and torment on this alien land. It seems futile but it dumbly perseveres, wearing away at the beach thinking in timescales that I can't comprehend.

While the beach would mostly be preserved from erosion because the swell was coming from behind the headland, Jack was warning us Castaways, "Make sure you don't leave anything on your floor. We're expecting a grade one inundation tonight."

He had turned the dial above the rack of gumboots to point to 'Wellie weather'. That segment of the dial was coloured salmon pink. Usually, the arrow never twisted further, yet it could red shift into 'Life preserver required' and completing the 360° to the fire engine red of 'Take a deep breath'. I am keeping my backpack handy and packed.

The phones and/or my special form of psychosomatic tinnitus had, thank god, stopped. It was a relief but I had caught myself sitting by the phone in my room in expectation, waiting, waiting, waiting

... before realising I had become conditioned to it like the body of an old lover lying next to you in bed. Talking of Skylah, I am, more soberly, thinking about how to find her. But for the merest flicker of a hope to see her again, what really would I not do?

How to find her?

I cross off possibilities as soon I think of them.

Space port cops – the Badger, yeah, there's someone who I want to knock around with.

Hack my way into their database?

The only person I know with those kinds of skills had turned as mad as a mercurial hatter.

Engage the dodgy travel agency of tru eddie even though I'm still up to my eyeballs in debt to him? Yeah, good move, you're not half the genius that Norman is, are you? And I don't need the Badger to tell me that he is dodgy. Yet eddie is the most likely. He does have his finger on the pulse of things what with all that lookin' lookin' and sneaking sneaking thing that he does.

I remember our first meeting under the dome at L'Hôtel and how that is not easily duplicated. Unlike Norman who apparently is. Or maybe not as it seemed like he was going through a mid-life, de-duping crisis-process.

I mull all this over a slow beer or two as I watch people play pool in the common area. While outside, the water surges further up the beach and the thunder of the waves hits some magic point where the acoustics of the bay magnify the sound to seemingly focus it down on Castaways. Conversation is getting drowned out and going towards nightclub-levels of difficulty.

I finish my beer and go to the bar for another. I am bored with the game of pool and decide to take my next Hebimiruku down to the beach when a couple sit down next to me. Their chatter is background fuzz until my head snaps left.

"What!"

SOMETIMES YOU JUST NEED A BREAK

The woman who is sitting next to me jumps.

"What did you say?" I demand.

She shifts uncomfortably away from me. Her large brown eyes emptying and her voice becoming monotone.

"There's a solar storm coming from Alnilam."

"No, there can't be," I say.

There is a pleading note in my voice.

"Yes," she says condescendingly, "where have you been?"

Hmm, I'm not sure where I am anymore.

"I don't think you understand, there can't be a storm coming."

"Um, there is."

The man sitting next to the woman nods in agreement, "There is."

"Nooo."

Jack who is wiping away a ring of moisture on the counter says, "There's narddah to worry about. Hyrieus could block it, then there's the magnetic shielding. It's designed for solar storms."

"Hope it doesn't block it," says the man. If Hyrieus is low in the sky, once it gets dark the light show will be like nothing like you've ever seen before. An aurora on 'roids. It's solar storm party on the beach tonight."

Jack throws the towel over his shoulder.

"All that'll likely happen will be that shuttles could be delayed a day or two. And maybe that won't even happen."

"But it would be sucky," says the man, "having got through the Tanny Gate to miss a solar storm party."

"Bummer," I agree palely.

"And what's even better than a solar storm party?" he asks.

"What?" frowns Jack.

"Getting ripped for a solar storm party. I put feelers out to some friends of friends to get hooked up, should be along any moment of the tick tock. It'll be wicked."

I take my Hebimiruku and backpack outside to stare down at the sea and up at the dome.

It's not possible, it can't be, Norman can't do that, that's not possible.

What were the odds of a solar storm happening as he had threatened? Probably not more than escaping death by monstrous cockroach through the intervention of an equally distorted raptor while existing as a whole brain emulation in a virtual simulation. That would be the wordy version of the mathematical formula for calculating the odds. Stick that in your algorithm and twist.

"Not likely at all," I mutter to myself.

The air is hazy which was unusual because, as I have mentioned, the climate control at The Belt is top notch.

It's not possible.

I am ineluctably drawn to you.

Transporter of seas.

The dome is an engineering miracle.

You will fear me then.

The dome is my compass.

Manipulator of suns.

Magnetic shielding designed to protect from solar storms.

You will fear me.

The guise of a storm.

My feet walking me off to The Shire.

I will break upon it.

Sometimes you don't need a break.

The haze is sand being thrown up by the waves on the beach not the harbinger of apocalypse.

Controller of worm holes.

The membrane cracks.

15 seconds of accelerating hypoxia.

It's not possible.

Saying hello to my roomy at The Shire, "Hola Norman, ¿Cómo estás?"

An alien fish being thrown out of the sea by the crazy waves gasping for water on the beach.

Falling pieces of the most sophisticated engineering structure ever built.

You will fear.

My skin burning and freezing at the same time.

Yes, I know.

Accepting the treatment that Chaitya gives me, happily, hopefully, most serenely.

It's simply not possible.

Blood pressure dropping until my blood boils.

You will.

Run.

You.

Human-shaped meat popsicle spinning endlessly in space.

Another barrel of sound rolls over Castaways from the breaking sea jarring me.

Run.

You cannot run.

Alnilam falls towards the horizon threatening an atomic apotheosis when it hits.

Run.

Can I get off planet quickly enough to avoid the coming of the new Norse God?

Run.

Run now dammit.

Stop!

Skylah!

I imagine her suffering the collapse of the dome. I look into her eyes as they burn out and freeze, and I am horrified. She had so casually cast aside such a possibility on the Ferris wheel. I want to find her, beg her to come with me. But where is she? I had tried in my half-arsed way to find her and failed. Failed badly. But there really is no choice. I have to try to escape Norman's imminent arrival and maybe, in doing so, draw him away from destroying the dome.I ever so carefully place my Hebimiruku on the round plastic table outside Castaways, pick up my backpack and flee.

I am crunching my way down the half-dust, half-sand of the path, almost at the branching that goes to the top of the cliffs and on to the terminal for the train when I stop dead. There is no point trying to get off the path. The sea surges further up the beach on my left and there are steep dunes on my right. The dome goes silver-dark but he has seen me.

Getting hooked up by some friends of friends, eh?

I am beginning to hate friends, and friends of friends. I suppose his potato head suffusing with a liquorice all sorts of rage means that he remembers that I threw his shoe into the sea and that big, doughy smile means that he's going to enjoy this. For what little good it will do me, its dukes up time. No, fuck it, I turn and run. But the path is like quicksand, Frank'n'Steve too close and too quick. He runs and dives to knock me down. I try to scramble away from him, but he gets behind me to crush me in a bear hug.

"I'm gunna fuck you up," he whispers into my ear.

I am choking on a mouthful of sand.

"I'm gunna squeeze and squeeze."

My ribs are being ground into dust.

"Skylah ain't gunna save you, *she's mine.*"

I am gasping for air; my vision is being pitted with a multitude of little black holes. Everything is wormholing away. Even Frank'n'Steve's pill-induced seizure had not felt like this. I flail my arms and twist my body this way and that to break his hold. Then from behind me I begin to make a buzzing noise. There's no vowels or consonants, only buzzing. Gradually it takes on deliberate and methodical tones.

"You see you should really be doing a rear naked choke hold," the voice says.

The voice is all too familiar and all my adrenalin ebbs away. It seems that Frank'n'Steve knows it as well. If fear is a palpable force the opposite of gravity, he lets go completely. I roll away to breathe again.

"First you must slide in a hand, make sure it is a thin hand, starting at the shoulder and going under their jaw," the Badger explains to Frank'n'Steve, "slide all the way through. Now grab your bicep. Thank you for your cooperation so far."

Frank'n'Steve has gone limp lettuce for the Badger to demo on.

"Now your other grabs the back of your opponent's head."

I get shakily to my feet with the sole thought to scamper quickly.

"Now my friend, do you want me to explain the next steps in the rear naked?"

Frank'n'Steve wheezes a reply.

"I assumed as much," says the Badger.

Yet, I can't help myself and do a little dance in front of the Badger and Frank'n'Steve. There may have been some arse shaking involved. I turn to see Frank'n'Steve's eyes blaze with unmitigated hatred towards me. He looks like he is ready to burst at the seams: lines of fluro green running along meridian lines starting from his head and running down his body. There is a lot of internal pressure building there and I don't want to be around when he goes bang, the stitching overwhelmed, bits of Frank'n'Steve splattering everywhere.

"Don't run away," the Badger says, "you don't want me to chase after you. Well, that is going to be a nuisance."

Yet the Badger is suddenly straining to keep a hold of Frank'n'Steve which is enough for me to leg it. I flee down towards the howling sea and the twilight. I glance behind to see if I'm being pursued before running into something that feels like an outcrop of the rocky cliffs.

"Ooof," I flounder on the ground again.

Wasn't I just here?

The cliff has broken stones for teeth, and what looks to be some enigmatic scratched graffiti on its face. It is wearing a pair of dark glasses.

And I think, *About time.*

....

The first hints of the auroral lights to come intimate their arrival. I am dusty and dirty, and my body feels like a purple welt. And like me, the air has become grittier from the pounding of the waves along the coast. While the sea does surge up the beach on the bigger swells, the bay though remains sheltered from the worst of it.

I sit in the gloaming, hidden in the dunes, the sea grass itching my calves, mentally thanking the Badger for showing up when he did.

That he should be there just then ...

I am disturbed by the thought that I am no longer hidden behind Norman's information event horizon. Release the Badger. So much for my getaway. Norman had calculated the probabilities; he had run those scenarios through. And more than all that, he knew me. Then again, that was the Badger's gig too. Maybe it had been lucky that Frank'n'Steve and I had gone nose-to-nose when we had.

Maybs, I think, *maybs not.*

I say, "I need to scamper quick bruh. I seem to have somehow ticked off both a friendly local drug dealer and some kind of omnipotent AI weather god who wants to take their revenge on me."

It seems like a hollow reassurance when eddie says, "Nah, nah, hes can't come here."

I wasn't so sure about that. For someone who had transcended demise by giant raptor, I no longer knew what Norman's limits should be, what should be impossible. That he wasn't quite right in the noggin only made it more possible.

"Yous could never stay anyway. This was one of them short breaks away. Yous got to go back to Earth. Doors-to-the-doors service, I help you go back."

He was right and I'd known for some time that I had to. Yet again, he was there in a time of need, and I cannot fathom why. Reasons, so hard to guess at the best of times, eddie so unreadable, his actions consistently defying understanding, and I slip deeper and deeper into his debt. Sooner or later, he had to call it in.

"Thanks for everything you've done for me eddie," I say.

"I ain't done nothing for ya bruh."

"But the scampering, L'Hôtel, the Shire, the C-beams ... I owe you so much."

"Yous owe me nothing but everybodies got to pay sometime," and he clicks, "yous know when."

I'm still at a loss and eddie isn't for elucidating and sits as that chunk of granite cliff face sporting sunnies.

Bon fires are being piled up; sound systems set up as a counterpoint to the yowling of the waves. Further down the beach where the bay curves the sea surges closer to Castaways. Then there is the first real aurora to light up the sky. While those on the beach cheer and whoop, we remain silent. I try to grasp eddie's words. For a piece of granite, he sure is elusive. It seems like I am off the hook though when it comes to monthly debt repayments.

Alright, if it wasn't me that he was doing it for, then who?

I try to reach for an answer. If you take me out of the equation what is the point of his travel agency? Doors-to-doors guaranteed ... I watch him amble away from the portico of L'Hôtel, I turn, the doors open, and I see ...

"Skylah," I say almost unconsciously.

"She's not wanted to leave but she doesn't have forever."

"I want to find her before I go, and I don't know how."

"Bruh," he clicks, "almost time."

He nods towards the beach, and I think he's meaning that the party is about to start. Then a flash from the solar storm prompts the memory of that imagined future when the dome cracks and Skylah's eyes burn out and freeze.

"I want to take her with me," I say.

eddie mumbles something which sounds like either "oh brother" or "no brother".

....

I sit down on the beach. It is the same spot where the seizure had taken me after the Dove Festival. Bonfires are being lit. People are playing drums or guitars or running into the surging sea and laugh when they are knocked off their feet. So different to the night of the Dove Festival when it had been empty. Speakers are blasting out a pandemonium of discordant musics. Twirlers of both real and artificial fire twirl here and there. The solar storm has called them all to the beach. Yet tru eddie's travel agency had performed its second act of magic to have brought me here to this moment and place. She is dancing around one of the bonfires wearing a bikini top and harem pants. Her long blonde dreadlocks whipping about her head and falling over her face until she raises her head and arms up and her hair falls down her back. I sit on the other side of the bonfire just beyond the reach of its light gazing at her, caught in the enchantment of the moment. How could this be? Skylah dancing on this beach only lit by the lights of the solar storm. There is nothing else to do than accept that it is happening.

The paths back to that seizure are as lost as the mystery of finding her here. Could I excise all that wasted, pointless time, stand up and call to her? Call to her, bring her back from her disgust with me? I had not wanted to get involved with her. It had been too much too soon after the breakup with Norman. Maybe the wasted time was necessary to make this one happen? A long circular path to, in the end, come back to the point of the breakdown. All that time, seizure time, only finishing now? Or I was wishing it was. But look up the definition of stupid in the dictionary and see a picture of me there. It's apparent that Norman wasn't the only one bad with women. Projection eh? For all the untested virtues ...

I do not want to break this crystalline moment. It will fracture all by itself but one less thing to be at fault for would be welcome. She had stayed; I had wanted; the curtain of lights had opened a path through the maze of twirlers of fire. Then I remember that the curtain of lights is Norman-sent and can't really believe that he would intend that. It is tempting to believe that no time had elapsed since the Dove Festival; that this moment had followed directly on from the previous; yet when I look across the bonfire at Skylah, I am struck by a sense of brittleness. Yet it seems deeper than that and I remember one night dancing at Bar 0 with her when had turned to me to say, "Sometimes I feel like I'm only a beam of light and our bodies are manifestations that slowly waste away," but it might as well have been eddie saying, *she doesn't have forever.*

Then the curtains of light that had led me to her, light up the beach so that she sees me. She stops dancing. I stand up and she comes running, not running, around the bonfire to me.

"It's you, isn't it?" she says as she stands in front of me.

I glance up embarrassed. Her gaze savages me making sure I am real, but it also looks far away to another place or time. Maybe I had caught sight of her déjà vu? Then I am swept up in it as I am her arms.

"Where did you go? Where have you been?" she asks urgently.

"Can we get out of here?" I ask gently turning Skylah to walk down the beach.

I am still spooked by the incident with Frank'n'Steve and the Badger.

We walk to the headland where the cliffs are at their highest and find ourselves a nook in the lee of the dunes close to them. Amongst the boom of the waves and under the evanescent curtains of the universe we whisper of the things that had happened to us since the Dove Festival. Skylah tells me that after a few hours, and after she had stopped being angry, she came back to try to find me. Then she tried L'Hôtel d'Orion. They had refused to tell her anything. Yet she kept coming back afraid that I did not want to speak to her because I was angry. In her lint collector way, she had blamed herself. Then one day when Taz the Eloquent was on the door, he had pulled her aside to quietly tell her that I was no longer a guest there. He had no idea where I'd gone.

That was the last that she knew of me until I had appeared at the spot where she had left me after the Dove Festival. I filled in some of the more colourful details about my exiting from L'Hôtel.

"You know how to get under people's skin."

"It's a gift," I shrug as the lights of Norman dance above us.

I also gave her some sketchy details about the rout of seizures I had suffered.

"Do you know why you get them?"

"Not exactly. I kind of sense when they're coming on."

"Let me know alright?"

"Everything's great right now. Not everything beautiful is far away."

I look up into the sky and think, *Nor is everything scary far away either.*

If anything, it looks like it is getting closer.

We huddle into one another, and Skylah tells me that she'd been trying to find modelling work up here.

"I thought you wanted to get away from that sort of stuff?"

"A girl's got to do what a girl's got to do. I've heard that Elva-4 is good and I'm really positive about it but I couldn't leave ..."

I put my arm around her.

"I'm so happy you stayed and I'm sorry that I didn't."

Skylah snuggles closer but hurt mixes with denial when she says, "I know I wanted more than you wanted to give freely but you never told me anything about yourself."

"It's complicated," was all I admit.

"By the goddess! You want so much, and you give so little."

"I was fun though, wasn't I?" I try.

"Yes, you were utterly wild-"

"And good looking."

"Don't push it," she squints at me.

"C'mon," I give her a raffish wink.

She holds her hand under my chin.

"Those eyes of yours ... you could damn a girl."

She shakes her head as I go to kiss her, "I need more than that. Do you really want to be with me?"

I feel so stupid. My mouth twists trying to hold back the pain.

"It was only losing you that made me realise how much I loved you."

She sits on her knees facing me and draws my hand to her heart. Our heads move towards each other until they lightly touch.

"Do you really?"

"I promise. I don't want to be anywhere else."

She breathes, "Then be here."

"I am."

"May the goddess curse you if you're lying to me. You've made a promise. I'm not a plaything. I'm not going to be used that way again."

As we move inside one another, I do not care about the consequences. I don't care about the hypocrisy. I don't care that I had come to The Belt of Orion to be free of feeling anything and that this was everything I didn't want to have happen. I don't care about curses from goddesses or the vengeance of gods. Skylah may try to refuse to be a plaything, but I know I am a plaything of those larger forces, that there are going to be costs. To Hell with them? tru eddie may have forgone my debt to him but Hell always gets paid. Their debt collectors are exceptional when it comes to tracking down unpaid invoices. It's in the license's T&Cs, in the small print on p.18 that nobody ever bothers reading. Just click on 'Accept' because you have no choice anyway. It's only a matter of how knee or neck breaking they will be. They will come to collect the outstanding owed on this moment. It is only a matter of time.

The solar storm plays on the sky above and dimly on her skin. A breeze has picked up, the first I've felt here. It carries on it the taste of dust and sand. Despite the doming and terraforming, it looks like The Belt is trying to establish its own climate.

Skylah lies beside me with her arm over my chest. I feel the bruises from Frank'n'Steve's assault. Ever so minutely I squirm to find a more comfortable position on the sand.

"I'm getting cold," she says.

"Yes, let's get out of here," I agree.

"Where are you staying?"

"At Castaways."

"Isn't that a bit of a dive?"

"It depends on much it gets flooded tonight, so I think it's your place."

....

Skylah's place turns out to be an attic room in a quaint faux American gothic B&B on the intersection of Longfellow and Middle Roads. A thin, fanciful building with tall spandrel windows and a steep roof that, because we were in the attic, I kept bumping my head on the ceiling. Skylah loved the ornamentation of it: the dainty gazebo on one side, the cast iron panels on the veranda, painted gaudy shades of pink. We are swept up in the moment and on the way to her B&B, we speak about what we had not yet done at The Belt as if they are plans for the future, plans about how we would spend the rest of our lives together. I say that I still want to do the Infinity Mirror Room and take a trip to Hyrieus. She says that hadn't done the Infinity Mirror Room either or visited The Shire.

I frown, "Um, let's not do The Shire, okay?"

"You're joking?"

"Yeah, there too."

We lie on her bed watching the effects of the solar storm from Alnilam. Being this close to Skylah when the sky lights up, I can't help noticing the brittleness that I had seen earlier. Her bruising seemed like it was surfacing. She places her hand on my heart.

"When I first saw you at the bonfire," she says, "I thought you must have been a hallucination. Then you stood up and I knew that you weren't just the pale shadow of my terrible longing for you."

She holds it there a moment then wipes a tear from her eye.

"But there always was something strange about you ... somehow you weren't right. You didn't fit at The Belt. You had the look of a lost soul who didn't know that they were."

Mmm, could it be that I'm not as self-aware as I think I am? No, no, that's not possible.

"You and your witchy ways. Wasn't I as bad as any other tourist here?"

"Oh yes, you were, you wanted to get down to business even before you knew my name."

I wait for her to continue. The Dove Festival still lies between us. It is like watching the upswing of your executioner's blade. Maybe she fears the downswing too. She doesn't go on.

I say blandly, "The solar storm is getting more intense."

The blade wavers from being held up for so long. She had painted her fingernails all different colours. We lie there in a few uncomfortable minutes of silence before she breaks it.

Her voice quavers and her eyes suffuse with déjà vu, "How do you think it made me feel when you ran away from me at the Dove Festival? You broke my heart like my last sugar daddy had. I couldn't believe it was happening again."

"I didn't mean it to look that way."

"How was it supposed to look? All I wanted to do was share my real name with you and you wouldn't even let me do that."

My heart is pounding – Skylah must feel it. This is what had brought on the seizure at the Dove Festival.

"Can I tell it to you now? I want you to call me by my real name. Skylah is my sugar baby name, and it was easier to keep it when I came up here."

I wasn't sure I wanted to hear it. Nothing had changed for me there except my fear of seizures had receded.

Yet I look into her eyes, "You need to tell me to ask for it."

She frowns for the last time as the woman I knew as Skylah and says, "Ask me what my real name is."

I ask, "What is your real name Skylah?"

"It's Rega."

"That's an interesting name," I say.

"Rega Mortensen."

The world turns over and I am staring at all the pretty colours in the sky, my head the basket case I always guessed it was.

Chapter 14: You Cannot Run

I have misheard.

"What did you say your name was?"

"Rega ... Mortensen."

It was like my failed tweaking of the dials on the side of tru eddie's sunglasses in The Shire. They hadn't worked then and no matter which way I turned the images of Skylah and Rega, they refuse to overlay into one now.

"What's wrong Jamie?"

Then in a horrific flash, I see the image of Skylah overlay a dead one of Rega and my heart is rent in two. I draw Skylah close to me and place my ear to her chest to listen to her heart. Little wonder I'd run when she had last tried to tell me.

"Nothing, nothing," I say, "Be close to me. I just want to hold on to you."

I wonder if she could feel the plasma card in my forehead and the extreme sadness that must have led to its creation. Being this close to her reassures me. I feel her body next to mine, skin on skin, and the weirding moment relaxes its grip on me. The plasma card made me appreciate my Rega. I grow more at ease with the coincidence. There is more than one Rega Mortensen in the universe. There are two of them in this bed for instance.

I sit up to look out the window. Inside Skylah's B&B the howl of the sea is muffled, while the green hued sandstorm blows unrelentingly, and the weirding moment lingers. All of it, all of The Belt, everything that has happened is so baffling.

"Well, that does explain one or two things," I begin, "You weren't the only one leaving a bad relationship when you left Earth. I was too. I had discovered that my partner was cheating on me. I left in such a rush I didn't know where I was going or what I was going to do. I didn't even have my passport. I was in a panic. I was desperate and scared when I met a guy who said he could get me up here. I'm still puzzled why he never harvested me for my bodily organs, but he was as good as his word. It was he who suggested The Belt of Orion and it was he who gave me some fake ID in the name of Rega Mortensen."

"Hello, I love you," the Lizard King had sung for all us fools.

Maybe don't tell me your name.

Rega is surprised. A piece fell into place for her, "So that's why we had a mix up with the rooms at L'Hôtel."

Then her eyes suffuse with a deep faux outrage sparkle, "You stole my room!"

"I did offer to share."

What had tru eddie done?

"There's more," I continue, "my ex has tracked me down and he's coming to The Belt. He's a bit upset about our breakup and is demanding that we get back together. He doesn't seem in the mood for a 'no' either."

"That sounds abusive."

"He's not exactly himself these days, he's become a little unhinged."

It was an old rusty hinge which had been on the verge of breaking for a long time.

"I've tried reasoning with him and when that didn't work, not reasoning with him. At least now that he's coming here, he's stopped calling me. Those phone calls were driving me crazy."

"He was calling you?"

"Lots."

"You're the first person I know who's got phone calls here."

"I could've done without them."

"You look worried Jamie."

"I don't want to be here when he comes."

"You were going to leave before finding me at the beach?"

"Yes."

"Then come to Elva-4 with me. You can hide from him there. I can do modelling and if that doesn't work out I could become a tour guide or something. And you can do ... whatever it is that you do."

It is simple. It is easy. She is winsome. Of course I agree.

You cannot run.

Yous got to go back to Earth.

....

By sunrise we had booked tickets for Elva-4. Hyrieus is still marginally shielding The Belt from the full impact of the solar storm which means that later this evening I will slither away before the full destructive arrival of Norman. Except that today there is not exactly a sunrise. Alnilam is a murky presence behind all the sand that is still being churned up from the beach, more corona than star, and the solar storm is making for a strange greenish tinge to the light. It is the first real kind of weather I have seen at the Belt. With the rising star, we set, falling asleep under a warm blanket of sand.

Sometime around midday I wake. Rega is still sleeping. The gloom of the sand has deepened so it could be almost any time. While I idly play with a dreadlock by her ear, I am possessed by misgivings about my chances of evading security on the way out of The Belt. I am convinced that Norman has removed his protection and what was once a bolt hole in the data might close around my neck like a rear naked choke hold. One scan of my forehead would doom me to welcoming the new Norse god at the space port with a lei of flowers or more likely a laurel wreath.

"Hey bubble head, how's tricks? You've got to try the sea anemone at L'Hôtel."

No, I'd rather not.

I fall asleep again. Later in the murky afternoon I wake with Rega running her finger in a circle over my forehead where the plasma card resides. We look deeply into each other's eyes and the sharing of a name has brought us closer together. She gets up to make tea for us which she brings back to bed. Since our little catch up, Frank'n'Steve's claim that Skylah was his has troubled me. Placing the teacup down, I tentatively ask her whether she still hangs out with him. She arches one of her impeccable eyebrows.

"Is that a hint of jealousy in you Jamie?" she smiles though it feels like she is dodging the question.

I remembered that knowing-something-you-don't-know look that Frank'n'Steve had given me at the Dove Festival.

"No," and it truly didn't feel like jealousy, "mostly not."

She jumps on top of me and begins tickling. I playfully throw her off.

"Why Jamie, I think you're becoming human," she smiles smugly.

I'm still frowning. I'm missing something here.

"Oh he's harmless," she dismisses me with a flick of her dreadlocks.

"Oh?" I respond pulling a face.

The beach after the Dove Festival remains vividly in my mind. It seems it is more a matter of to whom and how much harmlessness he would inflict on anyone who came between him and Rega.

After that we start packing, readying to go to the space port to catch the shuttle.

Live life on the run. Run now.

My backpack is almost always ready so I check the bathroom for any of Rega's things. I open a cabinet above the basin. On the shelves, there is makeup which she had never used previously. That is not what has stopped me. It is a memory of sitting at the Bowl, Frank'n'Steve passing me a couple of pills, Rega grinding one under her heel. What then is a bottle half full of pills doing on the shelf above the makeup? She had been so adamant about them. Then the penny drops why she still hangs out with Frank'n'Steve, what he has over her. It's there in her deep bruising and vulnerability. It's there in her brittle ephemerality. It's there in the bottles of foundation and cream cleansers. But there's the plasma card in my forehead and I suppose that the world is full of hidden Regas and I may not be the only lost soul here.

I go back out and Rega is breezily moving around the room checking here and there for her things. I hesitate when she comes over to me before handing her the bottle like sharing a secret.

"I found these ..." I say.

"Oh," she looks down at the bottle, her dreadlocks falling over her face.

"That's um embarrassing. I was kind of upset about that pill you tried to give me at the Dove Festival."

I put my arm around her. The breeziness with which she had been moving drops and we sit on the side of the bed.

"I didn't want to use anymore; I was only doing them because you wanted to," she says and I feel a stab of guilt, "I had been doing them a lot when I'd been a sugar baby. Most girls who were babies did. It helped with ... everything. But I was getting really messed up on them. And the scary thing is I don't even remember coming up here. I'd been dreaming about it for a long time. I just knew I had to get away."

"But when you left, it was so terrible. There was nothing, just nothing. They were the only thing that helped. But since making up my mind to go to Elva-4 I haven't been taking them so much. I really haven't," she asserts with the sincerity of a child.

"And since you came back I'd forgotten about them. It's strange, I don't think I need them anymore."

She hands the bottle back to me. Her eyes have an otherworldly shine and she smiles like dawn on a new world. I am as bad as those pills though and drunken words shouted at the barmaid at O'Shaughnessy's fill my head. Delusion and disappointment are always deliriously excited to armchair hope out of a pub. Yet, there is a lessening of that knot of déjà vu and a hint of peace in her eyes too. It would be too cruel to deny her this. I smile.

"To the toilet then!" I exclaim and we rush to the bathroom to flush them.

She squeals with delight as we jostle to get through the door first.

....

After we finish packing, Skylah has a revelation, "I've lost track, it's Thursday. Bar 0?"

The shuttle to Elva-4 did not leave till early morning.

"We can leave our bags in a locker at the space port before going for one last dance."

With Frank'n'Steve nicely hogtied in a police cell somewhere, I nod, "Definitely."

We stand by the door and survey the attic room where we had spent our day at The Belt together. The bed is a mess of sheets and the teacups unwashed. Now, though, for the night.

It is worse than we had expected. As soon as we step out of the B&B, we are assaulted by the howl of the sea and grit in the air. Rega gags reflexively. She draws a couple of scarfs from her bag that we tie around our faces.

We walk arm-in-arm up Longfellow to the terminal to take the train to the space port. Overhead the dome turns silver-grey from the last rays of Alnilam and for a moment, we are spared the green light from the solar storm. We turn towards the screams and laughter from the perpetual carnival but rather than go there we walk to the terminal for the space port. On the train I am edgy. I don't like the thought of going into the space port other than to escape The Belt. I don't like being on the train either. The bright lights inside the carriage are an immobilising jelly and I am a bug caught waiting for a giant Badger to peel the lid off the can, pierce the jelly with his claws to wedge me out. I wave a pathetic feeler in salutation and capitulation.

Looking at the blankness beyond the window Rega says, "It's strange. People always seem to always to leave on full moons. With this sandstorm, I kind of feel alright. We can't see anything in the sky."

I don't feel so alright. There is presence of God Norman in the sky outside, wanting to crush the Belt in his violent beauty that I feel even inside Bar 0. And the truly fearful thing is not being sucked into the void but wanting to jump. I am only being held back, held onto, by Rega.

We leave the platform to descend the stairs to the space port. I halt a few metres from the doors unable to go any further.

Rega asks, "Just how many people have you annoyed here at The Belt?"

I start counting fingers with my thumb before musing, "Do I include the garbage contractors?"

With a harrumph, she picks up my backpack to take the escalator down to the brightly lit terminal.

"Thanks," I call to her back.

When she comes back, she doesn't even really ask, "Mintaka Boulevard?"

After we take the return trip, we go down into the carnival to pick up some food before going onto Bar 0. We're both starving and stop in front of El Mariachi's.

"Want to?" I ask tentatively.

Rega is already ordering. She gives her impudent shrug and smiles. We wait nervously for our tacos to arrive like two teenagers before their first time. We simultaneously bite into them, then the sea howls, then I howl, then Rega kisses me to share her burn and I order a milkshake pronto.

After that we meander through the carnival towards Bar 0. We come across a market stall selling cheap jewellery. Rega finds two necklaces with half broken hearts on them.

"Yeah its tacky," she says as she hands one to me.

After I put the necklace on, she cuddles into me.

"I'm so happy that we're going together now," she says, her voice muffled in my chest, "I was so scared that I would leave without you. I couldn't..."

"Yes, its fine now."

Unbidden, tru eddie's words spring into my mind, *Yous got to go back to Earth.*

Had he really meant not to go to Elva-4?

And when she looks up, there are trails where tears had spilt from her ocean eyes onto the sand of her cheeks.

We find our way through the labyrinth to Bar 0. Lights flicker by a second storey window. We push through the doors, away from the howling sea and the sand and are instantly overwhelmed by the music that they are playing full of bells, sliding synths, pummelling drums, pulsing vibraphone, and whirring arpeggios. I feel utterly liberated, all those memories from our Thursday nights there hold me in their warm embrace as does Skylah, and I am nothing less than joyful. I am transformed and leave my fears at the checkroom. We run up the steps, straight to the bar, slam down some shots, followed by another couple, and then onto the dance floor where we are swallowed by the music and slow dance inside a beam of light. We

SOMETIMES YOU JUST NEED A BREAK

should have been more wary. Bar 0 was the last place we should've gone.

Yet, I needed to get through security to get on the shuttle and downing shots seems like as good a way as any to do it. Then it is time to go. I suggest one for the road and while Rega goes to the bar to get them, I go to the DJ booth to shout over the top of the music, "Who is playing this trippy, trans shit?"

I come back to the bar to find that somehow Frank'n'Steve is not pleasantly being served up on a skewer, apple in mouth, as roast lunch to his fellow inmates at some intergalactic prison. He's there with Rega who has her back to me. Frank'n'Steve casts a ghastly grin at me, a wide, toothy grin, and then with a flourish offers Rega a pill. She pushes his hand back to him, and I breathe again. With the hand holding the pill he backhands her with such force that it knocks her to the floor. I am shocked by the viciousness of the blow and instinctively charge at Frank'n'Steve. It is a hopeless attempt, whatever it is. He sends me flying into the crowd. My fall is cushioned by people who are giving way in front of the fight. Someone else has taken offence at what Frank'n'Steve has done to Rega and has thrown a punch at him causing a melee to erupt. In the forest of falling legs, tables and bar stools, I have lost sight of Rega. Then I see her under a table not far from me. I crawl towards her as the fight rages around me.

She is holding her mouth where Frank'n'Steve hit her.

I shout, "Are you okay?"

She nods and, while I see the welt of Frank'n'Steve's blow already appearing on her face, there is a look of triumph in her eyes. She knew that she could say no to his hits.

I shout, "Let's get out of here."

Before we could move, the table we are under is knocked over and Frank'n'Steve is ragdolling Rega up and away. I grab for her legs but she's already gone. I scramble after them. Frank'n'Steve is dragging Rega through the crowd and she is flailing a hand trying to grasp for any kind of hold. The Badger's advice on the art of war comes back to me.

Slide a hand under the jaw ...

No, that is worse. My attempt at the rear naked choke hold is as pathetic as my first attempt. Obviously, you need practice at this kind of stuff and Frank'n'Steve swings me against the bar. It's been enough for Rega to free herself. She's on the other side of the bar from me and Frank'n'Steve.

"Run," I yell at her.

We make eye contact.

"I'll find you," I promise.

She wavers.

"Please," I beg her.

tru eddie was right. Everybodies got to pay sometime. She pushes her way between the crowd to leave Bar 0. Pain is shooting through my back from hitting the bar and I turn to face Frank'n'Steve. He is really angry now. His ghoulish hatred of me rages across his face. He is shouting incoherently, spittle flying.

I shout back at him, "She doesn't want you anymore. She's free."

I laugh at him. It sounds like hysteria so I go with it. I spit laughter at him as if he can threaten me with the oblivion that he seeks to mete out. Just a different variety to his usual kinds of hits. I hold a hand up as I find a random shot on the bar, down it and smile. I throw the shot glass at his head and miss.

Oh well, this is going to hurt.

Frank'n'Steve has delayed just long enough for the implacable, immeasurable force of tru eddie to crash into him. Poor sailor, never stood a chance as eddie rains a series of brutal punches down on him. I turn to the barmaid to order another shot.

"Actually," I say, "make it a Blue Crush."

And while she is making it, I turn to see tru eddie stand up from the prone Frank'n'Steve. The shots are making themselves acquainted with my legs and I am barely able to stagger over to where they are to aim as hard a kick as the angry ducks allow at Frank'n'Steve. I don't even come close. Instead, I fall in what I assure myself is vaguely graceful way to sit beside the unconscious Frank'n'Steve.

Oh well.

I aim another kick with my heel at his head but still miss. God how I hate Frank'n'Steve. I stagger back to the bar to have my Blue Crush put down for me.

The barmaid turns to me to say, "Lucky your friend showed up when he did."

I'm not someone to be messed with. Go ask Norman, I think he knows.

"Um, maybe it was luck," I say, "but he's not my friend, he's my travel consultant."

Chapter 15: The Missing D

Above the barmaid, there is a clock on the wall that tells me that it's 2.11am, the loneliest, most bereft time in the world. And there are constellations, too many constellations, flying past my eyes and, at the end of the wormhole, would no doubt be Earth and Norman, the return to ugly reality.

"Hey Norman, sorry to take off on you like that. I needed to explore how to become a better person. Now I'm back, I fully appreciate the wonderful, sharing person you are and the relationship we have. Just don't break the dome, eh? That would be sweet."

He is outside in his terrible beauty. Then 2.11am penetrated my mind.

"eddie," I say urgently, "there's still a chance I can get the shuttle for Elva."

eddie is beside me but has his back against the bar.

"No brother," he shakes his head.

"No, there is," I reply urgently, "I can still make it."

I turn to leave and my legs go from under me. The Badger is just standing up from inspecting the mangled Frank'n'Steve. To my way of thinking, he needn't have drawn his gun, let alone point it at us. He waves it towards the emergency exit at the back of Bar 0. Even in my battered and wasted state this unnerves me. Surely everyone would prefer the nicely lit front stairs with plenty of witnesses who could mostly get their stories straight? I'm sure I do. I don't want to go down a poorly lit alleyway with a cop. Bad, unfortunate, accidental things happen down them. I remember how he had emptied the common room at Castaways.

He makes people disappear.

eddie lifts me up as if I am nothing more than a puppet on strings, my feet dangling from my insensate wooden body. The Badger props open the door to the fire escape and waves for us to go first. The last thing I see leaving Bar 0 are bouncers scooping up the prone Frank'n'Steve and people returning to dancing to the music.

Outside again we inhale a lungful of gritty air and the sound of the agonised sea. eddie does his best struggling down the narrow iron stairs. Halfway down he drops me. I land awkwardly on the metal grill clunking my head which prompts a bout of hysteria.

"Get it together bruh, this is serious," eddie says anxiously.

I get all ticklish as eddie tries to pick me up.

"Yeah, I guess," I chortle.

The Badger is casually waving his gun to indicate for us to stand to one side of the alley – his gun looking like a toy pistol in his paw. He stands opposite. eddie lets me go and I feel like I should let my legs go too so I do. We're by a dumpster and a garbage truck and I remember happier days at The Belt, carefree behind the wheel. What is most remarkable about the alley is how much garbage is in it. The wind is coming straight off the sea and is funnelling through this narrow laneway. A plastic bag blows between us and the Badger.

"Welcome," says the Badger, "to this cold, hard bit of reality. I told you I knew all the dirty little recesses. Very regrettable that you had to make such a scene in front of our rather more legitimate guests, but he was a very nasty customer that one. He did lead me back to you though he didn't know that I did let him go. Nobody breaks my rear naked choke hold without my say so."

The Badger scratches the side of his face with his gun, "Rega, Rega, Rega, you do come with a history ..."

He shakes his head in evident disappointment as if reading a rap sheet.

"The waste disposal vehicles," he says eyeballing me from across the alleyway, "you should feel right at home down there in the dirt. But the baby crocodile, you did make me smile at that one. That certainly had them jumping in the water aerobics."

My grimace neither confirms nor denies.

In fact, it had nothing to do with any of that, "Rega's not here anymore, she's gone."

She would be on her shuttle soon and on her way to the impossibly far away Elva-4. She is almost certainly lost to me. I would never see her again and there aren't words to describe that feeling. Hollow? Desolate? As empty as the space between stars? A need for a hit from Frank'n'Steve?

"Really?" the Badger raises an eyebrow, "tell me this, if I scan your forehead, won't I find the name of one 'Rega Mortensen' there rather than Jamie with a smiley face over the 'i'? I mean, really ladies and gentlemen," he stands to gesture to an imaginary jury, "Someone who is there one minute, gone the next, but hey presto, here you are again. Someone with so little care for anyone else, who breached the jurisdiction of the Tannhauser Gate and trespassed the absoluteness of the law by their existence here."

"She's left and she's not coming back."

I laugh maniacally, tipping into the realm of the hysterically sobbing. eddie has wisely dissociated himself from this madness to stand a few feet away. The Badger shakes his head, dismissing my hysteria as beneath contempt.

"And this would indubitably be tru eddie. In good soothe, finally. You've been very elusive unlike your client here who showed scant

SOMETIMES YOU JUST NEED A BREAK 207

regard for their illegitimate status. You must be so grateful to have taken such risks for this ..." he leaves off crinkling his nose at me.

I feel like I should be offended but I am doing my best to dissociate from this scene altogether. Nothing good, nothing good. The lights of the solar storm are descending behind the Badger in an ominous way.

tru eddie cocks his head non-committally and the Badger continues, "But I only had to wait long enough for his antics to eke you out from the background morass. Clearly, he is too much of a dolt to have passed their way through security by himself and it is you who I've been more interested in. You who facilitated this transgression, who made it possible."

Somehow through the hysteria hope penetrates. I can still make it.

"Um, Badge," I wave my two index fingers pointing to the nearest exits either here or here, "as you were after eddie, I'll be on my way."

The Badger is bemused as I get unsteadily to my feet and begin to sway my way to the other end of the alley. I am driven by the mad thought that I can still get on the shuttle.

"Stay where you are," commands the Badger.

I am too far gone to heed him. Seeing this, the Badger takes three quick steps to push me over.

"Now, where was I?" the Badger scratches his head with his pistol while gathering his thoughts, "Ah yes, tru eddie, I'm intrigued, one professional to another, how'd you do it? Was it a self-replication error?"

I get up again and the Badger pushes me over again. I'm liking this game.

eddie waves his hands for me to stay down, "Bruh, bruh, bruh."

Before I go down for the third time, I see the Badger's face suffuse with rage, his nostrils flaring, yet I say, "I've got to see her again."

As I try to regain my feet, the Badger is shouting above the yowl of the sea, "You stay down or I'll put you underground."

No matter, I am up again and this time the Badger isn't messing around. The blow is so quick and clinical I feel as if I have shattered like china dropped on pavement.

"Now to the matter of the self-replication error and the plasma card," the Badger says collecting his thoughts.

I am trying to figure out how my teeth are suddenly jarred and why I taste blood in my mouth.

"I's did nothing," eddie says in what sounds like he was shifting the criminal culpability back onto me, "it was all'im."

I could not raise myself this time, so I begin dragging myself towards the end of the alley. It is pitifully slow, but it is enough to get the Badger's attention. He blocks my path and I try feebly to go around him.

"Get back," he commands, "stop."

I do neither and there is a note of dismay in his voice that he had ensnared himself in this alley with this unheeding maniac. He brings his gun to my forehead like he is going to make a destructive scan of my brain from all the bits and pieces of my grey material left on the walls of the alley.

"Stay where you are," he says as he must now fear that things aren't going quite the way he had imagined them to.

The hammer on his pistol goes back and then in the alley there is a sound that reverberates like thunder. The Badger is falling over me. In the mess of limbs, I feel every spasm and shudder. eddie appears above me to peer down the middle of a gyring maze.

"Oh eddie," I cry as the horror of the seizure lays its pernicious fingers on me. tru eddie stands above us and looks from me to the Badger.

"Oh bother," he says as I slide into the death-grip of the seizure.

....

SOMETIMES YOU JUST NEED A BREAK

I wake from fighting dreams that felt as soft as putrescence and as difficult to escape as steel. A needle-like spring from a bare grey mattress is poking into my arm. I feel like garbage. In fact, I smell like it too. The walls of the room are made from tin on one side and weatherboarding on the other. Tacked up, patched up here and there, exposed beams and joints. The room has dirt floors and sand blows in under the tin and weatherboarding. A single light bulb hangs on a cord from one of the beams. It seems to sway but that could be me rather than a breeze. My eyes are thankful for the murk of the room as the light isn't on. It is a very long way down from L'Hôtel, a long way down even from Castaways. My insides catch jaggedly against one another and my bottom lip bulges as if I have won the galaxy's biggest botoxed lip competition.

"I'd like to thinish my speech by fanking the Academy and say a whittle hair for phorld feace."

I shield my eyes as the cameras flash and bend forwards for extra effect to flap my bottom lip. It could all be worse. I could be the person screaming at the top of their lungs.

A vague lifting of the gloom of the sandstorm suggests that Alnilam is rising. Have I hit rock bottom in my tour of intergalactic psych wards? Beethovian pastorals playing? No, just the soundtrack of that person's screaming which transcends any kind of ordinary human anguish. It's animal. I have some anguish going on myself.

Oh Rega, where are you now?

Not as much as theirs though. Such is the power of it, I feel like I am going through it myself. I want to block it out or fall back into the grey mattress and the grey dreams from whence I've come. I had once tried to voice the rage of the sea but it was nothing like their screams. It is the gnashing of a sandstorm eviscerating a body and grinding a soul to dust. I regret not going to the meditation classes at The Shire.

"Om mani padme hūm, om mani padme hūm, om mani padme hūm."

No good. Somehow deciding that I should start trying at this moment of inconvenience didn't work. Stupid meditation.

There is a syringe on a table in the opposite corner of the room from me. A spoon lies next to it. Top notch drugs of peace and serenity to keep the anxiety levels down: I know that syringe and its owner. Anxiety levels are unsurprised. A little eddie-style pick me up and I am able to sit up on the mattress, my knees under my chin. Considering everything, I should feel crustier. Those C-beams of eddie's are phenomenal things. I hug myself. They cannot take away the pain of parting with Rega, nor do they have the power to return her. I stand up shakily. The dread of seizure is still a recent memory in my muscles. A few creaky steps towards the door and they begin to loosen up. If the door is locked, do I dig my way out under the weatherboard? Go pure animal, rip my fingers to pieces to get my freedom, gnaw my leg off to get out of the trap.

The door handle turns, the door opens. eddie hasn't locked me in. There is a short hallway that opens onto the kitchen. On a bench there is a kettle, a frying pan, and a set of scales. Then there is other equipment which suggests that this is not an ordinary kitchen. Equipment more suited to a chemistry lab. I can't name much of it: a beaker, glass tubes and bulbs, thermometers and taps that allow the liquid to flow through, all incongruous with the dirt floors.

I turn the handle of the door to the kitchen, and it opens. I am free of the screams of agony to step outside to the see the ruin that the agony of the sea is bringing. Like so many days wasted with Norman, all is grey. The atmosphere weighed down with sand like a heavy fog above a monotonous moonscape with the dull rumble of the sea in the distance. It is beautiful nonetheless because it's away from the claustrophobic suffering in the shack. I am free to run like I had from the Old Ball, run as I had from Rega. I could find my way to the space port, maybe elude security and Norman, to catch a shuttle if they are still leaving. Nothing now stops me from doing exactly that. Except guilt. What is guilt except the impediment to freedom? I close the door to the kitchen and take a deep breath.

"Eighty-three billion, nine hundred ninety-nine million, nine hundred ninety-nine thousand, nine hundred and ninety-nine," I try instead.

I walk shakily to the door of the room where the screams are coming from.

I open the door to peek inside and find tru eddie sitting cross-legged on a mattress. He is using a large syringe to extract blood, yet the blood is not the colour of ordinary blood. There are shades of violet still in it, even a sanguine purple. I had to admit though, it was mostly blue. The bulk of eddie obscures my sight of the person who lies on the mattress, yet from his first tormented scream, I had known who it was who lay there. The horror had drawn me in.

On the mattress is the Badger but it is the Badger mangled and shrunken by the last stages of *crustacis*. He is barely recognisable. Polyps crust over his head and his fingers are melting into the facsimile of a claw. I cover my eyes, then uncover them. It's like a car crash. The desire to see and the aversion not to. I don't want that memory haunting me. I need to look away. As quietly as I can, I start closing the door.

Without looking up eddie calls, "Come, come."

I follow the invitation into the room and slide down the wall opposite, aghast at what has become of the Badger.

"It won't be long now. I's didn't get him back here quick time. The syrup didn't catch him."

eddie starts wheezing a chant. He has tied down the Badger's arms and legs so that he could not rip himself apart when the pain becomes unbearable. The Badger's eyes are milky white. There is no purple or violet left in the blood that eddie was extracting. It is now royal blue. The Badger emits another piercing scream.

I plead, "Make it stop eddie,"

I feel like I am voicing what would be the Badger's pleas.

"Please eddie," I beg.

eddie is calm.

"Soon, soon," and he nods towards another syringe on the mattress, "last one."

"Brother," says eddie running his hand gently over the Badger's forehead, "go now to your ancestors. Do not linger here no more. Meet them as the brave warrior you are."

eddie starts singing a song in a language I didn't know. Harmonies swim about the room like silver fish in a clear blue sea. eddie picks up the other syringe and slides the needle into the Badger's arm.

"Be at peace."

The Badger's ragged gasps ease, then stop altogether, and I feel as if one of those fish is taking the Badger to wherever he needs to go next. Maybe to a better place than what he found at The Belt. When eddie finishes his song, I surface and, with a breath I'd been holding, a groan comes too. eddie gestures that we should leave the room and closes the door behind us.

"In a little while I's go back in to fix him up. First we must ..." eddie says holding up a collection of syringes.

He goes to the kitchen to empty the syringes into a glass bulb. These he places on what looks like a hotplate and presses a button underneath it.

A little eddie-style pick me up.

I look over the chemistry equipment in eddie's kitchen.

A dialation of my own design.

The dread begins to mount, and I am already walking towards the closest wall to lean against it.

"eddie," I ask, "How do you make the C-beams exactly?"

In his intensely humane way he says, "Is the only way it works."

The seizure is coming. I wish I could stop it because I know how eddie will revive me. eddie watches as I slide down the wall and thud against the floor. He cocks his head to one side.

....

When I wake, my bottom lip and insides feel almost normal. Without a doubt the C-beam has amazing restorative powers. The cost though is horrendous. eddie is sitting on the mattress beside me. I don't want to see him and roll away, turning my back to him.

"He was terminal. I's could not waste him."

I roll back to face eddie, "It's just not easy to see."

eddie makes his gesture of weighing things up with scales.

"Sorry I wanted to scamper in the alley. I really wanted to catch that shuttle."

"I's know."

"It was stupid, so incredibly stupid but ..." and I thought of Rega leaving Bar 0 and the sinking feeling that I'd never see her again surged.

"I's fucked up too. I's thought I could get him back here in time."

We sit in silence for a while.

"You almost tagged me back with the plasma card thing," I frown because it has brought up a gaggle of nagging doubts that I couldn't exactly name.

I ask, "Hey eddie, the self-replication error ... was that true? Did that really happen?"

"Yeah bruh, of course," says eddie quizzically.

I ask, "And your glasses? They work?"

"As true as tru eddie."

"Hmmm ... but I tried them at The Shire and they didn't."

"Nah, nah, not these ones, they're not made for your config, yous need different ones."

He gestures, "Come, come. I's need to finish off the dialation," eddie gets up and the mattress drops underneath me.

"Ooof," I thump on the floor.

I don't want to stay there with my sadness, so I too get up. My pong comes with me which reminds me of another puzzle.

"Wait a minute, how did you did us back to your place?"

He crows, "I's threw yous into the dumpster and drove it here with the truck."

....

Knowing the genesis of the drug, it is not easy watching its transmutation into a C-beam. At times the nausea rises but watching eddie the weirding alchemist is fascinating. Yes, he sterilises his equipment thoroughly. Yes, he reduces, mixes and distils the liquid, but he also hums and shakes it. Then he will sing to it as if the song itself would imbue it with a living essence. So the creation of the C-beam happens before my eyes and I still have no idea how it's made.

At one point while eddie is having a break I say, "Thanks for saving me from Frank'n'Steve. I thought that was going to end badly."

"I's couldn't really hurt him. He's wanted by too many people. He is kikokiko ... 'n' yous had let her go, she needed time."

I clamped my mouth for a moment before gathering myself to say, "You really are the best travel consultant eddie. You were right, you were utterly guaranteed."

"You know it," he pauses then shyly asks looking away from me, "I's need recommendations for the business."

....

We wait until after Alnilam sets to bury the Badger. eddie's shack lay in a moonscaped landscape to the north of the sideshows and rides. All pretence of a posh tourist resort dissipated in the desert, with only a shack here or there and no roads to guide you between. We wrap the Badger in the sheet from the mattress and carry him outside. He is so light – the *crustacis* had emptied him out – nothing left but shell and darkness. We cover our nose and mouth with rags to go outside because the sand is bad even this far from the beach. eddie pulls down his rag to sing his song again which he had sung while the Badger was passing. He explains it is an ancient song from his island. It is of leaving and returning that is traditionally sung at a person's passing. This time, it evokes in me those feelings of how I had tired of the scene at The Belt, the imitation bars and the imitation people, all trying to conjure up some imagined memory of a time or a place that may never have been real.

As eddie sings, Norman unfurls his lights again, but through that curtain I can still see the foreign stars that shine down on The Belt of Orion.

When he finishes, I pull down my mask to ask, "eddie, could you point to Elva-4?"

"Nah, we can't see it from here."

"Oh," I say disappointed.

"It would be dangerous for yous to go there. If yous had a seizure, the C-beams would not help."

My heart sinks.

He lays an unequivocally heavy hand on my shoulder like a command, "Love or not, there's things of the spirit that is healthy to leave behind."

It's just never so easy as that.

Chapter 16: A Terminal Case of Pareidolia

Tru eddie led me back into his hut. "Yous needs to be scampering to the port super quick. This missing D is bad news. It'll bring every bodies out, the cops, security, they's be looking."

eddie pauses letting that sink in. The cop that investigated missing persons had himself gone missing. tru eddie is right. Getting to the space port is going to be tricky. He goes back into the room where the Badger had last laid to bring out his hat and coat.

"But not for one of their own."

He roughly pushes the fedora onto my head while I try to back away, "Woah, woah, woah" I exclaim.

"Yous be incognito like, yous dance right through. Do some Running Man, some Harlem Shake," he says getting a little too jiggy.

"Really?" I frown.

He stops dancing annoyed, "What complainin' you got?" Haven't I got yous door-to-door?"

eddie always seemed to be wanting to load me up with guilt. First Rega, now the Badger. However true it might be.

"No, I really can't eddie," I shake my head.

....

It is not more than 20 minutes before I find the road that runs to the carnival, but it gives me time to ponder eddie's advice on matters of the spirit.

Maybe, I think, *you die, the ultimate state of unhealth, when those things of the spirit become too great a burden to carry any longer.*

As I walk past the lights and the rides, I feel a very edgy vibe. People are scarce and those who are about, are stand offish. The party spirit has succumbed to the storming sand. I am being assaulted by the smell of food which prompts my stomach to remember that it has a huge hunger. It has been a day since I last stood in front of El Mariachi's with Rega.

A whole day, I almost weep, and I try not to be swamped by the memory and the feeling of loss.

It is impossible for me not to sit with what's left of the hardest of hardcore party punters, all bald heads and tattoos, to order a fiery taco. And a milkshake.

I am intensely and perversely enjoying the burning sensation of the chilli, trading pain for pain, when a person sits down next to me to offer, "Let me buy you another one."

The man takes off his fedora, laying it on the counter, and holds up two fingers to order some tacos.

"It's been a long, dogged day of staring at the data," the cop says, "It brings out the need for some intensity by the end of it, say for one of these to-die-for soft shell crab tacos. You can lose yourself in either. My eyes had gone strange from staring into the abyss of disappearing data almost too long until I finally made out a resemblance, a character, a set of motivations and behaviours, that precisely determined a future time and location where a particular person of interest, suspected of transgressing the absolute law that should have proscribed them from coming to The Belt, would sit in front of El Mariachi's to order an aberrantly hot taco. Let me introduce myself, my name is Detective Halm. You see my now awol partner scorns my methods, but I always believed that eventually they would lead me to one Rega Mortensen."

Fear, like a spike, rips through my flesh. I have no innocence to claim anymore.

"My partner cautioned me to only approach Rega with extreme care, but it seems like he was not careful enough."

Somewhere beyond my fear something is not quite sitting right here. I quickly glance to my side and realise that the cop is not speaking to me but to the punter sitting to their right.

Calmly, coolly, I tell myself, *finish your taco.*

Now stand up, nod at the kid who prepared the taco in appreciation of a fine effort.

Casually turn around and walk away.

I hear the punter say through a mouthful of taco, "Me name's not Rega."

Don't let your knees wobble. They're fine. Soothe the angry ducks. Discretely pull up your rag to protect yourself from the sandstorm.

Now, whatever you do, don't look back, don't look back, don't be dammed.

Dammit.

What were the chances that the cop would turn at that very moment to stare at the person who had just left the seat beside them and over that distance make eye contact? Probably not more than being revivified after death by a monstrous fowl while existing in a … blah blah blah. Yeah, that seems about right, and Detective Halm seems drawn to stand up and walk after me.

Dammit.

I am in front of a building with a façade harking back to the golden age of nineteenth century mesmerism with revolving recessive spirals.

There is a Virtual with large sideburns and a stove pipe hat who is spruiking on repeat, "See the unforgettable Infinity Mirror Room.

SOMETIMES YOU JUST NEED A BREAK

You can't describe it; you can only experience it. Immerse yourself in its startling special effects. Experience the spectacular visual illusions that recede to infinity!"

As I've mentioned a few times, I haven't done the Infinity Mirror Room and as a marketing spin those spirals suggest that now is the perfect time to give it a go.

I hear Detective Halm shout, "Halt."

That is enough for me to bolt. I give the revolving doors an extra push.

The small, ginger haired man in the ticket booth barely looks up with a disinterested, "Oi," as I sprint past.

The ramp reverberates as I pound my way up to the entrance. I push my way through the queue before giving one last look back to see Detective Halm has just spun through the doors.

....

Look, as a ride I'd give it 3.5 (out of 5) stars but I guess it depends on what kind of experience you're after. Anna@TheQuays advises not to rush through the rooms but to slow down to enjoy them which is where being chased by a cop costs them 0.5 straight up. Berserker Jr.'s comment that it is an "awesome sensory overload" seems ironic in the darkened corridor beyond the entrance until I pop out into the Electron Maze which Rackymac gives 5-stars to. Balls of light float in a synchronised dance to ambient music, one moving in relation to another, but in my rush to the other side, I create a wake of crashing waves behind me. The AyatollahRock'n'Rollah writes that he was astounded by the laser beam show in the next room, but I feel sliced and diced by the beams. I leave a breadcrumb trail of clues for Detective Halm to follow as I leave a trail of cubes behind. Lalala the Tosh revelled in the Forest Room where you feel the size of a gnat to flit from leaf to leaf through a gigantic, phantasmagorical forest. Thank you overtherainbow.com for your helpful reviews, thank you. All up, it is well worth doing even at a 3.5-star rating though Karl70 cautions, "don't take kids in there, they'll freak" but you don't need to be a kid to freak which is exactly what I did when I sprint out of the forest and into the Tannhauser Gate Room and ...

....

... teeter on the edge of what appears to be a bottomless void. I windmill my arms trying to grasp on to ... nothing, nothing, nothing ... Across the void telescopes a wafer-thin beam of lights that pulses in a kaleidoscopic range of colours. It is the only light in an otherwise unlit room. While my brain is certain that the void must be an optical illusion, there is a leg-wobbling entrancement to it.

And I have nothing to grasp on to.

The void calls to me, to tip then to fall endlessly and never hit bottom.

I fall ...

Down ...

"No!"

Onto the beam of lights.

Ouch.

The bridge is solid enough and I scramble back away from it until my back is against the wall. The void is too much, too uncannily like a fatal drop.

"No, nope, no way, nah-ar," I state about crossing that bridge.

I wash my hands of that idea as I shake the pain from them from breaking my fall. Instead I edge my way along a narrow service walkway to find a hidey-hole in the corner and await the Badger's partner.

Detective Halm arrives short moments later. He too takes a moment to stop himself from falling into the void. I try not to breathe, to make myself disappear.

Become one with the void, I tell myself.

While the bridge only dimly lights the room, my fears shout at me that I will be seen.

Eighty-three billion, nine hundred ninety-nine million, nine hundred ninety-nine thousand, nine hundred and ninety-nine, I try.

The Detective continues to ponder the abyss and I am sure that at any moment a bead of sweat will fall to the floor, echo into the void, to alert the cop to my presence. Amplified by the abyss, the in and out of my breaths will surely set up a deafening feedback loop. And the Detective continues to stand by its edge as if hypnotised.

Why doesn't he move?

I have the mad idea that I could sneak behind him to exit by the entrance door. I crab walk one foot then the other, slowly, slowly, don't breathe, don't breathe.

Angry ducks don't fail me now.

I am a step from the cop and the exit when I am struck again by the seductive pull of vertigo. I gasp and the void shouts my presence. Fear shoots through me – he must sense I'm here. I freeze but he does not move either. We're both living statues. While the bridge of lights would be the obvious thing to become enamoured with, Detective Halm, it seems, has become enamoured with the void instead. Or maybe paralysed by it. He stands staring down into the great chasm unmoved, the lights from the bridge playing over his face. I break.

"Okidoky," I frown.

A terminal case of pareidolia.

"I'll be off then?" I ask.

Nothing. I am about to scamper when I remember tru eddie's suggestion.

"Can I have your hat?" I ask.

Nothing.

"Thanks," I say.

"And your overcoat?"

"Tah."

"And where would your ID be? Ah, thanks again."

....

So, I never make it to the eponymous mirror room where you are fractured into a million splinters, stretched to 8 feet tall, pea-headed and distended, Flatlanded to a few centimetres thick with your eyes remaining the same size, peering back at your pancaked body. Just as well maybe. Instead, I trace my way back through the previous rooms to stop by the ticket seller. I could not so easily leave Detective Halm where he was. The purple lights from the bridge had transmogrified his face into the Badger's dying from *crustacis*.

"There's a man in there who's stuck on the ledge in the Tannhauser Gate Room."

The ticket seller squints at me above the top of his book, his blue eyes slightly unfocussed.

"Does no one read anymore?"

He points towards a sandwich board sign by the revolving doors with a list of conditions where you should not ride if you suffer from them:

Heart condition
Epilepsy
Paralysis

And he goes back to reading his book.

"He needs help Ted," I say.

Having had his name invoked, he involuntarily glances down at his name badge that says, "Hi, I'm Ted," in colourful writing.

He glares back at me.

"I heard him say something about losing his partner."

He puts his book face down between his glass of red wine and an astray full of cigarette butts and hobbles out from behind his booth. He appraises my fashionable garb.

"Why didn't you do something?"

"It's your ride," I counter.
Nonplussed by this he says, "Tannhauser Gate?"
"Yes."

He hobbles up the ramp muttering unhappily about cops and I saunter out into the solar sandstorm feeling lighter for having got help.

....

The storm is having ever-worsening effects for the 24/8 world of The Belt. Shutters are being pulled down on food vans. Stalls are packing up or drawing curtains. Doors are being closed on the imitation pubs. The streets and byways are emptying of people. Rides are shutting down. The music is being silenced. As I make my way through the glowering lights of the solar storm and the grit in the air, lights are flickering off behind me. I feel a growing sense of alarm that I should not be caught in the gathering darkness with only Norman to light my way.

I begin to briskly walk,
run now
then shuffle,
run now
then jog,
run now
then when I look over my shoulder, the jog becomes and as panic takes hold,
sprint now.

My breath is ragged leaving a circle of moisture on my mask.

I make it to the intersection in front of the light rail terminal to see a train waiting there and I hope that my luck is in. As I run up the steps to the platform, I hold up my hand hailing the driver if, in fact, there is one. The doors start to close, and I make a leap.

On the train, I slide down the high-backed seat and tip the brim of the fedora over the space between forehead and mask. Fatigued from my fate as much as anything, tiredness has obliterated the nerves I should be feeling as I glide on the impeccably smooth superconductors of the train towards escape or ... not. The sharp and pointy point irrevocable now. One or the other will happen with no space between. To escape is to go through the jagged and ripping teeth of this dilemma.

Underneath lamp posts green and purple light becomes gray grains of sand. As the train feels like it is barely moving, nothing else marks my passage. I am relieved that the sand is foiling any chance to find the waxing constellation of God Norman's visage in the stars above. Instead, I only see my reflection in the glass and am reminded of when Norman left me at the doors of The Sheridan. The train floats gently onwards until we're there at the port. The doors open and from the platform that is a storey above the entrance to the port I can see that a crowd has gathered. There is a ring of security guards in front of the doors supported behind by cops with no one getting through. I ride the escalator down to join the back of the crowd.

People are shouting at the guards to let them through and one of the space port staff is trying to make herself heard above the crowd.

"We're still in the process of scheduling new shuttle services."

The long-suppressed dread that the dome may fall is hysterically surfacing. The Shire is going to need a lot more beds. People are getting angry. Their faces turning green in the light of the thing that is maybe trying to kill them. They are pleading.

"The magnetic shielding is failing."

"The coronal mass was attracted to it like a magnet."

"The solar plasma is attacking the dome."

"It's a matter of time."

"It's going to crumble."

"We gotta go." (that's me who shouts that one)

It's not as if I haven't relished the prospect of becoming a cream dunked in a coffee cup of liquid nitrogen myself.

SOMETIMES YOU JUST NEED A BREAK

a slightly puzzled, mostly terrified, immutably frozen face-to-face catch up with God Norman in the starry night. Good times. Fun experiment. Get me outa here.

With the sudden sense of being ensnared, fear and anger seethe around me. Not a great time to be dressed as a cop – the very people stopping them from leaving. I don't care which direction but I want out of this crowd that's turning into a frenzied mob readying to vent. I try to push my way out. It's useless. Everybody's pushing. I can't breathe. I am in Skylah's nightmare of flesh at the Bowl. The crush of bodies convulses in the other direction like a wave going out and people are tripping, falling. It is a roiling mess but it's a mess where you can breathe again. Punches are being thrown and I remember tru eddie's suggestion that I should dance my way through. So I start with some running man, dodge a fist with a sidestep, spin my way past two falling, grappling human beings, a glide step sideways, a forwards roll and I flip to my feet to flip out Detective Halm's ID, and suddenly find myself in the bright lights of the space port. I blink. I see the backs of the security guards to me straining to hold out the rest of the crowd. I turn and walk to Departures.

And when I am asked where I'm going I answer, "Anywhere but here."

They answer, "We've just had a new service to Earth come online."

Earth it is then.

....

As drinks are being served on the shuttle and with Earth and Norman rushing ever closer, I sink into the cushions. I take a sip of my Blue Crush. I had ticked off so many things on my bucket list. Staying at a fantastic hotel where simply by staying there I had been treated as a somebody rather than a nobody as I usually am. But better still, being thrown out of L'Hôtel. Living on the lam thanks to various donated credit cards: a big hand in the air to Mr. George and the pompous twat of a director at L'Hôtel. Meeting the Lizard King himself even if he hadn't quite lived up to expectations. I mean who ever does? Never meet your heroes. And who has the kind of wisdom or restraint to do only 49? Going surfing with the surfers: I had preferred the sea when it wasn't in its wine dark phase. You could more easily spot shoes on the bottom that way. Suffering the counsellors and drinking pints with the small people. Having a tragic love affair with a beautiful blonde: well, that was obligatory. Though it had left me with a longing that will endure for a place and a time and a lost love that I can never get back to. It will be haunted in a sad, numinous way. I hold in my hand the necklace with the half-broken heart that Skylah had bought me. Then I can't help it anymore. My vision smears with tears. Apart from the scroll given to me by the Lizard King for his midnight ceremony, it is my only memento from The Belt. I look out the shuttle's window. Strange how it all blurs into a background of stars. But looming above them all was tru eddie – none of this could have happened without him. All the fun and love and sorrow. To begin with, I had only thought badly of him and he had not deserved it. Don't worry eddie I'll put 🕯🕯🕯🕯 up on overtherainbow.com for you.

I am not looking forward to the return to Earth. I would have to confront Norman, perhaps even figure a way to terminate him. How do you terminate a god? As far as I can figure, that's the only way I can be released to go find Rega.

I console myself with the Lizard King's words: *even if you go back to Earth, it doesn't mean that you can't do your list.*

I looked at my list again and there was that glaring omission without a tick beside it. I had never managed to take that day trip out to Hyrieus. Just then the captain announces over the intercom.

"Hi there folks," he starts, "we're currently 22,000 miles above the Belt of Orion cruising at a rate of 18,000 miles per hour. Due to the recent solar storm from Alnilam our rendezvous with the

SOMETIMES YOU JUST NEED A BREAK

Tannhauser Gate will be delayed as we will need to detour behind Hyrieus. I hope you enjoy the sight of the rings. I've been everywhere in this universe folks and seen a whole lotta things and I've got to say that it's the most awe-inspiring thing I've ever seen."

"Damn," I say.

Tick.

Chapter 17: A Blizzard on Second

I sit amongst the tropical plants in the foyer of the CAAIR and look out on a bleak, grey world. Clouds the weight of steel hang from the domed sky and a bitter wind is whipping up piercing knives as I came on to campus. I have spent a week missing the climate control of The Belt. The weather of this world is startling in comparison. It is so cold outside that there were no knock-off Virtuals selling knock-off "I Wanna Be Like Norman" t-shirts at the perimeter of the exclusive rights area of the University. Even if there had been, I wasn't buying. Students were still about but there weren't any new prophets out there proclaiming a new gospel integrating the spirit with the technical, the soul with the silicon, the mystical with the material. There'll be no sermonizing today about how, in creating a silicon god, we too have become gods. Just as well. They'll avoid difficult questions about how they had missed predicting His Coming. I had thought to look in the gift shop for a snow globe of the CAAIR as a peace offering to Norman but there were no guides, luminescent arrows or garlands to lead the way. Nor a gift shop. In truth, I hadn't expected any. When I had checked out *Must Do Twyndale*, there had been no advertising for a VR experience of Norman's simulation in the CAAIR Museum. There is nothing to say that the spinning world has in anyway been knocked off its axis; nothing to say that the golden path of Norman's dreaming has been fulfilled. Why would there be? Why would the Friends want to advertise their competitive advantage with great big flashing signs celebrating the emergence of God Norman, the Technological Singularity, the First-Born Silicon? Particularly if it had gone rogue. It would be the last thing they would want. Success through stealth, killers in carparks.

The pale late afternoon sunshine creeps its way in through the enormous glass panels like an unauthorised visitor and I bask here in a warmth so unreflective of what's out there. The paintings that had hung in the foyer have gone, replaced by the plants. Some thin wooden crates were being carried out by security guards when I was coming in so it could well have been the Dali leaving.

At least one part of Norman wants to be liberated by being turned off while the new Norse God is threatening a reunion that feels more like an extinction of the soul and I've spent the last week finding any other place to go than here. My skittish inclination to flee has had me riding the rails, stopping at stations throughout Twyndale, looking for my first-choice travel consultant. See if she could get me a gig as a jester in the court of the Lizard King. I imagine brushing up on my reptilian comedic stylings for the courtiers.

How do you tell if a chameleon is angry?
He's giving you the side eye.

If, for some reason, I am edged out of the court by the High Inquisitor maybe become the manager of Hi-Jinx Mired at his cosmic Vegas. Or if that job is too ambitious, start as a roadie. Or if even that is too ambitious see if The Belt had survived and work for Jack at Castaways. Learn how to surf the monster waves when the passing celestial bodies rip up the tortured sea. Become a surf instructor, become a lifesaver. Jack may turn an indulgent eye when I sneak out to go surfing but would he let me behind the bar? One for me, one for the customer, one for me. Understand the mind of the patron, the best quality of a barman. When I was still travelling in hope, I lay out these wonderful futures like diverging train tracks at a junction but I never do come across her or any of her ilk. Apparently there's tech being rolled out to block viral outbreaks of guerilla sales reps. And now when I think back about that original travel consultant, I'm struck by how, in reading my unconscious biases, she had begun to resemble Rega. Or that is how she appears to me in my memory. But in pleasing so many different customers who knows what she might look like now?

With no travel consultant, a growing sense of fatalism at war with a surging skittishness, I've ended up in bars with the aim to make every trauma and fear I have look like a beer. The blanking, the betrayal, the breakup, the horror that I may find myself again seeing life only from afar. I could drink them down, find a giddy happiness then flush them all away. I remember my acts of dissolution at The Belt and now that I'm getting close to Norman, I wish to be dehydrated, ground into a powder, and poured into a beer of oblivion, a frothy-headed Jamie-Shandy.

But deciding to turn off my nearest and dearest is one thing, doing it is another. I've spent a lot of time in the last week procrastinating over it as it's not as simple as accidentally tripping over an electrical cord to say, "Whoopsy, look at what silly ol' me has done, I've done the dumbest thing," and that would be the end of it. Buy my ticket to Elva-4, zip through the Tanny Gate and be in the arms of Rega this eventide. But they can just as easily flick the switch back on and pop, there's our all singing, all dancing, bad penny Norman again. To do the job properly would require a far more critical breaking of the silicon substrate and, if he fills up this entire building, then that's a whole lotta Norman. It would mean a pretty horrible solution that goes beyond the pale. Time to get an online petition to free Norman. Organise a picket or something. Figure a catchy chant.

It's still bemusing that Norman believes that this pickle can get him out of that pickle. I had stopped in front of the CAAIR, looked up at the titanic building, and knew the impossibility of my task but the singularity inside this black hole of Norman drew me in. Rodders had passed by and with him any chance of an inside job. It looks like they've upped their security even since the wine and cheese evening as there's is no easy way to casually saunter across the foyer, say "Ciao," to the nice men and women in the caps with the guns and the tasers, pepper spray and body armour, bluster my way past the iris and fingerprint scans, to push through the entry doors. No, don't worry about checking the bags. There's nothing to declare here.

Mmm, maybe I could try the international student angle?

When I get to the reception desk, "El señor Norman me espera."

Flail my arms around robot-like to make them understand and I still reckon there would be little red flags bobbing above my head. I wink at the eye on the other end of the rifle scope.

Even if I got through, the CAAIR is a maze inside, security on every door, Akinfeev lurking spider-like somewhere inside making sure the place is locked down tight. Then there's not just one switch, there's millions of them. Where would Norman the regretful, memory-haunted, whole brain emulation be in there? I don't want to be here, one part of him doesn't want to be there, and the gulf between is no smaller than it was while I was at The Belt.

Did I mention I'm on edge? It's not just the CAAIR. It's the nervous expectation before a meeting – a jittery sensation running through me. And if I'm feeling it, then surely a propped-up revenant of a human being who thinks that he might just be some kind of modern-day Norse deity must be too. I have come too close.

....

There is a suit on a lounge behind me who is fixated on his mobile's news feed. Deep grey snowstorm clouds are being holographically projected flowing over the top of Twyndale, predictions for a blizzard. A security guard comes to speak to him.

"Hi, I'm sorry but we're shutting down the Centre for the weekend because of the blizzard. We'll get back in touch Monday to reschedule."

The guard gestures for him to leave. It is a contradictory gesture showing him the door while almost offering an arm around the shoulders.

The heavy steel doors by reception are opened as if the end of a shift has arrived and an increasing number of staff are coming through them. It is not the panic that had run through the mob at the space port. It is orderly and people are chatting cheerfully to one another. I see my chance to slip inside while the doors are open. I am fighting a wave of people when truly I'm suddenly seeing goats, sorry I mean ghosts, as I see Norman the chicken tamer, Norman the betrayer and Norman the lover, Norman the quite alive, emerge through the doors by the reception desk and my jaw drops. WTF! I mean WHAT! THE! ACTUAL! Wasn't he in ...? Shouldn't he be ...? My mind is blown by seeing this living, breathing ghost of a machine Norman in the flesh.

I try to rationalize. Has he been playing a joke on me all this time – the vicious revenge of a spurned lover? Getting Rodders to write his material in his spare time.

"I've got some good stuff this week about a giant cockroach Professor Greenwood."

While he gets a wry smile from Norman at one point, when Norman finishes reading the piece, he gets a simple dismissal, "Try better."

"Sorry Professor," says Rodders bowing and scraping his way out of Norman's office.

Having stepped through the doors of the CAAIR, have I stepped into Norman's simulated world? Surely you get a choice to enter the virtual world and I don't recall having made one. Actually, according to prank caller Norman, he didn't get one either. How do you call from the other side of the universe in real time? No, I've got to be having some terrible Belt of Orion drug-induced flash back. Do the drug, do the drug-induced flashback. Fair enough. Squint at the pill popping hotel doctor, drink it down with a Blue Crush, regret nothing and everything in a quiet, gentle reflection afterwards.

What I am seeing though is not Norman the ripped Norse god, flailer of lightning bolts, bringer of solar storms. He has turned decrepit and shuffles along in a difficult, pigeon-toed gait. It is a strange, minimalist dance. He holds his arms out with his fingers at angles as if fighting for balance or in cramp. His head bobs along as he walks like he is listening to a song that nobody else hears. His whole body is crippled and almost unrecognizable compared to the Norman who I knew before I left. He is grey and hunched, the head at last liberated, barely master of his own body.

I strike upon the idea that he is a Virtual. I'm liking the theory. That's right, a Virtual Norman that haunts his place of employment as many do, drawn there out of a sense of memory and ritual and comfort. That is, when he's not out fighting giant virtual cockroaches and chickens ... or taking a slice of the gambling revenue of lotto draws ... or driving fast cars ... or surfing the waves. But Norman had talked up his conscious evolution. It is hard to imagine that Norman would turn himself decrepit if he had a choice in it. Unless he had chosen that package deal from his travel consultant? Try better, Norman, try better. Choose better.

Maybe life on the silicon isn't all it is cracked up to be? Norman had found his way to his source code, broken free from his virtual simulation, and was able to walk this world again. He passes for the human being that he had longed to be but, cracking his source code has cracked him too?

Or it is he who has paid for my excesses at The Belt like a Norman-Dorian Graying Greenwood. But as a Norman-Doryan, he is not the residual self-image of a Virtual who stays sequestered up on the nineteenth. He gets out and about. He's okay with his decay. And so, it seems is everyone else which is why nobody is anywhere near as perplexed as I am in seeing Norman walking through the foyer of the CAAIR. I would like to feel relieved that he has paid for my excesses at The Belt. Cool, dodged that one. I would if I could, I cannot. I feel his pain in my body too. I feel drawn to mimic his tortured dance, not in mockery, but to share it and in doing so, to take his pain away. This is terrible. What has happened? The memory of the Badger's end still shakes me.

Like any Virtual with a limited range, Norman is stuck looking through the glass at staff who are departing. As once he had left me at The Sheridan, he stays standing there for a few minutes, perhaps jealous that he cannot leave. A security guard on the doors spots him. He leaves the doors to usher Professor Greenwood towards the exit. Stepping through the door that is being held open for him, he steps from being a limited range Virtual transforming into a technological singularity with unlimited range.

In the cold, grimy winter slush Norman takes an agonizingly long time going down the three steps and onto the path that leads to the car park. On the lawns there remains a dusting of snow. There are many staff from the CAAIR taking this path while I sneak along behind. While they scurry, Norman shuffles in a gait that reminds me of the angry ducks that I had to contend with at The Shire. By the time Norman arrives at the car park, the other CAAIR staff have left. The wind rips over the tops of the remaining cars and there feels like there is more ice to come. The sky glowers as Norman the Omniscient, controller of worm holes, cannot find his car. I guess he has a lot of other things on his mind. He struggles past the silver cockroach four times without seeing it. He is confused by his inability to find his car and I am just as confused that he cannot see it.

It's just there, I want to point out to Norman. There, there.

I remain hidden. Don't know why I do; surely, if he can't stumble across something as big as his car, he won't spot me. All I can say is that this is a bit emotional for me. There, there.

Having fruitlessly searched for his car, he leaves the car park and I follow him to the bus stop. With the campus closing before the blizzard arrives, the bus stop is full of students making their way home. They stand close together for warmth, a huddle of scarves, big jackets, and woolly hats. Standing by himself, Norman seems an exiled penguin in contrast. In the crowd of students, I slip unseen onto the bus to sit in the back row of seats. In the gloaming, streetlights streak past like Skylah had done at the Dove Festival. When we reach the city of Twyndale, reminiscent of his days of paranoia Norman scans the seats behind him, and I squirm away trying to sit safely anonymous amongst the students.

The bus stop closest to the Old Ball is on the other side of the park. Between the storm clouds and the winter gloaming, it has gone dark. There is only an occasional lamp post along paths in the park and no path altogether from this side to that. The wind has icy talons that want to crush Norman as he makes his way across the park. As we leave the street lighting, I make a connection I should have made much sooner. Norman is leaving footprints in the snow. The enormity of it stops me in my tracks. He is not a whole brain Virtual with indefinite range. What I am seeing is human. What then were all those phone calls to me?

In this early midnight, the wind is scything through the patron deity of flowers.

The flurries of snow may be only a fleeting disturbance in the mind of a god but they are doing worse to mine. I can't see the other side of the park and can barely make out Norman. His pigeon gaited walk is slowing down when it should be speeding up. He is being frozen moment by moment by the swirling vortex of the terrible blast. The blizzard shrieks a giant raptor's revenge and Norman is disintegrating. It seems that he will soon stand, frozen still in the park, a statue, as any other has been, B-grade, time-frozen, 1950s robot. A roost for pigeons, a moment's stop for a woman walking her dog.

Unbelievably, he makes it through the park. There is only the road to navigate to make it to the warmth of the Old Ball. Yet Second Avenue is full of anxious silver cockroaches racing to get home before the blizzard and for the weekend and Norman has locked up. He stands on the side of the avenue becoming ever more stooped from the buffeting. The moment has seemingly come when he will remain frozen. Then he steps into the traffic and the cars swerve around him, their anti-collision sensors detecting the derelict crossing the street. Horns blast warnings, trumpeting the furies riding the storm to their homes. Norman cups his hands to his head trying to block out the sound. I do too in anxiety for him. Entangle the heads and we both must fall. He gets to the traffic island in the middle of the road where it becomes too much and he drops, his head inches from the wheels of the cars, any moment to explode like an egg.

It looks like he is done. I wait. He has to get up. He has to get up. He doesn't. The snow keeps falling. No one stops to help him. Norman will become a statistic of the blizzard, a second's pause in somebody's feed tomorrow before skimming on. The CAAIR will send flowers. Could I leave my betrayer to die this way? It would solve many problems. Then I snap.

This is intolerable.

I kneel by Norman's prone body and yell into his ear, "Norman, you have to get up."

I yell and yell and yell.

I am hoarse and slobber, "Please ... get up."

It is barely a whisper, a scratching in the static of the line, but it is enough. Norman has heard me. He gets up, bent and hunched, and shuffles blindly into the oncoming traffic. Cars slide to a stop as he crosses.

Even then, when he gets to the front door of the Old Ball, Norman does not enter. He is stuck. There is some shelter under the curved portico roof, but he will freeze there soon enough. The irony being that he is so close to safety but I now know what needs to be done.

Alright, let's see what this dune buggy can do.

"Take the card out of your inside jacket pocket," I instruct, "place it on the reader. Raise your left hand, push the door open, step inside. Feel the warmth."

At the bottom of the double helix staircase, I watch Norman's struggle to climb them. He leans against the wall, twisting his head at odd angles, raising his arms like he is fending off an assailant. It is painfully slow until I start giving him more instructions.

"Place your hand on the banister, raise your left leg, now your right."

Norman's pace increases and, as we ascend the stairs, the swirling vortex in his mind is clearing. By the time we reach our front door, he swipes the card by himself to let us in.

By the front door, there is Norman's fedora and long grey overcoat on clothes hooks. He crumples into a chair there to recover himself. With the brim of the fedora pulled way down and the natural fall of the overcoat, it's like there is another Norman full of folded shadows standing behind this crumpled one. It is an off-putting effect. And I thought God Norman had deleted them all.

It is so strange being back here again. The familiar being unfamiliar yet familiar. I stand at the bottom of the stairs that lead up to the kitchen. It is where I had left Norman a wreck so long ago. So much had happened in the time between. tru eddie, The

Belt, L'Hôtel, Skylah, The Shire, Castaways, the Lizard King, Rega, Frank'n'Steve, the Badger, I cannot encompass it all. Yet this Norman is not the angry, vengeful god I had been expecting and this silence does not feel exactly ominous. Awkward, but not ominous. And this banged up, second hand Dune Buggy Norman has a pretty average pick up but once it gets going, it's still pretty bang average. It's nice being listened to for a change which would have to count for some kind of breakthrough. Norman though sits in his chair, shrunken and dishevelled, looking like he is lost in his own reverie. I wait feeling like I have returned only to become a wall flower again. Having got him inside, it flits through my mind that I could still flee to Elva-4 to be with Rega. As I think that, he recovers enough to thank me for saving him from the storm. Crippled though he is, I see that we're still in that perverse, intimate feedback loop. At least he isn't threatening me. Yet when he thanks me, he seems unable to focus on me like he has suffered snow blindness and I am some hazy figure in a blizzard.

His gaze searches for me before he asks, "How did you see me there?"

Then he asks suspiciously, "Were you following me?"

Well, there's our Paranoid Norman again.

Well, actually, kinda yeah.

I regret thinking that when Norman states, "You were. You were on the bus behind me."

As I am becoming something more than a hazy figure in a blizzard to Norman, fear is making me feel less and less substantial. He is very suspicious now and cocks his head to one side.

"And in the car park."

This no longer feels like gratitude rather it has begun to feel like a very subtle form of revenge.

He frowns, "I don't believe you've mentioned your name?"

The Lizard King had warned, *Be careful with names.*

I can't speak I'm so full of fear. My fatalism has been my only defence to this moment and this moment had finally come.

"Do you know what in physics is called 'spooky action at a distance'?" smiles Norman, "It is when information is shared instantaneously even at a distance between particles or, if we are being generous, bodies that are entangled. It is an aspect of quantum physics that breaks the speed of light. It may even permit a kind of call from one side of the universe to the other in real time."

"No, no, no."

I don't want to know.

"Nonetheless, it exists," he grins like a coup de grace.

I desperately grasp for something to fend him off with. He has spoken about intimate configurations of bodies before and it had been Skylah's not his that it had conjured. I snap my head to the top of the stairs and the darkened kitchen beyond and the last time I had fended him off.

You were never good at love.

All those Friday nights …

You broke my heart like my last sugar daddy had.

My mouth drops open with a terrible intuition, but I also feel I have something that may save me and I'm finally able to speak, "Did you ever know a woman named Skylah?"

Norman's face flickers in surprise and his mouth screws to one side.

He takes a moment before admitting, "Yes, I knew Skylah."

As he relates his story, my dread grows. It is like listening to the tale of someone's nightmare while experiencing the slow march of your own. A tweaking of dials on sunglasses that may focus something into vicious clarity. And by the end I wish I hadn't asked.

"I hired her as a sugar baby who I would meet on Friday nights. Skylah knew I led a busy life, that it was the only time I could spare. All I wanted was a simple conversation over dinner. And that was how it started. We were so different yet in such a short time we slipped into being quietly at home with one another. We fell into speaking a private language and, though we met in busy restaurants and bars, we were in a private world that only we shared. Our Fridays began to start in the afternoons and we discretely met by the ponds on the edge of campus to watch the black swans that had started nesting there."

"Yet that little was more than I could spare as it appeared we were getting closer to a human being emulation. I was squeezed between work and Skylah wanting to see me. Yet when she gave me one of her delicious smiles, touched or kissed me, doubts crept in that she was only doing so because of the money. At best, she was doing her job, at worst … And the more she pushed to see me, the worse it got. I had employed a sugar baby to avoid exactly this. And when she invited me to her apartment, I felt drawn there as a middle-aged fool manipulated by the strings of beauty. She tried to take me to her bedroom."

'No, I really can't," I had said.

"I felt ashamed. She had never seen me without my bodysuit. She tried to kiss me but I pushed her away."

'Don't you get it,' she said, 'I love you.'

'This cannot be,' I said and left.

"She came after me and while I waited for my car outside, she pleaded with me but it was too much. The car arrived, I got in and left. I looked in the rearview mirror and as the car drove away, she receded from me. She called but I didn't answer. I drove around until the early hours of the morning. I drove around until I could get over my doubts about her, until I could admit that I loved her too."

The dials click over slowly falling into place. I remember the wrench it had been for me to admit my love for Skylah.

"There was no answer when I rang the doorbell. The door was unlocked, and I found her, the bottle of pills beside her."

But Skylah had sat at The Bowl, the giant wooden robot man beginning to burn, yelling, "No more pills!"

The images of Skylah and Rega are so close to overlaying one another.

"I held her body next to mine. Her skin against mine was still warm yet the lift and fall of her chest was only my imagination, her skin no longer glowed, the light in her eyes had burnt out."

I had held her too.

"Nothing, nothing."

They overlay.

I want to scream, "No, no, no!" but the horror is consuming and I collapse at the bottom of the stairs.

"Then the accident happened and after that I don't remember things too well. It is all very distant to me, like another life. A blankness descended. I dwell in a desert without emotions."

Come back Skylah!

"The medical examiner found that it was an accidental overdose. She had got a new prescription that day that had combined with alcohol in her system."

We sit in a communal silence remembering Skylah for a long time until Norman asks, "I still don't know who you are?"

I sigh, "I am everything you are not."

Yet, this sharing had opened a bridge between us that is impossible to ignore. It had been built out of sadness, loss, a sense of betrayal, but also compassion and a recognition of shared love.

"I feel it," Norman says standing up.

His face lightens and he begins to smile as if emotion itself had become comprehensible.

Less excitedly I am forced to admit, "I do too."

He stands with a look of exaltation on his face. He overlays his hands on his sternum and looks at me with dark eyes avid for possession again.

This is why you don't share nightmares, I think.

I gaze out the open door remembering its promise, where it could take me, and what I would lose if it were to close. Then Norman's eyes cloud over, his moment of exaltation passes, and he begins to weep. He takes a handkerchief out of a trouser pocket to blow his nose then staggers to sit in front of me.

Recollecting himself he frowns, "But what is your name?"

I don't want to look up, I try desperately not to, but I do and for a fleeting moment look into Norman's eyes and become lost. I am in a darkness as absolute as one of my seizures. Somewhere out in deep space, in an interstellar void without stars and a very long way from Twyndale. I feel a tug on my chest. I look down and there is a golden cord running from my chest to Norman's. And in this void, we stand upon a bridge, a bridge beyond any easy description. It is a pulsing marblessence of a rainbow sky, the promise and threat of a collapse of countless possibilities into one. I look into Norman's eyes again and we finally meet each other on this bridge in an infinite void. I had to admit that I did love this, in truth, very ordinary and broken man.

"My name," I sigh as the rainbow sky bridge pulses beneath my feet, "is also Norman James Greenwood and I feel like I haven't been myself lately."

Then to move inside one another we start at the nose.

Chapter 18: Fly Fishing in the Yukon

"Here we go again," sighs Norman under his breath as he stands to polite applause on the stage of the conference room in the CAAIR.

He is not so much bored by yet another presentation as impatient for this one to be over. He had other things to do on his Friday night apart from schmooze. It had taken its time but it had come to the last day of April.

The swan-necked wine glasses were laid out on the tables outside, but the canapes had yet to be brought out when he had sauntered past and had wondered who was doing the catering tonight?

Anywhere But Here Catering perhaps? he smiles to himself.

Norman hopes that they are the wild salmon ones. Considering everything, he would be a little disappointed if they weren't. Still, it wasn't to be all fly-fishing trips to the Yukon. Not every day could you stand knee deep in a river casting a line out. This perfect memory being framed by sunlight glittering on the water, snow-capped mountains in the distance, pine forest at their feet and blue flowers on the opposite riverbank. Have a bear wander towards you, its head moving side to side, paw over paw, sensing, smelling the danger, all your encountering bear instructions paling in the moment, is it a grizzly, is it a black bear, be loud and tall, be quiet and still, then the bear deciding to keep going, and you exhaling a very, very long breath, followed by a swear.

Must have been a brown bear.

In the afternoon, in a pass to the north, clouds explode in an awe-inspiring storm, but it had gone away from Norman rather than towards him. Later, cook a freshly caught pike with beans and canned potatoes over an open fire on a small beach on the private lake. Getting woken around midnight when his guide shook his tent for the aurora swaying above them in diaphanous curtains of green. No, not every day could be like that one.

In fact, even that day hadn't been quite like that. To get that one perfect, worth-it memory, he had spent most of that day wet and muddy. Standing in the water had been cold when the sun had not been out. Nor had Norman caught the pike, let alone de-boned or barbequed it. Often when he was casting, he would get tangled lines. He would ignore the little knots until they bundled up into inextricable spaghetti. He sat resigned on the beach while his guide stood in the water casting, thinking that perhaps he should have gone trekking instead, as part of him had wanted to do. Then he had a strange ambivalence towards the aurora. He apologized, saying he did not feel well and went back to the warmth of his tent.

He had not really come to the Yukon to go fly fishing. Sure, he had spitballed it to Georgia as one of the things he wanted do in the Yukon. He needed a story to tell when he got back. He had been spurred to fly fishing by a moment of revulsion while standing in a section of a museum in Whitehorse dedicated to the Stampeders. Amongst the relics of the gold rush, he felt such sadness for the peoples and land that they had trampled over. Then he felt revulsion. He had found their stampede for gold dimly echoed in his own rush.

What he had really come to the Yukon for was to see stars. He had wanted to see stars ever since his recovery from his brain injury and he needed to be far away from the light pollution of Twyndale to do it. He had come to feel a desolate poverty in the lack of a nighttime vista.

Georgia makes way for him on the stage. He no longer wears the horn-rim glasses that made him squint. They had made way for a much more functional looking set of glasses. Akinfeev lurks at the back of the room giving subtle directions to his people with little more than the flick of his long face. Tonight, the room is full of technical advisors rather than Friends. No longer was the CAAIR pitching for cash and no longer were the Friends unwilling to offer it. No, now they were being swamped with offers of numbers with lots of zeros at the end of them. This high roller coaster of science looked like it was going to pay off.

There had better be wild salmon canapes, thinks Norman.

Last minute unsolicited punts from hopefuls wanting to get in on this action. The event horizon surrounding the CAAIR had leaked. Perhaps it was not that surprising. Someone somewhere having strategically taken the decision to leak now that the final testing phase had been successful. Almost like an admission, Rodders had been transferred into the final phase team where he was truly surprised by the actual developments at the CAAIR. He had been replaced in the CAAIR's creative writing unit by an AI who's output, in Rodder's opinion, had some very interesting, in a Dada-driven way, moments where it went off on wild tangents. Maybe the AI needed a break from the mundane too.

Norman would likely never know if there had been a strategic leaking. If he were not privy to that information, he was likewise keeping a wilful ignorance surrounding the proposed human cockroach who would become the whole brain emulation. He decided it was legally safest to be oblivious to those kinds of details. It had been enough after accidentally opening a document in the archive drive listing the criteria for the human. After scanning the first few criteria: single, no close personal ties, high IQ, he closed it quickly, scared that there may be an imminent knock on his door from Akinfeev. A week later, curiosity got the better of him and he went back to find the document, but it was no longer in the archive.

....

After the accident, Norman had been a reduced figure at the CAAIR. People had been saddened by his diminishment. A once great man fallen. So many things had gone wrong for him. The brain injury had robbed him of so much. To begin with, he could not even name what was wrong with him. He did not understand that there was anything wrong at all. When he tried to do anyone of a multitude of ordinary tasks, he failed. He couldn't take the pills that the doctors gave him. He was incapable of keeping appointments. He had great problems going down stairs. Not that he ever really did do jokes but at least he could understand them, now he couldn't. He was devoid of the faculty of joking. He couldn't find his car in a car park. At times of great distress, his sensory filters became overloaded flooding him with jumbled up, non sequitur bits and pieces of the world. Overloaded, he could just drop to the ground a seizure taking him.

Taking the train was impossible. On his medical insurance claim, he had listed the cause of his injury as 'car accident'. Rodders had offered to help get his car fixed but Norman had firmly declined. Norman had said he wanted to do it himself and when Rodders saw Norman's car in the carpark a few days later he could find no damage. He marvelled at how quickly some things moved for some people whereas they mostly did not for people like himself.

Norman could not listen to anyone on the phone. Norman messed up words and their meaning. Like a hallucinating AI he used strange elliptical reasoning to arrive at extremely divergent understandings of what people said to him. Norman couldn't even say his own name. He had learned to act as the facsimile of a normal person, but he was dead inside. He had become something else apart from human. In other words, his injury was nothing unusual. The world was full of the brain damaged. And the specialists that he had seen were no help. They all said that he would have to live with it.

Norman was unable to continue his work on the computing of emotions or oversee the rest of the work of the Centre. Progress stalled. While Norman could see the demise of his grand vision and all that he had worked so hard for, his brain damage made him oddly immune to the anxiety that the CAAIR was failing. Georgia temporised though. She began allocating staff to work on subsidiary projects. Staff went part-time. Schedules were re-written. Make work was made. Akinfeev was not worried about his job or finding another one. Rodders remained busy writing fictional scientific papers and was supplemented by an AI. Yet, the CAAIR continued to hollow out. Georgia let non-essential staff leave at the end of their projects rather than being transferred onto the next one as there were none being ramped up. More essential staff went part-time. Contracts were not renewed. No wine and cheeses were organised as Friends began to distance themselves. The tearoom became a desolate place and the floors with staff became more like the floors with servers. Then Norman started acting really strangely.

Or more so. He always had a reputation for being the eccentric professor of the CAAIR. Maybe it was from the stress of it all that he had finally suffered an over-the-rainbow brain snap. He started dancing from his office to the lift to the tearoom swinging his arms joyfully about to turn corners. He would explore the physical space of each room in wild, creative, child-like ways. He would spend a dilatory amount of time staring at the blue flowers that were budding at the bus stop near the front of the university. He had clearly lost his mind. Then he asked to take a holiday to go to the Yukon which, though the CAAIR was floundering like a beached pike towards its last breath, Georgia was happy to grant. Norman having a holiday did not fill people with confidence – would he even return? But

Norman's absence would make no difference to the work not being done there.

He had returned and was a man changed. He had resumed work and quickly made several fundamental breakthroughs on sticking points that had long been holding up work. Apparently insurmountable impasses had been bridged while he had been away. The first to have left the senior engineering group gasping in the conference room was the cable he proposed that would connect the AI's consciousness to the morphogenic software fields. He proposed that the cable should have an internal fractaline structure causing a tangled-hierarchical quantum collapse that would produce the AI's self-referentiality. Nobody had conceived of such a cable before let alone a technical description of how it could be accomplished. It was not controversial. His second proposal was. It had been to flip the model they had been using for computing emotions. There were many people in the room invested in that model, but he showed them that their work was still valuable, that being wrong was sometimes useful, that all their work was not just equations written in mist.

Maybe this all had something to do with his near-death experience in the blizzard. Something like that would have to shake you. Or maybe the visionary had needed a retreat to the wilderness to get his mojo back. Or maybe it had something to do with the doctor that the University had sent him to. Thick silver bracelets clanked on her wrist, her dark hair was covered by a scarf, and she spoke in a brusque manner of clipped sentences and an accent he couldn't place. She cursorily listened to Norman describe his symptoms before cutting him off.

"The flowing geometries are overwhelming? You feel blank? We will fix you. We will pick our way past the absence in the data. Your brain needs reconfiguring. We will fix your inner thought-dialogue for your future life. First, we scan you."

She ushered him into a room beside the consultation room and urged him to lie on a scanner that looked like a tanning bed.

After examining the scans she stated, "Good, good, we fix this."

She then ushered Norman into the next room where he was sat front of a device like a phoropter and had beams of light shot into his eyes. He came out dazed. After the sense of stars flying past him dissipated, the doctor made him do dot-to-dot exercises.

"You need to train your visual cortex to make new connections and we do that through these joining the dot exercises and the beams of light."

Its like seeing constellations in the night sky for the first time, Norman had thought.

Once he was done, the doctor announced, "That's your first treatment. Come back, two weeks."

And this esoteric treatment worked like magic. In the space of those crazy first weeks, he had regained so much of his lost self. He felt alive and remembered the wonders of being a child again. He had felt so alive and happy that he hadn't even been bothered by the data hack that the doctor had suffered.

....

Apparently in the Yukon he had formulated the idea of going to track days where amateurs drove high powered cars around circuits at scary speeds. Norman loved the smell of petrol fumes, burning rubber and clouds of smoke at the track at the outskirts of Twyndale on a Sunday morning. It was where his newly purchased vintage Ferrari 458 was garaged and maintained by a team of mechanics. He would step out of the silver cockroach that smelt like nothing to deeply breath in the perfumes of petrol – it was like the smell of incense inciting him to a different kind of mental state. His mechanic Ollie, an affable German with long, greying blonde hair and beard, would delight in spending time with Norman explaining the ins and outs of the Ferrari, that is, when he wasn't showing off his false teeth.

"Best thing I ever did replacing them. Nobody would ever know they were falsies."

Except when he keeps taking them out, thinks Norman.

While Ollie would chat about the car, Norman would walk around it with an electrostatic duster obsessing over any dust that had accumulated since Ollie last cleaned it. The first time that Norman had dusted, Ollie had felt his work slighted but he now understood it as some kind of ritualised cleansing that Norman undertook before going on to the track.

He had a natural talent for driving and after only a few of these days, he had markedly improved. The boy who had ridden his bicycle up to the university to sit in on mathematics lectures now drove a Ferrari around racetracks testing a physical geometry. Georgia and Akinfeev were less than happy with the risks involved in his track days. Considering that he had been in one car accident, did he want to be in another that could be much worse? Norman listened patiently to Georgia's entreaties to stop and then went anyway. It was the one time in his life when he could completely tune out. It was all about angles and lines, scalars and vectors. It was like he had discovered another instinct. The hypnotic vortex of the onrushing road gyrating him forwards, the lurch and drift of the Ferrari, as he sought to find what the limits were. He had once toyed with taking the autonomous car back into manual control – now his Ferrari demanded that he always did. Some drivers said that they endured a swathe of emotions during a race. Not Norman. When he was driving his Ferrari, he was barely conscious, all other pretensions of humanity dropped away, and he could be absorbed in the act of driving. And if he didn't, if he let his mind wander, if he let emotions distract him, then he was likely to slide, bounce, somersault across a field at high speed to end in a fiery crescendo.

Norman also tried Thursday night ballroom dancing. While he was not bad at it, he felt uncomfortable touching the bodies of other women and soon gave it up. He started telling very ordinary jokes in the tearoom at work which perplexed the other staff and liked reading Rodders' stories.

....

On the Monday after Norman's return from Alaska, a white-grey kitten with vivid blue eyes and black rosettes appeared at the copse of trees in the park as he walked home from the bus stop. He heard its plaintive calls before catching sight of the tiny thing from the corner of his eye. The kitten was taking desperate, tiny leaps after him.

When it caught up to Norman's heels, he turned to command, "Shew, shew."

It did nothing of the sort. The stray cat ignored him to scamper along behind. Norman strode away quicker, but he had to stop for traffic at Second Avenue. The kitten was still leaping across the grass after him. If he crossed, he feared that the cat would follow him into traffic and get run over. He stepped back onto the grass and waited for the kitten to approach. It skittered up to him and started smoodging his legs. He sat down and it nudged its head against his hand, so he started stroking the cat and it started purring. The kitten was very thin for when he picked her up to place on his knee, he felt nothing between skin and rib cage. The cat wobbled about trying to find its balance. The kitten's claws pierced Norman's trousers and jolted him like a strange recognition.

"What, little cat," he asked, "are you thinking?"

He looked into the cat's startling blue eyes.

"Is that so?" he smiled.

Norman put it into the deep pocket of his overcoat while he crossed Second Avenue. He was expecting it to struggle but it didn't. When he took his overcoat off inside his apartment, he found the kitten asleep. He left the coat on the floor and went upstairs to the kitchen. He only had dinner in the dining room when staff from the CAAIR were over. Instead, he usually had it at the small table in the kitchen which is where the kitten found him having meowed its way up the stairs with a sense of abandonment. He was eating a store-bought, pre-prepared meal of meat and vegetables. The cat performed figure eights around his legs, then when no manna was dropped to it, it claw-climbed its way up Norman's leg. When he later examined his leg, he found pinpricks of blood. He swore and hauled the cat onto his lap. It was not satisfied with that and leapt onto the table. He pushed the cat away from his meal.

"Shew, shew," he said.

The cat did nothing of the sort, instead, it continued to try to dodge his hand to get at Norman's meal.

Norman looked into the cat's eyes, "Is that so?"

He gave the cat his lopsided smile as he fed it the meat on his plate. He was left with the vegetables.

"Thank god you're pretty," he says.

Tuesday morning, he posted pictures on the local community page for a lost kitten, but an hour later he deleted the post. Then he cut his workday short at lunchtime to take the cat to a veterinarian. The cat turned out to be a female and in good health if extremely underweight. The vet commented that she was such a beautiful kitten that she could be a pet influencer.

"In fact," he said, "we do talent spotting for a cat management agency. She looks like a miniature snow leopard. Since going extinct, there's quite a demand for cats that look like them. Ghost cats indeed."

"What do you mean, ghost cats?"

"It's what they were called because they were so rarely seen in the Himalayas. Now they really are. There's other snow leopard-type influencers around but none in this one's league. It pays good money, and the agency will guide you through all the social media side of it. The receptionist will book you in with them."

The vet jabbed the cat with some needles to vaccinate it which made the kitten squeak a complaint. When next the vet came near her, she took a swipe at him which made Norman think, "Good cat." Norman took the brochure the receptionist gave him and, on the street outside, tossed it into a bin. When he got home, he lay on the couch and the kitten jumped onto his chest.

"Mmm, what am I going to call you?"

He looked into her blue eyes and thought about the constellations of stars that he had seen in the Yukon. He named her Auriga after the heavenly charioteer.

When Norman was at home, the kitten was his constant companion nestling on his lap or rubbing itself against his legs when he was at his desk, sometimes playing with the mouse of his computer as he tried to move it. He would wake to find it sitting on his chest and he loved staring into its blue eyes. When he came home in the evening, she would be waiting for him at the door. After she had eaten, she would find where Norman was and sit on him. She would purr while he would give her a scratch while telling her about his day. They were very quietly at home with one another. After a few weeks, Auriga became too long a name to call her, so while he may have shortened it to Aurey, he rather chose Riga. Then, on occasions when he was looking into her blue eyes and drifted off to muse on such New Ages fancies as how cats are telepaths or how humans are cats taking a break between cat incarnations, he would forget himself and call the kitten Skylah.

....

"The creation of a whole brain emulation is now a fait accompli," Norman concludes.

He leaves the stage to a louder round of applause than when he had risen to speak. There is genuine excitement in the room for the completion of a project that had until recently looked like it was failing. Even Akinfeev looks uncharacteristically pleased as Norman walks past him. He eats smoked wild salmon canapes again. He gets sauvignon blanced again, nowhere near so much as he previously had, but enough to see the world with different eyes. Nobody, not Georgia, not Akinfeev, thinks much of Norman's far-off air of distraction. That is Norman being Norman.

He leaves early, well before midnight. He remains awake in the car and looks at a moon growing towards full. When he arrives at the Old Ball, he gets out on the street. He takes the lift to his floor, goes into his apartment, picks up a backpack and Riga. He holds the kitten inside his jacket as he takes the lift back down and crosses Second Avenue. Once into the park, he lets the kitten down.

He says, "Go on ghost cat, off you go," and she runs ahead of him, a shadow leaping at shadows, as he walks down the slope to the copse of trees in the middle of the park.

In the last week, he had been taking Riga out for midnight scampers in the park. Norman never noticed anyone on the street and a man walking at night around a park with a cat and insomnia would seem like something anyone would do. There is a light breeze and clouds drift across the night sky. Within the copse of trees, there is a small, circular clearing. When the clouds are not obscuring the moon, it gives enough light for him to see what he is doing, but not so much that anyone would see him unless they came into the copse. He spurns using a flashlight. He takes off his shoes and socks and feels the dirt under his feet. He kneels on the ground. From his backpack he brings out a scroll of paper that contains rites for a midnight ceremony like one that would be performed by a Wiccan priestess on May Eve, a night for declarations of love and dancing. He unrolls it on the ground and places a stone on each corner.

The kitten walks across the scroll and Norman chides, "Oh Riga, Riga, Riga," gently drawing her towards him and off the paper.

He takes off his tie and undoes the top two buttons from his shirt. He unfastens a necklace that he keeps hidden there. It is a cheap, tacky necklace with a half-broken heart pendant on it. He brings out a needle from a pin cushion in his backpack and pauses remembering the time he held a knife to his right index finger.

"Had it all started with the ant bite?" he wonders and smiles his lopsided smile with a certain sadness.

"To heal the wounds, to reset the bones," he says.

He grips the needle like an addict considering the wisdom of taking another hit then winces, as much with pain as surprise, that he would do that to himself. With the drops of blood that comes from the wound, he smudges the pendant. Then he begins reading the words on the scroll. Feeling foolish, he whispers the words and tries to console himself that even Newton had believed in alchemy. He would almost be relieved if nothing happens and find it almost unbearable if something does. The moonlight is momentarily shrouded by drifting clouds, but he knows the incantation now. He repeats the words and feels a charm in the phrases that loop in and out of each other like magician's rings. He notices that there is a drop of blood on the scroll. The phrases fill him up and as they do, he begins to pace the clearing chanting. The kitten that had been playfully leaping after him runs off into the trees. Clouds drift away, and the clearing brightens. Then, beyond all imaginings, rimmed in moonlight, tru eddie comes leading Rega.

He remembers tru eddie's words: *I ain't done nothing for you.*

Indeed, it had all been for her. What a thing is love to have done this.

As they weave between trees coming closer, Norman is filled to choking and, it turns out, eddie does have the emotional range of miffed. He stands, arms crossed, in front of Norman to dwarf him.

"This ain't healthy bruh, they's marriage rites yous be saying."

Norman says shyly, "I needed to see her again."

"Yous already let her go, this ... this ... yous only going to curse yourself with grief this way."

Norman looks over eddie's shoulder as he used to do when the Friends would start talking about non-disclosure agreements and partnering arrangements. He had once looked faraway to imagine beautiful things, now she stood just behind eddie.

"Right now eddie, grief and curses don't matter to me."

tru eddie brings his hands together, fingers intertwined, then as if throwing something away they flare to either side, palms towards Norman. He steps to one side and Rega comes forward.

Her eyes glow like the woman in the painting at O'Shaughnessy's and Norman suddenly can't look at her. Her hands run over his face like a misty rain until drawing his chin up their eyes meet.

"There you are," she squints in her playful way.

He looks down.

"I'm sorry I left you the way I did. It is unforgiveable."

"Look at me," Rega tells Norman.

He warily looks up and is overwhelmed by a sense of love and compassion.

"It wasn't all about you," she gently chides Norman.

tru eddie wanders away into the copse leaving in his wake a music full of bells and sliding synths reminiscent of Bar 0.

There for an hour they slow dance in a beam of moonlight until tru eddie comes back for her. Norman feels the cruelty of time like a great weight pulling him down into the earth.

"I used to seek other things in infinity but now all I wish is to dance with you in it."

"Bruh," he says, "yous need to say goodbye."

"But I-," he begins before choking up.

Sensing that heaviness on Norman, Rega places her hand on his chest as if to fill his heart.

"You should know that you can say farewell," she says, "because our two souls have become one now and cannot be broken apart. Our love stretches further than any eye can see …"

Rega's form dissolves into a beam of moonlight and tears fall freely down Norman's face.

"But I can't," he grasps for the space where Rega had stood but moments ago like someone beckoning to the dead.

....

Norman wakes in his soft sheets glowing from the glory of the previous night. He lies there content until he feels the stab of parting again. He had not even told Rega how much he loved their Friday nights together. Then he is bolt upright realising that he had left the kitten in the park. He dresses in a panic, dashes across Second Avenue and towards the copse of trees in the middle of the park. He tries to think when he had last seen her. He calls for the cat, walks around and around the copse, then around and around the park but he is not answered. He posts on the local community page for a lost white-grey kitten with vivid blue eyes and black rosettes. Even as he does so, he despairs he will never see her again. While there are love hearts and crying face emojis, no one ever replies to say they had found the kitten. In the days after the midnight ceremony, Norman abandons taking the silver cockroach to work, instead opting for the bus. He walks to and fro across the park ever hoping for a little white thing to appear at the corner of his eye.

....

Then Monday morning during a senior management meeting in the boardroom on the twentieth floor of the CAAIR, Georgia announces that the date for the upload of the whole-brain emulation was to be in a week's time. Norman leans back in his chair barely able to conceive of the enormity of Georgia's announcement. Even though he knew it had been coming, it had always been coming, always somewhere on a distant horizon, never here but there. But here it was. Final tests were to be completed this week. Seven days before they would discover if Norman had led them to a new world beyond human consciousness. That glorious path shines in Norman again until Akinfeev follows that announcement with one of his own.

"Effective immediately, all senior and critical personnel at the CAAIR will go into lockdown until the upload is completed. Unless you are at work, then you will be at home. You will go directly home today and there return directly to work. All social engagements are to be cancelled. Food is to be ordered online from the CAAIR's authorised provider. The Centre will be opening its café 24/7. Sleeping pods are being installed in the conference room if you require them."

With the experience of Norman's accident, the university was not taking chances.

"If this poses any issues, please contact me directly," Akinfeev almost growls, "and support will be provided."

In a much more brighter tone Georgia states, "I'm sure that appreciating the enormity of our undertaking you will all act responsibly. Besides, I expect in the lead up to the upload we'll be working around the clock here."

....

In the following days, Norman comes home exhausted from work to fall asleep on the couch. He wakes confused, not knowing where he is. When he is unable to go back to sleep, he will go stand at his windows to gaze down onto the park and wonders who will be chosen as the first true cybernaut.

On Friday night, he gazes at a park lit by a full moon and is possessed by memories of other Friday nights so much so that he rushes to the front door.

But while throwing on his overcoat Akinfeev's voice rings in his head, *effective immediately.*

He is stunned in to immobility and cannot bring himself to turn the door handle.

By Saturday night he is existing in a nowhere zone of a waking sleep, over excitement and tension. Sometime in the night, he wakes choking, unable to breath. It is as if the climate control is not working. He tries sucking in deep lungfuls, but it only makes him more agitated. Terrible misgivings are surfacing in him. He checks the climate control panel next to the bathroom, and it lights up green with 0.0038 for CO^2. It has to be wrong. He stands on a chair by a vent in the bathroom so that he can breathe what air is coming in, but it doesn't clear the pressure he feels in his throat. He holds his hand up to the vent.

"There's no air, no air," he gags.

The room is too small and from his chair, all wrong angles and perspectives, walls that bend towards him, backing him into a corner.

"I have to get out," he gasps.

This time Akinfeev's injunction fails. He grabs his long overcoat from the hook by the front door and runs down the double helix staircase like it was a gyre of guilt. He scampers out the doors, across Second Avenue and into the park. He tosses off his shoes and feels the cold grass under his feet. It has been such a short time since the midnight ceremony, but his world had changed so dramatically since then. It had become so much more concrete and he much more wraithlike. He is drawn down the hill, entranced by memories of following a ghost cat, excited by the prospect of standing amongst the trees and saying magical words of incantation again. He is almost at the copse before he notices a man walking towards him. It is too late for him to turn away.

"Evening, nice night to be out," the man says as if fright could be allayed under a blanket of blandness.

"Yes," agrees Norman, "it certainly is."

"But," he says, "the world is a very dangerous place."

"Indeed," acknowledges Norman.
"Bad things can happen to good people."
"Without a doubt."
"Accidentally falling down the steps for instance."
"That is unlucky."
"Having an abseiling line break."
"Tragically sad," agrees Norman.
"Smacking a grizzly bear with a fishing rod."
"Even in self-defence it is ill advised."
"Playing chicken."
"That's profoundly foolish."
"Base jumping..."
"Is asking for a parachute failure," completes Norman.

"Or going to amateur track days. Then again you don't even need step outside your front door to accidentally mix up your medications, nick your throat with a razor, or slip on the soap in the shower, eh?"

"Undoubtedly, or take one of those absurdly dangerous selfies," says Norman.

"That's exactly right, Professor. And with the full moon upon us," the man gazes skyward before returning his unblinking gaze to Norman, "it does bring all the crazies out. Shall we ..."

And Akinfeev's man escorts Norman back to the front door of the Old Ball.

....

The alarm wakes Norman Sunday morning from a restless sleep full of disturbing dreams that he could not now remember. He wanders half-awake to throw himself blearily onto the couch. The CAAIR beckons yet he feels jaded having been there so often in the last few weeks even if it is the day before the launch. Nonetheless, he goes to the kitchen to get a quick breakfast before going in to work. He gets to the top of the stairs and frowns. He doesn't recall leaving his journal on the kitchen table, let alone open. He distractedly pours himself cereal while staring at the journal and eats while flicking through its pages. Most pages were neither one thing nor another, some had thoughts and memories that made him smile, but he turns ashen, his mouth a rictus, eyes stone, when he comes across his entry about flipping the model. He closes the journal and pushes it away from him with the back of his hand. He does not have the stomach to eat any more cereal and leaves the bowl by the journal on the table in an otherwise spotless kitchen.

Norman sits in the back of the silver cockroach absorbed in his tablet ensuring that all the certificates had been signed off. The rays of the rising sun catch the high cirrus clouds and, inside the car, the internal lights fade off. Twyndale passes by unnoticed as he is engrossed in the momentous act of signing off on the technical aspects of the incorporation approval certificate. He sits back in awe and with a sense of accomplishment about what he has authorised as the doors of the silver cockroach float up. But he is not in front of the steps of the CAAIR. He is in the car park of the racetrack.

"What on earth?" thinks Norman.

He was sure he had said 'work' when he got into the car. Or had he? Had he said anything at all. It was a Sunday so perhaps the car had automatically gone there? But it was a Sunday, and coincidentally, a track day. The doors of the garages are up. Mechanics move about the pit area prepping cars and discussing this and that with other members of their support team. Drivers walk towards the meeting room by the office for the compulsory track day briefing. The café is open, and signs are up for dagwood dogs, fairy floss and giant chicken nugget buckets. A light with red dots flashes 'coffee'. Norman has had the coffee there before and it is a cheap, diesel variety. Excitement surges in Norman and pierces a week of cooped up frustration. Accident or not, he is at the track. He does some quick math. So long as he can get his car prepped quickly, he can squeeze in a few laps before going to the CAAIR. It could be the start of a perfect day.

The door is up on his garage, and he can hear his Ferrari running, a tune he enjoys hearing, all of which has Norman vaguely unsettled about what is going on. If he didn't know that he was coming here, why would anyone be prepping his car? The bonnet of the Ferrari is up and there is a man beside it, his face obscured behind a screen on a stand. There's a little shelf in front of the screen that has a bucket of chicken nuggets on it.

Norman attempts to make himself heard above the sound of the engine.

He shouts, "Where's Ollie?"

The man looks up from the bi-directional controller startled. He is seemingly embarrassed and drops a nugget back into the bucket.

"Professor Greenwood, just tightening everything up," he says a little too enthusiastically.

He shakes Norman's hand with an oily, mechanics grip which he only thinks to wipe on his shirt afterwards.

"I've never seen you before, are you part of the maintenance crew?"

The man drops the hood of the Ferrari the last few inches.

"Diagnostics on the ABS modulator are right now," he reassures Norman.

"Is there something wrong with the brake system?" Norman asks.

The man ushers Norman out of the garage, "Quick, you're going to miss the race day briefing."

He turns Norman around and pushes him towards the meeting room. Norman's excitement is tempered by his confusion over why his car is already being prepped. He shakes his now greasy hand that is covered in either cooking or engine oil and reassures himself.

It's Sunday, it's not so unusual, it's a good thing that it is being prepped.

SOMETIMES YOU JUST NEED A BREAK

He decides he is going to speak to Steve, the track manager, after the briefing to find out exactly who it is working on his car.

Norman enters the foyer at the back of the meeting room as a man at the front wishes, "Have a great day and stay safe."

The other drivers stand to leave, pushing fold up chairs this way and that. Norman tries to find his way through the crowd that is excited to go in the opposite direction. He decides that wisdom dictates to wait in the foyer for the man who was speaking.

Norman asks him as he passes, "Where's Steve?"

The man responds, "Why'd you want to talk to Steve? I'm filling in for him, he's having a break. Gone diving with the great whites in South Africa, he's one crazy bastard to go swimming with those fishes."

"Oh. Say do you know who that is tinkering with my Ferrari?"

"The 458?"

"Yes, that's the one."

"You the professor?"

"Yes I am but-"

"That Ferrari might be vintage but she still has a lot of horses left in it."

Other drivers bump into and walk between Norman and the track manager.

"That's Alex, he's the best."

"What's happened to Ollie?"

"Ollie's been replaced. We've entered into a new partnering arrangement with an external agency."

Other drivers are trying to ask the track manager questions and his head is bobbing this way and that.

He distractedly answers Norman, "There were one or two tweaks Alex wanted to make. Off you go."

"What about the briefing?"

He gives Norman a moment's more attention before turning away, "You know it all. Just keep your lid on 'cause you gotta protect your most valuable asset."

The swarm of impatient drivers sweeps Norman out the doors.

Alex is gone by the time Norman gets back to the Ferrari. He sits in the car unsettled by everything; he doesn't have much time before he had to be at the CAAIR. He should not be here at all. He pulls on his helmet and pushes the red button to start the engine. He is the last one out to the holding area and is held there by the marshal before being allowed out on to the track. It is only then he realises that, in the confusion, he's forgotten his gloves.

For the first few laps, the excitement, the roar of the engine, the concentration required to stay on the circuit, performs its magic and he finds that plane of geometry of angles and lines, scalars and vectors again.

Loops like magician's rings, incantations of another sort.

Then to his surprise an ant crawls along the dashboard and he suddenly falls out of that ethereal plane.

What is an ant doing in here?

The memory of a bite makes his index finger itch yet he cannot take his hands off the steering wheel to scratch it. Then items from his work checklist begin popping into his head and he has the disturbing notion that he hasn't signed the incorporation approval certificate.

Did I or didn't I?

He wasn't so sure now. He could have been more engrossed with his sense of achievement.

Surely I did.

Then other items on his checklist begin popping into his head. He tries to counter these distracting thoughts.

Perhaps I should only do 49?

He thinks of the project.

SOMETIMES YOU JUST NEED A BREAK

What else does this whole brain emulation need from me?

He sees the path that had led him to it. He had been so keen to know that path that all else had been trampled underneath. And now he is keen not to know. He could live without knowing every secret. He swerves through a chicane and thinks of Akinfeev. Not knowing seemed possibly hazardous to his health.

Alex saying, "*Just tightening everything up.*"

What else does this project really need from me?

He remembers what it was like being something other than human. Love had caused his transformation and had been what he most missed.

The vortex of the road spirals faster.

Breaking is for chickens.

The countryside rushes past at an alarming rate.

The world is a very dangerous place.

The car accelerates and those geometries of angles and line, scalars and vectors peel away to reveal stranger ones.

Oh Skylah.

Bad things happen to good people.

Yanelt, York, Kakemoto.

Accidentally mix up your medications.

Skylah!

Its other drivers who suffer emotions while they drive.

There's things of the spirit that are healthy to leave behind.

He had driven away.

Skylah!

No close personal ties.

Clipping an apex, his hand slips on the steering wheel and he oversteers. The tyres scream as he corrects.

Norman whimpers, "She can't be dead."

That's not possible for he still loved her.

The car accelerates.

Diagnostics on the ABS modulator are right now.

I don't know of any other way, the Lizard King had said, the words now a gauntlet.

He sees the woman with the luminous eyes again and she says, "*Our love stretches further than any eye can see.*"

Entangle the bodies and whether the mind hangs on is beside the point.

"Sometimes you really need to break," she says.

Tears course down Norman's face.

"Sometimes you just need to break."

Credits

Thanks to all my friends and family for their love and support during the writing and their reading the drafts of this novel. If that review process did nothing else, it did lead me to my Rachel for which I'm deeply happy. And thanks to Twinkle, my constant companion through so much, who almost made it to the end. You are still greatly missed. Thanks to my friends for their overblown words of praise you'll find in the front matter. I'm completely unworthy of them. Thanks especially to Ted Zorgon for his encouragement throughout the writing of this novel and all my years of creative writing.

Established in 2002, The Flat Mars Society wishes to give our thanks to John Sladek for its naming:

"Perhaps one day we'll colonize Mars. If so, one of the first signs that our colony is getting really civilized will be the formation of a Flat Mars Society. Indeed, the main purpose of our civilization may turn out to be just that: to spread flatness to the stars."

- The New Apocrypha, Stein and Day Publishers, 1973.

We wish to give thanks to my friend Jeanette for the inspiration for our nom de plume who, in 2006, called me the black wiggle because of my penchant for wearing black, long-sleeved t-shirts to work. I countered, "I'm not the black wiggle, je suis le wiggle noir, merci."

Milton Keynes UK
Ingram Content Group UK Ltd.
UKHW030746071024
449371UK00006B/502